ALL THE SHINING YOUNG MEN

The Price of Liberty Series

A Call to Honor
The Color of the Star

GILBERT MORRIS
AND BOBBY FUNDERBURK

ALL THE SHINING YOUNG MEN

WORD PUBLISHING
Dallas•London•Vancouver•Melbourne

Library of Congress Cataloging-in-Publication Data

Morris, Gilbert.
    All the shining young men / Gilbert Morris and Bobby
Funderburk.
        p.   cm. — (The Price of liberty series : #3)
      ISBN 0–8499–3496–6
      I. Funderburk,   Bobby, 1942– . II. Title.   III. Series:
Morris, Gilbert. Price of liberty: 3.
      PS3563.08742A79   1993
      813'.54—dc20   93–24235
                                              CIP

Printed in the United States of America

3 4 5 6 7 8 9 LB 9 8 7 6 5 4 3 2 1

To my mother—Norma Ellen Funderburk

a reservoir of love
a river of good deeds

CONTENTS

Part 1

STRANGER IN A STRANGE LAND

1

CHERUB IN EXILE

Who's the old bag on the last row, Harry?" The tall, sharp-eyed man in white tie and tails stood in the center aisle, pointing to the woman who sat with her head bowed, a shabby black coat draped around her slight frame.

Harry blew his nose into a well-used handkerchief, the sound causing the tall man to flinch. "Don't know, Mr. Stringer. She came in while I was in the back. Been sitting there like that for an hour and a half. One time she read from her Bible a few minutes. Mostly she just sits there with her head down."

"Well she can't stay here. From the looks of her, I seriously doubt she made the Rockefellers' guestlist." Stringer smirked at his attempted humor and motioned elegantly with his long arm for Harry to escort the woman out of the church.

Harry looked at his scuffed brogans and rubbed his stubby, freckled hand across his shiny head. "Uh—I started to do that awhile ago, Mr. Stringer, but I—I just didn't have the heart. Look at her. Probably just a poor old widow woman."

"This wedding is strictly by invitation only, Harry! We most certainly can't have riffraff just walking in off the street." Stringer pursed his thin lips and shook his head as he walked smartly up the aisle, his hard heels ringing on the marble floor. As he reached the last pew, the woman on the far end, near the wall, slumped to her knees in an attitude of fervent prayer.

Harry blew his nose loudly, the sound reverberating in the lofty recesses of wood and stone. When Stringer glared at him, he shrugged his shoulders and waddled down the aisle toward the altar. Turning to his right, he disappeared through a side door.

The woman knelt on the hard floor, wisps of gray hair escaping around the edges of the dark mourning veil that obscured her face. Light filtering through the stained-glass windows bathed her in a gold-and-blue-and-violet radiance.

Well, she is on the last row in the far corner. How could she be a distraction to anyone? Stringer walked to the front of the church where he began adjusting the flowers and greenery of the elaborate floral arrangements.

The wedding proceeded almost as planned, with the proper balance of smiles, tears, and music. Great wealth was displayed with controlled and muted elegance in the gowns of the bride and her maids and in the wool, silk, stones, and metal that adorned the guests.

The woman in the last row sat at the far end of the pew behind her veil—inscrutable and silent. Her right hand moved to her lap from time to time as if something in the brown paper bag that rested there required periodic adjustments.

The bride was pledging her troth, the groom Cheshire-grinning with his perfect dental work, as a girl of five rose from her aisle seat unnoticed and slipped to the back of the church. With her ruffles, ribbons, and golden ringlets she looked like a cherub in exile. She eased between the pews on the last row, her hand squeaking softly as it slipped along the gleaming surface of the wood.

The face behind the mourning veil turned toward the child as she drew near. A gloved hand reached out, clasping gently the soft, pink one of the child. The two of them whispered for a few seconds. The child giggled musically. The mother, hearing her daughter, motioned brusquely for her to return.

"She's really very pretty, Mommy," the cherub whispered as she sat, legs dangling, next to her mother.

"Hush, child! She doesn't even belong here."

Ten minutes later the wedding party descended the wide stone steps of the church. Arrayed in rigid formation along the curb, Cadillac limousines—black, gleaming, and grand—awaited them like obedient family retainers.

Across the street in a small park, the woman from the back pew sat on a wooden bench, peering intently through her veil. The blonde cherub waved to her from the top step. She returned the wave as the child's mother led her down to the street.

Capped and coated chauffeurs, as stoic as any hobnailed Nazis, ushered their charges into the cars. The procession glided away from the curb—an oiled and shining armada of wealth—leaving in its wake the pedestrian gawkers.

*   *   *

"Hold on a minute now! That's a restricted area. You can't go back there." Gilmore Gibson stepped from behind the security and information desk, walking briskly over to the gray-haired woman in the tattered black coat.

The man's tan uniform was as neat as his crew-cut brown hair. His thought processes were slower than most, but he was dedicated to his job, which was the best thing to happen to him since he made the wrestling team at P.S. 111. At six-foot-two, he stood a foot taller than the woman attempting to violate his domain—the lobby and adjacent areas.

Dropping her brown paper bag to the floor, the woman turned to face him.

Gibson's eyes went wide. "Why—Miss Vitrano! Why are you wearing that getup?"

"Close your mouth, Gil. It looks like the entrance to the Holland Tunnel." Maria Vitrano snatched the gray wig from her head and shook out her glossy dark brown hair. It fell in soft disorder to her shoulders. Her eyes were large and so dark that the pupils were barely discernible. Beneath the slightly aquiline nose, a legacy of her Sicilian ancestry, her full lips curved in a half-smile. "This 'getup' is just a tool of the trade, the same as your muscles and nightstick and that *Police Gazette* you keep tucked away in the desk drawer."

Gibson flushed slightly. "Aw, that's just for when things get real slow. I don't read it much."

"Good literature should be savored, Gil," Maria smiled, turning toward the bank of elevators. "Take it home with you."

"Maybe you're right." Gibson returned to his desk, trying to remember what *savored* meant.

Maria stepped off the elevator into the bustle of the newsroom. It was immense—cluttered with scores of desks, cigarette burned and scarred from years of around-the-clock use by their transient and careless occupants. Ceiling fans turned slowly, recirculating the stale, lifeless air.

Wreathed in clouds of smoke, harried men in shirt-sleeves with ties askew typed frantically on their massive Underwoods. The heavy carriages of the typewriters chinged a discordant, incessant symphony as the men gazed at scribbled notes, rushing to beat their deadlines. Others leaned back precariously in their chairs, cigarettes dangling from their lips as they almost bellowed into telephones. Some hurried up and down the aisles between the desks, carrying folders and sheaves of papers.

The center of this productive disorder was the city editor, the heart that controlled the ebb and flow of news. Duncan Rourke sat at his huge desk in the middle of the room, almost hidden by the throng of reporters handing in copy or getting new assignments. His voice rumbled above the clamor like distant thunder.

Maria weaved her way through the bedlam toward Rourke. Jockeying for position, she finally managed to get five minutes with him.

"The wedding lasted longer than I thought." Maria spoke loudly, leaning reluctantly toward Rourke, whose breath spoke of too much time with coffee and tobacco and too little time with toothpaste. "You'll have to trust me to edit my own copy. I guarantee you this one will make the top fold. The society page won't hold it."

Rourke glanced at her ragged coat and scuffed shoes. "I know we don't pay much, Maria, but my housekeeper dresses better than that. And she's from Harlem!"

Maria ignored the remark. "What about it? Can I skip the copy editors? It's the only way I can get the story ready before we put the next edition to bed."

"What's the rush? This isn't exactly a breaking story. It's been in the news for months. Besides, every society reporter in town covered that wedding."

Taking a deep breath and holding it, Maria leaned closer, a smug grin on her face. "But only one covered it from *inside* the church."

Rourke looked again at Maria's disheveled appearance. "I'm not going to ask how you pulled *that* off. From what you've done in the past, my mind reels with possibilities."

"Nothing like that at all," she retorted. "I behaved civilly and with propriety—almost."

"Maria, we can't afford to keep a gaggle of lawyers on retainer to handle one libelous reporter."

"Just teasing," Maria saluted with mock gravity. "I took Law and Journalism. Made a B+."

Lighting one Camel from the stub of another, Rourke leaned back in his chair. "What makes this wedding different from any other silver-spoon nuptials?"

"Well, it seems that the blushing bride had more than one reason to blush. When the minister asked if anyone objected to the union, a former suitor did. And he proceeded to tell everyone why—from the altar!"

Rourke's gray eyebrows wriggled like two fuzzy caterpillars. "Well, you've never let me down before. Can you finish it before the ads are pasted? I'll take a quick look at it then."

"You got it, boss!"

Salvatore Como had noticed Maria leave the elevator and watched closely as she concluded her session with Rourke. Seeing her cross hurriedly to her desk and toss aside the coat and gray wig, he gave his slick curly hair a few touches with his comb, straightened his yellow silk tie, and sauntered toward her.

Maria saw him swaggering up to her desk as she rolled fresh paper into her Underwood. *What rotten luck! Why isn't this drugstore Romeo out doing some work?* "Can't talk now, Sal. Got to have this one in before the paste-up."

"All work and no play, Maria. You know what they say. Hey, listen to me. I'm a real poet."

Typing with a rapid, steady cadence, Maria only half-listened. "Sure, Sal. Robinson Jeffers can't sleep worrying about the competition."

"Who?"

"Robinson Jeffers. A poet. *Be Angry at the Sun* just came out. You oughta buy it."

"Aw, you lit majors give me a pain. Who cares about all that roses-are-red-violets-are-blue stuff? Anyway, there's a whole lot of artistic people in my family. I told you Perry Como's a distant cousin, didn't I?"

"Only three or four dozen times."

Como frowned, took his comb from his back pocket and ran it through his hair. "Whadda ya say we go out tonight and cut a rug? You need to get away from that schmaltz you listen to and hear some swing. There's a cat plays the eighty-eight and another one on the licorice stick who'll knock you out. You can't be an ickie all your life. It's time to get in the groove."

"What in the world are you talking about?"

"I'm talking about a jam session down at Duke's, Doll. Where the hepcats gather. We'll get knocked out."

Maria stopped typing. She glared at Como, her eyes bright with a growing anger. "Sal, don't you have some grisly murder or a crime of passion you could be out covering?"

Sal grinned. "Kinda slow now, Babe. I got nothing but time and a heart full of love."

Maria sighed. Taking a yellow pencil from the jelly jar on her desk, she scribbled on a pad, tore the sheet off, and gave it to Como. "Meet me here at eight."

"Now you're cooking with gas!" Sal glanced at the sheet of paper, folded it, and skipped back to his desk.

Maria gazed at the notes she had taken in the church, most of them without looking as she wrote, hoping not to draw attention to herself. *What a mess! Well, I guess I can decipher enough to turn out a decent article.*

As she unrolled the last page from her Underwood, Maria heard a commotion from across the room. Looking up, she saw several men gathered around Como's desk, laughing and teasing him good-naturedly. One held the directions she had given to him.

Anger coloring his dark face, Como stormed over to Maria's desk. "Hey, what's the big idea?"

Maybe this'll end it. Subtlety seems to have no effect on him. "Whatever do you mean, Sal?"

Sal punched the paper hard with his forefinger. "This address. It's the psychiatric ward at Bellevue."

"I should think the meaning would be obvious," Maria smiled knowingly, straightening the article she had just finished.

"I still don't get it. Why Bellevue?"

"Because if you think I'd go out with you, Salvatore Como— then you must be crazy!"

Como's face seemed to sag as if his aging process had leaped forward several years. His eyes glistened with moisture. Laughing half-heartedly, he wadded the paper up and threw it into the gray metal trash can next to Maria's desk. "That's a good one, Maria," he muttered as he walked away with a leaden gait.

She had expected anger—not this sudden, bright pain in Como's eyes. "Sal, I didn't mean to . . ." Maria let the words trail off. *I shouldn't have done that. He's not a bad guy. Maybe Mama was right. Maybe I do have a mean streak in me.*

Seeing Rourke's empty desk, Maria glanced at the glass-walled teletype room against the far wall. She entered the machine-gun clatter of the room and walked over to the bank of machines where the city editor was scanning the incoming messages from UPI. He squinted at the medium blue type; it came off the machines blurry and would smudge at the slightest touch.

Rourke glanced at her. "Looks like someone would invent a teletype that could turn out decent print."

Maria shouted over the din in the small room. "Why are you scanning the incomings? You've got to have better things to do with your time."

"Copy boy's sick again. Besides I heard the bell. I always like to look at those myself."

Peering over Rourke's shoulder, she still had to speak loudly to make herself heard. "Anything urgent?"

He waited a few seconds, then ripped off the roll of paper shifting out of the top of the gray metal box. "Let's get out of here so we don't have to scream at each other."

Heading toward the elevators, Rourke entered the side door into a small kitchen area. He poured steaming coffee from a large drip pot into two heavy white mugs and sat them on a long, narrow table, ringed with stains from years of sloppy drinkers. Lighting another Camel, he let the smoke drift from his nostrils and growled softly. "Well, they're really going to do it."

"Do what?"

He threw the rumpled teletype paper on the table and slapped it with his meaty hand. "That!"

Maria picked the paper up and glanced over it for a few seconds. "But they're Americans—just like us! How could anyone do such a thing?"

"Because they don't look like us. That's why!"

Sitting down, Maria spooned sugar into the strong coffee from a can crusty from innumerable wet spoons. She read a few more lines of the copy. "These internment camps. From what I hear, they're no better than prisons."

"'With liberty and justice for all.' Rounding up native-born Americans and herding them off to these camps! All in the name of protecting our hard-won freedoms."

Maria straightened the wadded teletype paper, reading a few lines. "'A Jap's a Jap! It makes no difference whether he is an American or not.' General John L. DeWitt said that. Who's he?"

"Commanding general of Western Defense. He considers the West Coast a battlefield. Even Walter Lippmann said that nobody's constitutional rights take precedence over national defense. Well, we never said this country was perfect . . . ," he said, pausing and looking off in the distance. Bringing his attention back to her, he asked, "What's that article of yours look like?"

"See what you think." Maria handed Rourke the article, sitting back to watch him as he read.

Rourke read through the article, smiling twice and making three corrections with his red pencil. "This is great stuff! You're the only society reporter in New York who could take a routine assignment and make a real story out of it. You work it just like the police beat."

Maria's cheeks colored slightly. "Thanks, Chief."

"Here, drop this off," Rourke said, handing the article to her, "and come right back. I want to run something by you."

Five minutes later she was back at the table with Rourke.

"I've got an idea," he began, folding his hands on his ample stomach. "World war comes to small-town America. What do you think about that for a story line? Most of our stories are based in the city. I think we need a different viewpoint."

"What's this got to do with a society reporter?" she asked, leaning forward with interest.

Rourke rubbed his chin, raspy with stubble. "Maria, for somebody with a couple of night classes in journalism, you're amazingly professional in your work. I guess your degree in literature gives you a certain eloquence most reporters don't have, but you keep your articles readable. The average Joe can understand them."

Maria felt the touch of excitement prickling at the back of her neck. *Maybe this is it. My chance to break out of this horrid world of afternoon teas and coming-out parties. God, deliver me from this before I'm smothered by boredom!*

"What I'm getting around to in my own convoluted fashion is that I need someone for a special assignment. Someone with a fresh approach. Someone like you."

"Well, don't keep me in suspense," she almost pleaded. "What's the scoop?"

"Liberty."

Maria frowned. "What's that supposed to mean?"

"It's what we're fighting for, isn't it?"

"So?"

"Liberty is also a town in Georgia," Rourke grinned. "A town where you'll go on assignment to write a weekly column on how the war affects life in small-town America."

"I—I'm kind of overwhelmed," she stammered. "I've never been farther than New Jersey."

"You've got the talent and the tenacity to make this a real feather in your cap, Maria. Not to mention selling a whole lot of newspapers for us." Rourke waited for her reply, knowing already what it would be by the look on her face.

"When do I leave?"

"How about day after tomorrow?"

Along with the excitement, a sharp chill of anxiety rose in Maria's breast. This was no longer a dream of success, but a true opportunity, all too concrete in its demands. She had never given much thought to the South, but considered it a sort of intellectual backwater—a region of antiquated social norms. She pictured dull-eyed rednecks, tobacco spittle running down their chins, and poverty-stricken, abused blacks. All in all, the South held no attraction for her, but she would do her job and make something worthwhile come of it.

"What about my column?" Maria mused.

"It's been taken care of," Rourke smiled. "Your flight's booked to Atlanta. You'll rent a car and drive from there."

Maria took a deep breath, leaning back in her chair, hands clasped and forefingers pressed against her lips. "One question."

"Shoot."

"Why Liberty? Other than the obvious mileage we can get out of the name."

Rourke got up and poured another cup of coffee. "One of my buddies at Harvard came from Liberty. Born and raised there. Knows everybody."

"How do you know he'll cooperate with me?"

"Talked to him this morning," Rourke smiled. "He can't wait to meet you."

Maria shook her head gently. "You think you know me pretty well, don't you? What's this guy like?"

"Comes from one of the founding families. Southern aristocracy—he says that means they wear shoes to church and formal dinners. Articulate, intelligent, sharp dresser. Graduated cum laude from law school. Takes an occasional drink and likes the ladies. Not to worry though; he's my age."

"What's his name?"

"J. T. Dickerson."

*   *   *

"Nobody'll ever come close to that record!" Carmine Vitrano sat on his stool behind the counter in his dingy, cluttered grocery store talking with his best friend, Avi Cohn. Vitrano's dark hair had gone completely white since his wife had died five years ago, and his back was bent like an old man's although he was only sixty-three.

Cohn brushed the cigarette ashes from his ancient vest and lit another Chesterfield. Sitting in the ladder-backed chair carved over the years with the names of customers, some long dead, his sad brown eyes watering from the smoke, he muttered, "For once I have to agree with you, my friend. No one will ever hit in fifty-six consecutive games again."

The two friends sat in the gloom amid the dusty shelves of canned goods, mesh sacks of onions and garlic that hung from the low ceiling, and odds and ends of clothing. They talked in the hushed tone used at wakes and hospitals. Since the death of Anita Vitrano, the store had somehow assumed the atmosphere of a funeral parlor. Long a gathering place for the neighborhood, the loud conversations, joking, and heated political discussions had given way under the dark, heavy grief of Carmine Vitrano. Old friends drifted away as the store drifted into ruin, but Cohn still came by almost every day.

Maria entered from the living quarters in back just as Tommy Dorsey's band began to play "I'll Never Smile Again." Even on the tinny-sounding radio, Sinatra's vocal, backed up by the Pied Pipers, was as smooth as silk.

"You get prettier every day, Maria," Cohn said softly, nodding in agreement with his own statement. "Just like your mother when she was your age."

"Thank you, Mr. Cohn," she smiled. "Hi, Papa. How're you feeling today?"

Vitrano smiled weakly at his daughter, remembering his wife—the smell of her hair after she washed it in the rainwater she caught in a pan in the alley—the touch of her skin when she came to him at night after his long hours in the store. It seemed to him that she had been dead for a thousand years now. "Fine, Maria. Just fine."

"Well, why don't you sweep this place out? Dust those shelves. Customers don't like to come in here anymore." Maria gestured around the store, her hands flashing whitely in the dark air.

Vitrano ignored the question, listening to the music and turning to his friend. "Now there's another *paisan* who's at the top of the heap. Sinatra—'The Voice.' Joe DiMaggio and Frank Sinatra—the two best in the business."

"Ah—Sinatra can't touch Bing Crosby. 'Where the blue of the night meets the gold of the day, someone waits for me,'" Cohn sang in a raspy voice that was only slightly off-key. "Now there's a song for you. This modern stuff is all brass and no sweetness."

Maria grabbed the broom that leaned against the wall and swept the wooden floor, slick from years of shoe leather, while the two old friends jousted with each other. In a short while, Cohn bade his friend farewell and left the store to the ringing of the bell above the front door and the sounds of a stickball game drifting in from the street.

"Papa, I need to talk to you," Maria said earnestly, sitting in Cohn's chair.

Vitrano leaned on the counter with both elbows. "Sounds serious. You getting married?"

"No, no. Nothing like that. It's about a job assignment I've decided to take."

Vitrano smiled broadly. "I'm glad you're getting out of that society business. They going to give you the government beat? That's what it's called, right? A beat."

"That's right, Papa," Maria nodded. "But this is a special assignment. In Georgia."

"Georgia? What's to report about down there?" Vitrano babbled excitedly. "A peach tree. A hillbilly. I think somebody's putting you on, Maria."

Maria explained the nature of her new assignment, much to her father's chagrin. "I won't be gone but a month at most. That's what Mr. Rourke told me."

"I don't know. I just don't know about this," Vitrano mumbled, shaking his head slowly. "They give the coloreds a hard time down there. Maybe they don't like Italians either. What if they got it in their heads that you was on Mussolini's side?"

"Oh, Papa! You worry too much. This is 1942. It's not like the old days when you came to this country." Maria got up and took her father's hand, hardened from years of backbreaking labor before he saved enough money to buy the store. "I'll be fine."

Vitrano gazed into his daughter's eyes, large and dark like his own, with the long curved lashes of her mother. "Maybe you're right. But you're all I've got left. I couldn't get along in this old world if something happened to you."

Maria knew her father was thinking of her brother, John, killed at Henderson Field by a Japanese pilot as he attempted to shoot down a Zero with a hand-held thirty-caliber machine gun. "I'll be back before you know it. Jimmy Dugan's going to come in and sweep out the store twice a week. I've already paid him for a month. And Mrs. Polito will bring your supper over every day."

"Give your papa a hug."

Maria walked behind the counter and put her arms around her father. She spoke comforting words to him, never letting on that she was more frightened than he was at the prospect of her trip into the Deep South.

2

SOUTHERN COMFORT

Maria pulled the 1939 black Ford coupe over to the curb in front of a small, wood-frame building with a faded shingle hanging out front. What was left of the black lettering on the white sign read, *T. Dickers , torne at Law*. A man in his mid-forties ambled out the front door, squinting in the noonday brightness. *Articulate, intelligent, sharp dresser*, Maria thought, remembering Duncan Rourke's description of his longtime friend, J. T. Dickerson.

The man, lean and about six feet tall, sat down on the front stoop of the law office. The sharp March wind blew his mane of light brown hair about his sad, cocker-spaniel eyes. He wore scuffed, brown brogans with the laces untied, baggy khakis, and an ancient Harvard sweatshirt. Incongruously, he also wore an expensively tailored navy blazer that needed laundering.

This must be the janitor. I suppose Dickerson gave him that jacket and sweatshirt. "Hello, I'm Maria Vitrano. I'm looking for your boss. Could you tell me where I might find him?"

The man took a silver flask from his inside jacket pocket and unscrewed the cap slowly. "Maria Vitrano. That's a mighty pretty name. Sounds Mediterranean."

"My mother was Spanish and my father's Italian, or rather he's Sicilian," Maria offered, stepping from the car and straightening her gray wool skirt.

"Spanish and Italian—a fiery combination." The man lifted the flask, took a long swallow, and shuddered. "Well, Maria Vitrano, what do you do? Fight bulls or sell bananas?"

"I beg your pardon!" Maria put both hands on her hips and glared at this insolent, ill-groomed stranger.

With a crooked grin, the man screwed the top back on the flask and put it away. "See—I was right. A fiery combination."

Taking her gray suit jacket from the car, Maria slipped it on against the chill wind and marched the few steps to the office. She was about to launch into a dissertation on manners when she noticed the sad, gentle eyes of the man reclining on the little stoop and the unmistakable intelligence that lay deep within them. "You're—you're J. T. Dickerson, aren't you?"

"At your service, ma'am."

"Why didn't you tell me?"

"You didn't ask."

Maria smiled and sat down next to him. "I guess I didn't at that, did I?"

"How's Duncan gettin' along—truly? Told me on the phone he's just great." J.T. took his flask out and offered it to Maria.

Maria shook her head. "He's overweight, overworked, and he smokes too much. A good wife is what Duncan Rourke needs. Someone to take care of him. But he's married to that newspaper."

"A good wife," J.T. murmured thoughtfully. "I expect you're right. Let's go out back and set a spell."

Maria followed J.T. into a small, dusty reception area with a desk and two gray filing cabinets that hadn't seen any use for years. An adjoining law library held a conference table cluttered with novels, volumes of poetry, and thick, leather-bound history books. All the law books were neatly arranged on oak shelves built into the walls.

"How 'bout a cup of coffee?" J.T. offered, entering the tiny kitchen that looked out onto an enclosed garden area. A cathedral-shaped radio sat in the open window. "Fools rush in where wise men never go," Mildred Bailey sang to the music of Red Norvo's band.

"Sure."

J.T. took two delicate china cups from the cabinet next to the sink, rinsed them out, and poured coffee from a white enameled pot. Handing one to Maria, he added a dollop from his flask to the other. "Outside all right with you?"

"Fine." Maria noticed that the trim on her cup was solid gold. *What an enigma this guy's turning out to be. I wouldn't mind doing a story just on him.*

Walking down three concrete steps, Maria found herself in a brick-walled garden area. Ivy climbed with abandon over the wall and onto several crepe myrtles near it. A three-tiered fountain, topped by a statue of a Greek water bearer, held green, slimy water. Wooden lawn chairs and wicker cocktail tables were spaced randomly about the brick-floored surface of the garden. Flower beds gone to seed lined the wall. Leaves rattled about with each errant breeze.

"Have a seat," J.T. offered, pointing to a chair; its white paint had been peeling for years.

Maria stared at the flaking paint, dust, and twigs on the seat of the chair.

"Where are my manners?" J.T. exclaimed. "I'm sorry. I don't get much company anymore."

Maria smiled at his embarrassment.

J.T. handed Maria his cup while he brushed the chair clean. When Maria returned his cup, J.T. took it with both hands, the fingers of his left hand brushing gently against the soft white skin of Maria's palm. She wore a plain gold band on her right ring finger and a silver cameo on her left forefinger. J.T. felt a pleasing sensation like a feather trailing slowly down his spine and he thought how beautifully Maria's slim hands adorned the rings she wore.

When they were settled in their chairs, J.T. cleared his throat. "Duncan tells me you want to do a story on our town."

"That's right. It seems all we've been covering is the big city. He feels we need to get the small-town viewpoint." Maria took a notebook and a short yellow pencil from her jacket pocket, crossed her legs, and opened the notebook.

J.T. stared at her heart-shaped face, the tingling sensation resting in the pit of his stomach.

"Could we begin now?" Maria asked. "Or I could come back tomorrow if it would be more convenient."

Startled out of his reverie, J.T. sputtered, "No—no. Now is fine." *What's wrong with me? I'm acting like a schoolboy.*

"Well," Maria continued, "what I have in mind is to build a series of articles around a couple of young men who are eligible for the draft now. First a little basic information on the town. Then get some background on the men—school, families, friends, jobs—take them through the whole process. Maybe do some followup after they're in the service—that is, if they make it that far."

J.T. felt himself drifting into the depths of Maria's dark eyes. "Ah—sure. Anything I can do. Sure you don't want to interview Ben Logan—only Medal-of-Honor winner in the town's history?"

Maria glanced at the puffiness of J.T.'s face, at the dark circles under his eyes. *I'd like to have known him when he was younger, before the drinking hit him so hard. Bet he was a nice-looking man.* "No, not Ben Logan. He's been on every front page in the country. You know what they say, 'Nothing's dead as yesterday's news.' No, what I'm looking for are ordinary, hometown boys, like Ben, on their way to experience the extraordinary circumstances of war."

"That doesn't narrow it down much."

"You're right, but there's an angle I'd like to work into these articles." Maria looked about the ruined garden area, thinking how lovely it must have been at one time. "Everything you read these days is about a bunch of gung-ho, fired-up men rushing off to join the service. What about those who aren't so eager to leave hearth and home for a chance to get shot at in a foreign land?"

J.T. sipped his spiked coffee. It tasted like wormwood. For the first time in years he felt an uneasiness bordering on guilt at drinking in someone's presence. "I can think of two boys who might interest you then. One's a tennis player who came up the hard way. Grew up working around the country club. He's about to break into the big time and doesn't want the war to ruin his dreams of glory. The other's a preacher."

"They sound perfect!" Maria exclaimed. "Oh, one other thing. No rich ones please. They always have ways to circumvent the problems we ordinary mortals face." Maria remembered the very wealthy families she had written about for her society column and how removed they seemed to be from the mainstream of life.

"Don't worry," J.T. smiled crookedly. "These boys know what it's like to work for a living."

"That's the kind I'm looking for."

J.T. glanced up at a fox squirrel scampering up the live oak that grew in a grassy area at the back of the garden. As it stopped on a high limb, the sunlight caught its fur, turning it the glowing red color of coals in a campfire. J.T. sat immobile, staring at the squirrel, his profile clean against the shade behind him.

"Are you all right?" Maria asked softly.

"What? Oh, yeah, sure. Just that squirrel, when the sun hit him—the color reminded me of something."

"Reminded you of what?"

J.T. finished the coffee in one long swallow. "Something about the last war. Everything's sort of fuzzy. Somehow it just came back. The night sky full of fire—and the noise."

"I shouldn't have asked. I'm sorry," Maria murmured, noticing the pain in his eyes.

"Don't be. I was only over there three months." J.T. felt again the gas searing his lungs, his mouth wide in a silent scream for air that wouldn't come. Felt rough hands dragging him from the battlefield amid the freight-train rush of the shells.

Maria remained silent, hoping J.T would continue.

"I think a lot about the boys from our town who've gone off to war. I see them in the uniforms of World War I, the 'doughboys,' because that was the war I knew."

Maria scribbled a few notes with her yellow pencil.

J.T. leaned forward in his chair, elbows resting on his knees, mumbling so that Maria could barely hear him.

> I sought my death and found it in my womb,
> I looked for life and saw it was a shade,
> I trod the earth and knew it was my tomb,
> And now I die, and now I was but made;
> My glass is full, and now my glass is run,
> And now I live, and now my life is done.

"That's beautiful." Maria lay her notebook aside. "I majored in literature, but I never heard that before."

"Not many people have."

"What is it?"

J.T. looked up and the years had fled from his eyes. "Just some lines a young man wrote to his wife a long, long time ago—the night before he died. But you're here for the living, aren't you?"

* * *

"I've seen him before!" Maria exclaimed, watching the lean man with the almost white hair rush to the net behind his second serve. "Last year at the national championships at Forest Hills. I can't remember his name though. Something unusual."

"Chance," J.T. replied, leaning back on his elbows in the five-tiered bleachers at the side of the court. "Chance Rinehart. He made the quarterfinals I believe."

Maria sat with her chin resting on both hands, enthralled at the speed, grace, and power of the two men on the grass-surfaced tennis court.

Rinehart pulled up halfway between the service line and the net, balanced on his toes, racquet poised for the first volley. His opponent, like a negative image of Rinehart with his black hair, drove a forehand down the line. Anticipating the shot, Rinehart took two quick steps to the left and angled a backhand volley out of reach.

Billy Christmas walked to the side of the court, plopping down in one of the folding chairs and toweling off. "What's J.T. doing out here? He never comes to the club anymore."

"Who knows what J.T.'s gonna do next?" Rinehart laughed, grabbing a fluffy white towel. "He sure is keeping exceptional company these days though."

"You better watch yourself with this one, Chance," Billy smiled. "She looks like she can take care of herself."

Rinehart glanced toward Maria, the sunlight gleaming on his tanned, sweat-streaked face. With its faintly hawklike features and smoke blue eyes, it possessed the drawn, hollow look of the Prussian aristocracy. He would have been exceptionally handsome but for the droop of the left eyelid and a jagged two-inch scar beneath it—a legacy bequeathed him by his father on one of his infrequent visits back home. "She's a tiny little thing, isn't she? But what I can see from here is all woman." *Think I'll turn up the steam a little and impress her.*

At eighteen, Billy Christmas was a top college prospect, but he was born to wealth, and tennis was little more than a hobby to him. His natural ability carried him along.

Rinehart, three years older, had thrown his whole life into the game as a way out of the abject poverty he was born to and had gone against the best players on the American and European circuits. At five-ten and 160 pounds, he was as quick as anyone playing the game and his timing was impeccable. Not quite tall enough for the booming, cannonball serves of a Bill Tilden or a Pancho Gonzales, he relied more on consistency and a first volley that more often than not won the point outright.

Billy won only one point in the last game, a perfectly placed ace down the center stripe on the first point. He hit his second serve deep into the backhand corner and followed it in. With a short backswing, Rinehart stepped across with his right leg, planted his foot, and took the ball early. Using the power of the serve to his advantage, he blasted a backhand down the line.

Caught flatfooted, Billy shrugged and returned to the baseline for the next serve. Unnerved by the rocketlike return, he double faulted. The next point was a long rally that he lost when he pushed a forehand long. At fifteen-thirty and following his serve in, he watched Rinehart's sharply angled forehand dip over the net just past his outstretched racquet.

At fifteen-forty, down two match points, Billy hit a flat serve down the center stripe. He knew it was another ace and turned to position himself for the next point. Incredibly, the ball floated back from Rinehart's block return, landing near the service line. Recovering quickly, Billy set himself for a forehand drive but spotted Rinehart already closing in on the net. *Too close to the net,* Billy thought, throwing up a textbook offensive lob. *Let him try to reach that one.* In the next two seconds Billy found out what it meant to be a world-class player.

Seeing the ball sailing out of reach, Rinehart spun around, his back to the net, and took three quick steps. Leaping high off the court, his back still to the net, he twisted in the air, his left arm pointing toward the perfect parabola of the white ball against the blue sky. His right arm whipped around from behind his back with the arc of the racquet closing perfectly with that of the ball until it exploded off the strings in a flash of white.

Billy stood mesmerized, watching the aesthetic beauty of the shot as though he were a spectator rather than a player. The ball caromed off the grass surface six inches inside the baseline, embedding itself in the chain-link backstop.

Walking to the sideline, Billy collapsed in a chair next to Rinehart. "How did you get so much better in just a year? I used to play you a pretty close match."

Rinehart grinned, his eyes crinkling in the late afternoon sunlight. "When you play with the big boys, Billy, you get better or you get on back home."

Slipping the cover on his Bill Tilden autographed racquet, Billy put the wooden press over it and tightened it down with the four wing nuts. "J.T.'s waving at us."

"Maybe he wants us to meet his girlfriend," Rinehart laughed. "The old rascal's been holding out on us."

J.T. rose from the bleachers, taking Maria's hand as the two combatants walked over from their arena. "I want you to meet Liberty's two star athletes, Maria. Billy Christmas and Chance Rinehart. Boys, meet Maria Vitrano."

Maria thought they looked like two statues come to life from the golden age of Greece. "Mighty proud to meet you," she said awkwardly in her clipped consonants. "J.T. told me that's the acceptable way of greeting people down here."

She shook hands with Billy first, noticing that he had the restless, guarded expression of those who are born to wealth and are never quite comfortable with it.

"Hi, Miss Vitrano. Glad to have you visit our little town," Billy mumbled.

Turning to Chance, Maria saw the gleam of a predator in the striking, smoke blue eyes. She felt drawn to him by a sheer animal attraction that caused her to tremble slightly, but she was repelled at the same time by an undefined fear.

"Welcome to Liberty, Maria." Chance spoke in the softly drawn-out vowels of the Deep South that Maria had already become fond of. "If there's anything I can do to make your stay more pleasurable, you just let me know."

"Why, thank you, Mr. Rinehart," Maria replied, trying to hide her nervousness.

Chance turned to J.T. "Well, J.T., nice to see you again. You're lookin' well."

J.T. ran his hand through his thick brown hair. "Chance, I took a good look in my shavin' mirror this morning. No sense in you lyin' about me. You got enough vices as it is."

Chance flashed his white smile at Maria. "Now, Maria, don't you go believin' everything ol' J.T. says about me. He knows I'm just a backward country boy tryin' to make it in a mean world."

"Maria's here to do some stories for her newspaper," J.T. continued. "She wants to talk to some boys with, ah—humble origins I guess you'd say. Billy, I'm afraid that leaves you out."

Billy forced a smile. "You're right, J.T. It leaves me out of a lot of things."

"Puts you in a lot of things too, Billy," Chance said, pointing to Billy's shiny black coupe parked near the club entrance. "Like that Cord over there."

This time, Billy didn't try to smile. "Nice meetin' you, Miss Vitrano. Hope you have a pleasant stay. Good match, Chance. Take care of yourself, J.T."

"Well, why don't we have something cold to drink?" Chance suggested, watching Billy walk away.

"I can't," J.T. replied quickly, not wanting to face any of his old friends who might be around. "Maria, you stay and get your story started. I think you'll be safe enough with Chance in the clubhouse with people around."

"Come with us, J.T." Maria pleaded. "You can fill in a lot of things about the town that Chance isn't old enough to know."

"We'll get together later," J.T. said, pressing Maria's hand between both of his.

Maria watched J.T. amble off toward the tree-lined street. "Does he usually walk everywhere?"

"Only since the mayor lifted his driving privileges. Seems J.T. hit about everything in town that couldn't get out of the way of that ol' pickup of his."

Maria felt an unexpected sadness, like hearing bad news about an old friend. *What a shame. Such a kind, gentle man.*

"Shall we go?" Chance offered.

Maria took his arm, feeling the smooth, tanned skin and the resilient muscle beneath—she felt another unexpected emotion.

* * *

"Now there's a real story for you." Chance pointed to a middle-aged couple seated across the clubhouse from them.

"Who are they?" Maria asked.

"Ellie and Hartley Lambert. Ol' Hartley owns the lumber company and about half of the rest of the town. He's hard to take sometimes, but he's a worker. I'll give him that much."

Maria gazed at the couple. The man was carrying on a loud, animated conversation with someone two tables away. His wife smiled placidly, sipping a martini and watching her bear of a husband dominate their section of the clubhouse.

"Ellie and J.T. were a real item back in high school. And for a year or two after, I think."

With her reporter's nose for a story, Maria's interest was aroused immediately. "What happened to them? Did they get married?"

Chance sipped his tall glass of ice water. "You really like ol' J.T., don't you?"

"He's a nice man," she replied tersely.

"Sure. Well, anyway, they were the perfect couple. The football star and the beauty queen."

Maria glanced at the quiet, blonde woman across from her, trying to picture her as a seventeen-year-old.

"J.T. was an all-state quarterback. Best this town ever saw. He turned down a bunch of scholarships to go off to Harvard and make a lawyer of hisself."

Maria sipped her Coke, fascinated by the story and by the soft, languid voice of the storyteller.

Chance remembered the national championships at Forest Hills and the girls of New York who had been intrigued by his southern speech and manners.

"This would make a good human-interest story," Maria remarked. "Wish I had time to do it."

"Just don't let on to J.T. I told you all this," Chance admonished. "Anyway, while J.T.'s in Bean Town hittin' the books and makin' the dean's list, Ellie's parents are makin' plans for their little darling's future. In the person of one Hartley Lambert."

"What was wrong with J.T.? A graduate of Harvard Law School surely has a bright future."

Chance shrugged. "Who knows? Maybe they thought J.T. would fall for one of those Back Bay beauties in Boston and leave their little girl out in the cold. Hartley already had piles of money and mountains of it on the horizon."

"They forced her to marry him?"

"*Persuaded* would be a better word, from what I'm told."

32

Maria thought of J.T.'s law office sliding into decay. "Does he still practice?"

"Now and again. When he's sober enough," Chance replied offhandedly. "The plot thickens now though."

"Well, go on," she urged.

"Enter our local war hero, Ben Logan," Chance continued, relishing the interest Maria had in his story. "He's head over heels for Ellie's daughter, Debbie—or he was last time I heard. I've been on the road playing a lot of tournaments lately."

"I think this is going to be an interesting place," Maria smiled, gazing about the room.

"We're just gettin' started."

"Who's that?" Maria asked, pointing to a sharp-featured man with iron gray hair sitting alone, reading the newspaper. "He looks like Blackjack Pershing."

"That's Billy's daddy, General Logan Christmas. Made a name for himself in World War I. Not as big as our boy Ben though. I think it kind of galls him that a poor boy like Ben, with a drunk for a daddy, turned out to be a bigger hero than he did."

"Is Billy going to follow in his father's footsteps?"

"Billy's dying to join up right now. He don't give two cents for being an officer, and it's killin' the general." Chance stood up abruptly. "Let's hear some music."

"Fine with me."

Maria watched him saunter over to the jukebox in the corner, his movement a picture of controlled power and grace. She gazed out the expanse of window that overlooked the tennis area. The last of the sunlight angled across the surface of the courts, giving a silverlike appearance to the manicured grass. She recognized the song from the first note, "I'll Never Smile Again."

Well, it's been an interesting first day in Liberty, Georgia, she thought. J.T.'s face came before her with his sad gentle eyes. She glanced over at Hartley and Ellie Lambert, then at General Logan Christmas. As Chance sat down across from her, she gazed at his tomcat smile and felt the pleasurable uneasiness of his company. Then it hit her. *He's told me absolutely nothing about himself.*

3

CHANCE

Maria awakened in her hotel room to birdsong and the pale gold light of early spring through the high windows—and the smell of freshly washed sheets, dried outside in the sun and wind. She stretched luxuriously, running her hand over the smooth, white linen. *They've been ironed! Who would ever have thought to iron sheets? Maria, you've got to see some more of the world outside Brooklyn.*

Someone knocked softly on the door.

"I'm coming. Just a minute." Maria threw back the brightly patterned quilt just as the door swung open.

"No ma'am. You jes stay right where you is. I wanted to make sho' you wasn't sleepin'." A short, stout woman with a round face the color of milk-whitened coffee waddled into the room carrying a white wooden tray. It was laden with a silver coffee service, china, and silverware. A single red rose stood in a slim vase of porcelain.

"Oh, my!" Maria exclaimed. "Is this the usual service or have I died and gone to heaven?"

The woman chuckled deep in her ample bosom, her white teeth gleaming in the bright room. "No ma'am, you ain't in heaven, but Georgia's mighty close. Everybody gits this service on de first day when dey rents a room for a week at a time like you done."

Maria propped her pillow against the headboard, smoothing the quilt over her green satin nightgown. "This is wonderful. I can't remember being so hungry at breakfast. Must be the fresh air."

The woman unfolded the legs on the tray, placing it across Maria's lap.

"By the way, my name's Maria Vitrano. What's yours?"

"Josephine, ma'am," she smiled. "I's glad you is hongry, 'cause you got fried eggs, country ham, grits, and my own special homemade biscuits—cathead biscuits I calls 'em."

Maria looked at the shiny metal cover on the plate. "Grits?"

"Yes, ma'am."

"I don't know about these grits, Josephine," Maria frowned. "I've heard about them, but I've never even seen any. Maybe I'll just try one to see what it tastes like."

"One what?" Josephine asked with a puzzled expression.

"One grit."

"One grit?"

"Yes. Why not?"

Something brightened in Josephine's eyes. She threw her head back, chuckling heartily.

"What's the matter?" Maria asked uneasily.

Josephine lifted the cover off the plate. "Dat's grits," she said pointing with her soft, pudgy finger.

Maria smiled first, then laughed softly. "You must think me a complete fool."

"No ma'am. It jes take you Yankees awhile to learn how to eat. I be back in a while. You take yo' time now."

As Josephine left the room, her starched apron rustling softly against her dress, Maria breathed deeply the aroma of the steaming food. She tasted the grits, drowning in butter, and was pleasantly surprised. Then she attacked the food, slicing off thick portions of the juicy ham. After buttering the hot, fluffy biscuits, she took her first big bite and thought she had never tasted anything so good. *I'll never be able to face another bagel after this.*

Maria stirred sugar into her second cup of coffee. She listened to the quiet in the room, the low, almost soothing hum of the small town coming to life. The tray looked like Mother Hubbard's cupboard.

As she sipped the coffee, she felt content in a way she had never experienced. *It's almost like—peace! That's the only word for it. Maybe it's being away from the hustle and bustle and all the noise. I'm on my own for the first time and it feels good. Not a bad beginning for a Yankee stranger in a strange southern land.*

Five minutes later Josephine returned with her broad smile and her broader skirts. "My, oh my!" she exclaimed, staring at the few crumbs that were left from Maria's breakfast.

"That was the most marvelous breakfast I can ever remember, Josephine."

"We done made a believer out of you ain't we, Miss Maria?" Josephine chuckled.

"A believer?"

"In our southern cookin'," Josephine explained. "De few northern folks I knows won't hardly eat when dey goes back home."

Maria smiled at the unfamiliar speech patterns rolling so smoothly from this jolly woman. "You know something, Josephine?"

"Ma'am?"

"I'm beginning to believe there's really something to this 'southern hospitality,'" Maria observed sincerely. "Are all the people down here so friendly?"

Josephine's smooth brow furrowed slightly. "Some is—some ain't. Like anyplace else, I reckon."

"J. T. Dickerson surely is."

"You knows Mr. J.T.?" Josephine asked.

"Met him yesterday. Seems like such a fine, gentle man."

"He sho'ly is." Josephine muttered, shaking her head slowly. "Po' Mr. J.T. Let dat woman ruin his whole life."

"You mean Ellie Lambert?" Maria remarked.

Josephine's eyes widened in surprise. "You sho' you ain't been here befo', Miss Maria?"

"First time I've been anywhere down south," Maria laughed. "I'm a reporter though, so I listen."

Josephine nodded her head, lips pursed in thought. "Well, I reckon you can't blame Miss Ellie for him takin' to de bottle like he done. Dat's what ruint him. He never let it make him mean like most I know though. Always helpin' folks best he could."

After exchanging a few pleasantries about the town, Maria decided it was time to get down to business. "Josephine, do you know Chance Rinehart?"

"Mr. Chance?" Josephine answered, taking the tray from the bed. "Knowed him since he was a little boy."

"What can you tell me about him?"

"Po' white trash is what he come from—if you know what I mean," Josephine replied knowingly. "Wudn't dat po' chile's fault though. His daddy was jes a no 'count and a drunk."

"Can you give me any of the specifics of his childhood?"

"Ma'am?"

"How much do you know about him?"

"Not a whole lot," Josephine confessed. "You want to find out about Mr. Chance, you ask Isaac Paul."

Maria took her notebook and pencil from the nightstand. "How would he know?"

"They growed up together. Both of 'em working out at de Pine Hills Country Club."

"There's another man I'm interested in for my story, Josephine," Maria remarked, finishing her notes. "His name's Jesse Boone."

"He's a preacher. One of dem holy rollers. Lives out north of town in de hills."

"What's a holy roller?"

"Dey do a lot of hoopin' and hollerin' in de church house. Roll around on de flo' sometimes, I heard." Josephine rolled her eyes. "Strange folks out in de hills."

Maria smiled involuntarily, laying her notebook aside. "Well, Josephine, you've certainly been a big help to me. I'm starting to feel right at home here in Liberty."

"We glad to have you, Miss Maria," Josephine replied, collecting the tray. "Anything you need, you jes ask for Josephine."

After Josephine had gone, Maria took a leisurely bath and sat in front of the antique dresser applying a touch of lipstick to her full lips, the only makeup she normally used. She brushed her dark brown hair until it fell in shimmering waves about her shoulders. Slipping into tan, pleated slacks, a dark brown blouse, and penny loafers, Maria slung her soft leather purse on her shoulder and left the room she would always remember for the splendor of that first southern breakfast.

*   *   *

"Isaac Paul? What in the world would you want to see him for?" Sylvester Hand looked like the maintenance supervisor that he had been for twenty-three years. He wore his gray hair cropped short and his green twill uniform neatly pressed. A short chain with enough keys to open a locksmith shop hung from his wide, black belt.

Maria took her credentials from her purse, flipped open the leather case, and showed them to Hand. He was dutifully impressed. *Guess Rourke knew what he was doing when he had this made up for me.* "I'm doing a story for my newspaper. I think Isaac Paul could give me some information that would be helpful."

"Yes ma'am," Hand agreed cheerfully. "Right this way."

Following him down the hallway toward the spacious lobby of the club, Maria noticed General Logan Christmas seated at a table in the dining area reading the *New York Times.* He wore sharply creased gray slacks, a white shirt, and a navy cardigan. As the white-coated waiter approached, he laid the newspaper aside and spoke with him. Pointing through the large expanse of glass toward a young couple on the farthest court next to an ivy-covered wall, the general listened intently to the waiter for a few seconds. Suddenly, his expression became fierce. He folded his paper neatly, slapped it sharply on the table, and, kicking the chair back, strode briskly from the room.

"Excuse me," Hand mumbled, clearing his throat. "I'd better see what that commotion was about."

Maria watched him walk over and speak with the short, stocky waiter. In a few seconds he motioned for her to join them.

"This is Isaac Paul, Miss Vitrano. Isaac's on duty so he'll have to keep workin' while y'all talk."

Maria held her hand out. "Nice to meet you, Isaac."

Paul glanced at Hand, who gave him a slight nod. He shook Maria's hand with the slightest touch of his own.

"You help this lady out, Isaac. She works for a big newspaper in New York City. We might get our names in the paper. Nice meetin' you, miss." Hand turned and walked briskly back across the lobby, whistling "Chattanooga Choo-Choo."

Isaac Paul put the chair back in place at the table, then stood, shifting about uneasily. He was only slightly taller than Maria and his ebony skin gleamed in the light from the expanse of glass that looked out on the courts.

"Do you mind talking with me, Isaac?" Maria noticed his liquid brown eyes and felt he was sizing her up.

"No ma'am. I have to go stripe court number one though," Paul muttered, his words almost lost in the empty dining area.

"You're going to do it in that white coat?"

"It ain't a dirty job," he smiled, walking softly toward the heavy glass doors that led outside.

"Mind if I tag along?"

"No ma'am."

As they crossed a flagstone terrace outside, Maria recognized Billy Christmas, who was obviously giving his blonde companion a tennis lesson. "Isn't that the general's son?"

Paul glanced toward the far court. "Yes ma'am."

"Why did the general get so mad?"

They were walking now on a narrow gravel path that led between the courts. It was bordered by cypress and landscaping timbers, and Paul knelt to straighten one, seemingly forgetting about Maria's question.

"Look, Isaac, I'm a reporter. Whatever you tell me will be confidential. You don't have to worry," she assured him. "I'm not interested in digging up any dirt, just doing a story about a small town caught up in the war. If people won't talk to me, how am I going to do my job?"

Paul lined up the timber at the edge of the gravel, pushing the wooden peg back into place.

"I guess I'm just a little nosy, too," Maria admitted. "My story's not about the general at all. It's about two young men who grew up here. One's Chance Rinehart."

Paul stood up and smiled for the first time, his teeth gleaming against his dark skin. "I'm twenty-four, Miss Vitrano. And I've had this job half my life. Mainly because I know how to keep my mouth shut. You'd be surprised the things people say in front of me—like I was a chair or a lamp."

Maria noticed that Paul's expression had become thoughtful as well as cautious. She also noticed that the heavy drawl he used in front of Sylvester Hand was gone.

"But I believe what you say. You just don't have the eyes of a liar," Paul grinned.

"Well, thank you, I guess," Maria smiled back.

After they had reached court number one, Paul went through a gate and opened the door of a small tin-roofed shed that stood behind a hedge growing along the fence. He brought out a hopper with spoked wheels, rubber tires, and a wooden handle, dumping it full of white power from a sack made of heavy brown paper.

Stepping back into the shed, he grabbed a ball of twine and pushed the hopper out to the net post at the side of the court.

Seeing the puzzled expression on Maria's face, Paul knelt and pointed to something in the clipped grass of the court. "See this? It's a nail stuck in the ground. They're at all the corners and where the lines cross. I stretch the twine between all the nails. Then all I have to do is push the hopper alongside the twine and the court's got nice new stripes on it."

"So that's how they keep the lines so straight," Maria observed, glancing at the faded stripes on the court.

As Paul went about his work, Maria followed along with him, not pressing for any information.

"The girl down there with Mr. Billy is Jordan Simms. Ol' Annie Simms's niece, but she raised her like she was her own chile. Live in that big ol' run-down house out at the edge of town—next to the cemetery." Paul pulled the twine taut, twisting it around a nailhead.

"I saw that old house on my way into town." Maria glanced at the girl with honey blonde hair moving gracefully on the court. "I'll bet it was a beautiful place in its heyday."

Paul nodded, unrolling the ball of twine as he walked to the next nail. "Anyhow they mighty po'—and the general's mighty rich. That's how come he got so mad when he seen Mr. Billy with Miss Jordan."

Maria followed him around in silence, allowing him to talk when he felt like it. As he came to be more at ease with her, he slipped into a less precise and controlled speech, but it never became the thick drawl he used in front of Sylvester Hand.

"Chance come to work here at the club when he was ten years old. He'd come in ever'day after school and on Saturdays. I 'member 'cause I had jes turnt thirteen. A teenager. Boy! I thought I was somethin' back then."

"What could he do at ten?"

"Anything needed doin'. Cut grass, clean off tables, mop, wash dishes. He was always a hard worker. His mama, Miss Dorothy, she done housework and took in ironin'. Them two had it pretty hard, I reckon. Hard as most of us colored folks. They even lived just across the tracks from the colored quarters.

"Ol' Kurt—that was his daddy—never give him anything 'cept that funny name."

"You mean Rinehart?"

"No ma'am, his first name. When Chance was born, the doctor tole somebody, 'Poor little thing. With a daddy like that, he ain't got a chance.' Ol' Kurt heard it and that's what he called the boy—Chance. He thought it was a good joke. I bet he ain't seen his boy more'n a half-dozen times since the day he give him that name."

"When did he start playing tennis?"

Paul looked up from the frosty white line he was laying down on the pale green carpet of grass that would darken as the sun moved north toward summer. "I believe it was the first day he come out here. He done all his work and was wandering around. Found a racquet somebody had left on the court and started swingin' it. From that day on, it jes seemed like a tennis racquet was part of his arm. If he wudn't packing a shovel or a broom, he was swinging a racquet.

"Mr. Hightower—he owns the department store—give him one of his old ones. I bet he's still got it somewhere too. That racquet meant more to Chance than anything."

Maria was filing all this away in her mind, not wanting to distract or make him uneasy by pulling out her notebook. "How did Mr. Rinehart learn to play tennis?"

"Picked it up on his own—at first. When he finished work, he'd pound that backboard with tennis balls 'til he couldn't hardly stand up. He watched the good players, too. How they swung the racquet. How they moved. The grips they used. Finally some of them give him lessons. Chance could make anybody like him."

"Surely he didn't get to the national championships with a few lessons from club players," Maria remarked, remembering the effortless grace of his strokes and the unshakable concentration in his match with Billy Christmas.

"No ma'am. The club pro saw how good he was. Said he had the most natural ability of anybody he ever saw. I heard him say it." Isaac carefully pronounced his words now, seemingly proud of the vocabulary he had accumulated around the club. "He spent a lot of time with Chance. Took him to tournaments with other clubs. He was some proud when Chance won the nationals in the boys' eighteens."

"Did he go to college?"

"One year. He made the semifinals at the NCAA champion-ships. Then he quit. Took off 'round the world with the Davis Cup team. Then he played the East Coast grass circuit, the National Clay Courts, over in Europe—anywhere he could get in a tournament. I seen him beat Bobby Riggs one time right here on this court." Isaac pointed to the court he had just finished lining.

"That's pretty fast company. Riggs won Forest Hills in '39," Maria smiled.

Isaac collected the string and pushed the hopper back to-ward the shed. "I read in the paper where he played in one of them ex'bition matches in California. Beat Don Budge and Fred Perry on the same day. 'Course that don't happen all the time. I got to go now, Miss Vitrano," he said, closing and locking the shed door.

Maria offered her hand to Paul again. "Well, you've certainly been a big help."

"Glad to do it. You say something good about Chance in that newspaper of yours," he smiled.

Maria stood in the shade of a willow next to the shed watch-ing Paul walk back down the gravel path. Then she slipped a small notebook from her purse and began to write. She finished just in time to see Billy Christmas and Jordan Simms walk across the flagstone terrace and into the clubhouse. *What a handsome couple they make. They look so happy. I hope the general doesn't ruin it for them.*

* * *

The early-budding trees of the Georgia spring were stained a brilliant reddish when Maria parked her rented Ford in front of Liberty High School. She looked down the broad street as the sun settled into the purple hills west of town. It flamed suddenly, as if giving a farewell burst of color to the world, then vanished in a soft, violet glowing of the sky.

Maria hurried up the front walk of the school between the gnarled old cedars, their trunks silvering in the dusk that settled about the grounds. Opening one of the huge double doors, she leaped back through the years as the smell touched her—the book, chalk-dust, and floor-wax smell that old schools have a patent on—

a smell like no other. She saw herself walking down a hall so very much like this one, hearing the voices and seeing the faces of her youth.

The worn and scuffed heart pine boards of the stairs creaked three times as Maria climbed them. She found the room and peered through the half-glass door. A desk lamp provided the only illumination. The man seated at the desk wore his brown hair unfashionably long, touching his collar. His gray tweed jacket hung loosely on his thin shoulders.

Maria tapped softly on the glass. The man looked up from his stack of papers, glancing at the door. He slid the chair back and pushed himself out of it with obvious effort, his right hand on the desk top. As he walked toward the door, she heard the soft slapping sound his right foot made against the wooden floor. In the lamplight and the light shining through the door from the hall, she saw his left arm swing limply at his side.

The door opened. "What can I do for you?"

"Hi. I'm Maria Vitrano. I work for a newspaper in New York, and I think you might have some information that would help me." She offered her hand.

"Leslie Gifford," he said, taking her hand firmly. "Come on in. I can't imagine how I'd be able to help you though. I thought most of the country's newsworthy events were happening in New York —there and Washington."

Maria stared at Gifford. His face had the appearance of youth with its clear, taut skin and smooth features, but the eyes were old. *Old and wise and kind,* she thought, *and with a strange light to them.* He looked as though he had seen the worst the world had to offer and had come away only slightly offended.

"Is something wrong?"

The words startled Maria from her thoughts. "No—nothing. I'm sorry. I didn't mean to stare. It's just that you have such an— interesting face."

"Well, that's probably the only thing you'll find interesting about me," he smiled.

Maria followed him over to the desk. *Why do all the people here seem so unique? They're southerners and I've never been south before, but it has to be more than that. Could it be the slower pace of life? They always seem to have time to talk to people. Even strangers.*

Maybe for the first time in my life I've slowed down enough to truly notice people. Whatever the reason, I hope it lasts awhile.

After pulling a chair over to the desk, Maria explained the purpose of her trip to Liberty.

"Chance was only an average student, but it's a wonder he passed at all. He spent so much time working at the club and later playing so many out-of-town tournaments that he had precious little time left for schoolwork."

"What can you tell me about his family?"

Gifford adjusted himself painfully in his chair. "He was an only child. His daddy left the family shortly after he was born. Passed back through town once in a while, but never saw the boy more than a few hours at a time. His mother died four years ago, right before he left for college. Poor thing. All she ever knew was work."

Maria listened, taking a few notes, but as Gifford spoke she became more interested in him than in the story she was doing. He possessed a kind of strength she had never encountered before. *And a peace,* she thought, *as though he's come to terms with the world.*

One of Maria's favorite poems kept coming to mind, Thomas Hardy's "The Darkling Thrush." She recalled its story of a man at the turn of the century who was "fervorless" in spirit. He heard the joyful song of a thrush, "frail, gaunt and small," burst forth in the dead of winter. She recited the final lines to herself, thinking that they captured perfectly the mystery of Leslie Gifford.

> That I could think there trembled through
>   His happy good-night air
> Some blessed hope, whereof he knew
>   And I was unaware.

Maria finished the interview with Gifford and drove back to her hotel still thinking of his strange, kind eyes and the mysterious light that shone in them. As she reached the stairs to her room, she heard the sound of someone singing and paused to listen. Walking down a side hallway, she saw a small, brightly lit room. Inside, Josephine was folding the day's laundry and singing a song Maria had never heard before. She trembled slightly as she listened.

My Lord, He calls me,
He calls me by the thunder,
The trumpet sounds within-a my soul;
I ain't got long to stay here.

Steal away, steal away, steal away to Jesus,
Steal away, steal away home,
I ain't got long to stay here.

Maria climbed the stairs, listening to the sound of Josephine's singing. It gave her much the same feeling that being with Leslie Gifford had—of being in the presence of someone who had learned to live with the pain and fear of the world—someone who had found joy in the song of a darkling thrush, who had somehow discovered the blessed hope of which she was unaware.

4

DARK MUSIC

She's a real nice lady, Chance. Treated me like I was just as good as anybody else." Isaac Paul tossed him a thick white towel as he stepped from the shower.

Chance walked over to his locker, toweling off and dripping on the concrete floor. "I'm sure she is, and I'm sure she did, Isaac. That's why I'm takin' her for a nice drive this afternoon."

"Where y'all goin'?"

Chance slipped into a pair of sloppy jeans, rolling up the cuffs. "Thought I'd take her out and show her the ol' swimmin' hole."

"Why you dressin' like that?" Paul frowned. "Where's them Sunday britches and nice sweaters you usually wear?"

"I got a feelin' this one is used to good dressers, Isaac." Chance put on a wrinkled white shirt, leaving the long tails hanging out. Sitting down on a long wooden bench, he stepped into a pair of dirty brown-and-white saddle oxfords.

"You look like a high school boy. The mo' messed up they clothes is, the better they like it."

"That's the idea, Isaac. The wide-eyed, innocent schoolboy look. Make her drop her guard." Chance stood up, striking a silver-screen pose. "What do you think?"

Paul picked up Chance's towel from the floor and dropped it into a hamper. "I think you look like Andy Hardy on a bad day. 'Cept you ain't got that innocent look about you like Mickey Rooney does in them movies."

Chance grinned crookedly, walked over to the mirror on the wall, and began combing his wet hair.

Paul sat down on the bench. "Chance, I knowed you for a long time. What you got in mind for Miss Vitrano?"

"Who? Me? Why, just showin' her a good time. Southern hospitality. She's gonna write about me in the paper, ain't she? I want her to say some good things."

"I knowed you a long time," Paul muttered cryptically, his dark liquid eyes holding Chance's.

"Yeah, you have, haven't you?" Chance sat down on the bench next to Paul. "You remember that time ol' Moon Mullins caught you snitchin' a little hooch from his still down by the river?"

"Sho' do," he answered, the hint of a smile on his dark face. "I jist wanted a taste for my granddaddy. He said whiskey with peppermint candy in it was the best thing in the world for a cold. I'd do anything for my granddaddy."

"I can still see the look on Moon's face when I lit that whole string of firecrackers," Chance laughed. "He thought every revenuer in the state was after him."

"He sho' forgot all about me," Paul smiled. "Never thought ol' Moon could run that fast."

"We had some times, didn't we?"

Over the years, Paul had become used to Chance's distractions. "You ain't answered my question."

"I ain't gonna do nothin' terrible, Isaac," he admitted grudgingly. "I just thought she might could help me out a little with the draft board. You know them big city newspapers like she works for carry a lot of weight."

Paul shook his head slowly. "You done tried everything in the world. Ain't no way they gonna defer you. No reason to. You healthy as a mule."

Chance scowled. "I know that. Maybe she could get me into special services or something. They do that for athletes sometimes."

"Why don't you jist go ahead on in and do yore part like ever'body else? We got to whip them Germans and Japs or this world won't be fit to live in."

Chance stood up, pacing back and forth in the locker room. "I ain't tryin' to shirk my responsibility to my country, Isaac. I believe we've got to win this war. I just don't want to give up everything I've worked for all these years."

Paul remained silent, staring at the wet floor.

"You see that, don't you? You know what it is to be poor. Well, tennis is my ticket out of this two-bit town where everybody knows what I come from. I got a chance to make the big time. But what happens if I lose an arm or a leg? It's the end of everything."

"I don't reckon your leg's worth more than anybody else's. Jist muscle and bone far as I can tell."

"I don't see you rushin' off to join up." Chance stopped pacing and glared at his friend.

Paul glanced up from the floor. "Went down two months ago. They said I was too short."

"Too short?"

"Yeah. Sergeant said they'd let me know if they decided to form a midget brigade."

Chance sat back down. "What do you want to go off to war for anyhow? You got a wife and two boys to take care of. How would they get along?"

"Allotment checks."

"That ain't enough for a family."

"It is when you come up like we done. Poor as Job's turkey. You oughta know. That little shack you and yore mama lived in wudn't no bigger than ours." Paul got up, took a mop from a bucket against the wall, and began mopping the floor furiously.

"You mad at me?" Chance looked sheepishly at Paul.

He mopped harder.

"Midget brigade, huh?" Chance smiled.

The edges of Paul's mouth turned up slightly. He stopped working and leaned on the mop. "That's what the man said."

"I can see it now." Chance stood at attention and saluted. "Mickey Rooney, Eddie Arcaro, Mayor Sinclair—and you."

"It jist might work," Paul chuckled.

"What do you mean?"

"Them Japs probably laugh theyselves to death if they seen *us* comin' at 'em."

Chance picked up his racquets and bag from the floor in front of his locker. "You still like me?"

Paul smiled. "We been friends too long for me to quit on you now. 'Sides, who else could put up with you?"

* * *

"Where does a tennis bum get money for a car like this? I

thought you were still on amateur status." Maria sat next to Chance as he drove his 1938 Buick Century along the blacktop just outside of town. A convertible, the car was pale yellow, long, and sleek.

Chance grinned sideways at her. "There's always ways to make a little spending money. Everybody on the tour does it. A little extra added to expenses here and there—you know. Then you have the—ah, ardent fans I guess you'd call them, who just love us boys in white. They sometimes drop a little cash on us."

"These ardent fans," Maria remarked slyly, "are they of the female persuasion?"

Chance laughed, turning his eyes to the road. "I'll never be able to pull anything on a big-city girl like you. I can see that now."

"You mean something like dressing up in that little boy outfit?" Maria teased.

The smile left Chance's face. "What are you talkin' about—little boy outfit?"

"It's really charming, but I doubt it's your usual getup. I picture you more as the slacks-and-sweater type."

This dame's got brains. I may have to do something drastic with her—like come right out and tell the truth. "Well, I have to admit I'm a little more casual than normal."

I'll bet you have an act for every occasion, Maria gazed at his patrician profile, his startlingly sun-bleached hair, and tanned skin against the white shirt. *Usually get away with it, too, I imagine.*

Chance pulled into the gravel parking lot of Three Corners Grocery. It stood on an interstice where a gravel road angled into the main highway. Constructed of rough-cut one-by-twelve planks, it was home to a red, gravity-fed Texaco pump—a Grove's Chill Tonic sign that vowed to fight malaria, colds, chills, and fever—a red-and-white Coca-Cola sign inviting them to try a drink that was "Delicious and Refreshing"—and a scattering of Prince Albert, Nehi, Camels, and other signs tacked to the building.

"Why are we stopping here?" Maria listened to the lonesome sound of the March wind sighing high in the tops of two massive pines that flanked the store. "I thought you were going to show me one of the town's landmarks."

"I aim to do just that if you'll hold your horses. We don't have a rush hour down here," he scolded her good-naturedly. "You're about to experience the true flavor of the South."

Chance went into the store, returning in a few minutes with a brown paper bag.

"What do you have there?" she asked.

"You'll find out soon enough."

They sped along the gravel road with rocks pinging off the bottom of the Buick and turned into a parking area that was nothing more than a small clearing at the side of the road. Ten minutes later, after walking down a leaf-strewn path through the hardwood forest, they came to the river.

"Why it's lovely," she almost gasped. "So pristine."

"Yeah, that's what it is all right—*pristine*," he agreed. "I thought you needed to see it if you want to learn something about the South. Every little southern town has one. The ol' swimmin' hole."

Maria was enchanted by the place. She stood on a beach of white sand littered with dry winter leaves. The clear, green water of the river sparkled in the sunlight, moving almost imperceptibly between the beach and a twenty-five-foot rocky bluff on the far side. To her right, the river shallowed, splashing over rocks and fallen trees with a musical, tinkling sound.

Chance scrunched upriver through the sand, carrying his grocery bag. Following him, Maria saw a huge boulder protruding from the sandy slope at the upper end of the beach. It curved smoothly upward, flattening at the base of a massive live oak, whose branches spread far out over the water. Sitting areas of natural stone were formed with parts of the boulder and the trunk of the live oak as backrests.

Sitting down on the cool stone, he watched her walk toward him with her pleated skirt swinging about her shapely calves. The rose-colored sweater curved softly toward her slim waist, complimenting her pale skin, dark eyes, and hair.

"You're in for a real treat now," he grinned.

"Better than all this?" she replied, sweeping her hand toward the beauty of the river and the woods.

"Different." He took two bottles of R.C. Cola from the bag. Laying the bottle caps against a sharp rock edge, he popped them off by striking them sharply with the heel of his hand. Offering one to Maria, he brought out the two remaining items.

She lifted the smooth, wet bottle to her lips, taking a big

swallow. "I have to be honest with you, Chance. My father sells these in his store. I prefer Coke."

"Bet you never had one of these." He handed her a round chocolate-covered cake in a cellophane wrapper.

"Moon Pie?" she read on the wrapper. "I thought that was something out of southern fiction."

"Try it."

She unwrapped the cake, took a small bite, and chewed thoughtfully.

"Well, how do you like it?"

Chewing a few more seconds, she swallowed. "Tastes like a chocolate candle."

He frowned. "You Yankees got no appreciation of the finer things in life."

"Guess we can't all have your sophisticated palate," she laughed.

Maria stood up and walked over to the edge of the boulder where it dropped off in a sheer wall of rock to the river. She could smell the water, the damp sand, and the fecund scent of decaying leaves from the forest floor.

Spotting a darker shadow beneath the shadow the boulder cast on the river, she watched it waver slightly in the current. A few feet downriver, where a swatch of sunlight blazed through the trees, she saw a redear bream gleaming in the watery brightness, its gills opening and closing slowly. The shadow streaked into the sunlight and just as suddenly disappeared, leaving a swirling on the surface of the river. The bream had vanished.

"You forgot this."

Startled, Maria flinched at the touch of Chance's hand on her shoulder. "Goodness," she gasped.

"Didn't mean to scare you," he said, handing her the R.C. "You sure were thinking mighty hard."

"Just lost in the beauty of the place, I guess." She stepped over to the base of the live oak, sat down, and leaned back against it. "It's so peaceful here."

"I bet you got a lot of important connections working on that big newspaper, don't you?" Chance asked.

Uh oh! Here it comes. So much for peace and quiet. "A few, I guess. Why do you ask?"

"Well, I kinda got a problem," he smiled sheepishly, glancing at Maria.

"Maybe you should see a priest."

Chance looked puzzled, then threw his head back and laughed out loud. "It's not that kind of problem, Babe—uh, Maria."

"Just what kind is it?" she asked, gazing intently into the smoke-blue eyes that affected her in a way she had to struggle with, in spite of knowing what was coming next.

"It's—uh, with the draft board."

"I could have guessed it was something like that."

Chance held his open hands out in front of him. "Oh, don't get me wrong. I want to serve my country as much as anybody. It's just that I don't want to waste all my training and experience. Special services is where I could do the best job."

"My only brother died at Pearl Harbor, Chance."

"I'm sorry to hear that."

"I don't say that just in passing," Maria declared bluntly. "It's to let you know how I feel about men who shirk their duty to this country—especially now!"

"I'm not tryin' to shirk my . . ."

"I think we've said all that's necessary about this matter," Maria interrupted. She saw a dark anger flicker for a moment in the depths of his blue eyes—then vanish.

"You're right," he said cheerfully, his easygoing nature back at the forefront. "Why ruin such a beautiful day?"

They walked along the river, Chance telling Maria the names of the trees and plants, showing her the trails and burrows of small animals. They came to a beaver dam and he pointed out the entrance to their home just below the water level.

"They dig their homes back under the bank after the dam raises the level of the water," he explained. "Out west they build lodges out in the middle of their ponds."

"That's the kind I've seen pictures of." Maria let him take her hand as they walked.

"I hope I didn't upset you back there. I had no way of knowing about your brother."

"No. It's all right. Let's just forget about it."

They walked back to the beach and stood together listening to the murmur of the river. The wind made a sibilant sound as it moved high above them in the crowns of the trees.

Chance encircled Maria's waist with his arm, tilting her chin back with the tips of his fingers. His smile was too perfect, the smoke-blue eyes too consuming.

Maria felt desire rising in her, coursing through her like dark music. "No!"

"What's wrong?"

"I never kiss on a first date."

Chance stepped back, slipping into his disarming smile. "You're kidding?"

"I have a very old-fashioned father." Maria took a deep breath. "It's the way I was brought up, and I'm not planning to change things now."

"I didn't mean to offend you, Maria. I didn't think one little kiss would . . ." His face changed slowly, clouding over. "We're still friends, aren't we?"

Maria thought of the small bream shimmering brightly in the sunlight—and of the great, lurking shadow. "Sure, Chance. We're still friends."

*   *   *

Chance walked along the gravel path that led to the rear of the two-story clubhouse. He noticed Billy Christmas rallying with Jordan Simms on the court near the ivy-covered wall. Jordan's tennis skirt bounced with her fluid motion about the court, the late sunlight flashing on her smoothly muscled thighs. *Attaboy, Billy. You got yourself a real looker there.*

Gathering the mail from his box at the foot of the stairs, he climbed to the small apartment he occupied rent-free for lending his name as the traveling pro for the Pine Hills Country Club, even though he was officially an amateur. As he thumbed through his mail, he found a letter marked *Selective Service*. He tore it open and read for a few seconds. Then he crumpled it into a ball and flung it across the room, muttering under his breath.

In the tiny kitchen, he took a bottle of Scotch from the cabinet and popped the cork. Pouring a water glass half-full, he walked to his balcony that looked down on the courts. From below came the metronomic sounds of the game. *Pock. Pock. Pock.*

Four hours later, Chance bumped across the rutted parking lot in front of Shorty's Saloon. Leaving the lights on, he stepped out of his car, directly into a mudhole, and fell flat on his face. He rolled over on his back, staring up into the night sky. The crescent moon sailed slowly across the sky on its back. "Looks like a martini glass without the stem," he giggled out loud.

A middle-aged man in a Stetson hat and overalls stepped out of the saloon. As he walked over to his Model T pickup, he almost stepped on Chance. Jumping back, he roared, "What in thunderation you doin' layin' down there in the gravel?"

Chance smiled pleasantly up at him. "I'm studyin' the stars—for my astronomy class."

"Yore what?"

"Astronomy class. You oughta try it. It's pleasant lying down here next to this mudhole. You get a different perspective on things." Chance giggled again.

"You plumb crazy!" The man stalked off toward his truck, muttering under his breath.

In a few minutes, Chance struggled to his feet and started toward Shorty's front door. "That's just what I needed. I feel much better now," he mumbled to the ancient cedar leaning crookedly away from the corner of the building. He opened his mouth to speak, gagged instead, and vomited onto the gravel.

A boy of sixteen, barefoot and hollow-eyed, walked out the front door. He stared at the white-haired man on his hands and knees, made a sound of disgust, and hurried off toward the road.

Chance called out to him. "Hey! I don't usually do this. Jes lost a bet. That's all." He got to his feet again. "Now that's what I *really* needed. Got room for some more now."

Pausing at the door, Chance noticed something glinting in the pallid light of the moon. Leaning close to the wall, he saw that a knife blade had been driven directly through the center of the metal Pabst Blue Ribbon sign. He grasped it with both hands, pulling with all his might, but it remained solid.

Three men sat at the bar inside Shorty's. One was unconscious. He slumped at the far end, his face flattened against the rough surface. Ragged breaths escaped his open mouth, which was partly covered by the bill of a red baseball cap that had twisted around on his head.

Shorty, who stood more than six feet tall, had come around from behind the bar and sat on a stool. His eyes were large and pale like those of fish who spend their lives in underground lakes. He turned toward the door as Chance entered. "Well, I'll be. Chance Rinehart. You slummin' ain't you, boy?"

Earl Logan sat next to Shorty, his overalls sweat-stained and greasy from a day of hauling pulpwood. His dark eyes followed Shorty's. "Hey, Chance. How you doin'?"

"Hey boys. Shorty, ain't you got somethin' on that jukebox besides Jimmie Rodgers? I'm tired of listenin' to his songs about lovin' mamas and lost women."

"You can't be *too* tired of it, Chance," Shorty snorted. "You ain't been here in more'n a year."

Chance stumbled across the sawdust-covered dirt floor to the jukebox. Glowing softly in the gloom, it stood on a small platform of scrap lumber. He leaned on it for a few minutes, scanning the titles. "Ain't nothin' on there worth hearin'."

Earl glanced at Chance's clothes, wet and muddy from his escapade in the parking lot. "I seen you lookin' better than this, Chance. You been in a fight?"

"Yeah," he mumbled. "With my uncle."

"Didn't know you had one."

"Oh, yeah. My Uncle Sam. He whupped me good," Chance grinned, plopping down on the stool next to Logan.

"How 'bout a beer?" Shorty asked, standing up to go back behind the bar.

"Yeah. What's that you're drinkin', Earl?"

"R.C." Earl muttered, looking away with irritation etched on his craggy face. The kidding he had taken since he quit drinking was taking its toll on his patience.

"Earl Logan drinkin' R.C.?" Chance goaded. "This'll make the front page of ever' newspaper in the country. Hey, Shorty, what do you think about this?"

Shorty took a dark bottle of Pabst from the galvanized washtub on the floor behind the bar. "I think it's Earl's business. That's what I think, Chance."

Chance grabbed the wet bottle from Shorty. Turning it up, he drained half of it before he put it down. "How's that war hero son of yours, Earl?"

"Ben's fine."

"I bet they got him mixed up with somebody else. He wasn't nothing but a skinny little punk in school." Chance's face was twisted with liquor and an undefined rage that sought to vent itself on anybody close at hand. "How could he be a hero?"

Earl Logan's lips grew thin and white, his jaw muscles working beneath the weathered skin. "You're drunk, Chance. Why don't you go home and sleep it off?"

Chance finished the beer. "Why don't you try and make me, you pious drunk?"

Shorty eased a black, leather-covered sap from the back pocket of his khakis. Taking one step, he leaned over the bar and thunked Chance behind his right ear.

The light went out in Chance's eyes like someone had thrown a switch. He slid off the stool, crumpling on the sawdust-and-cigarette-butt-covered floor.

"You didn't have to do that for me, Shorty," Logan muttered, gazing down at the limp form at the foot of his stool.

"I didn't," Shorty grinned. "I did it for me. I want Chance in good enough shape to get drafted."

5

FUNERAL

Maria was driving along the gravel road that led up into the hills, gazing out across the hazy blue valley when it happened. The black coupe suddenly felt as if it had broken free of the earth and was skidding sideways on a cushion of air. Without thinking, she hit the brakes and grabbed tightly onto the steering wheel, wrestling with it as she tried to regain control of the car. Abruptly, it began to spin as it careened toward the edge of the road and a steep precipice just beyond. She eased off the brakes and turned the steering wheel into the spin.

A sense of relief washed over her as the car straightened and angled toward the red clay bluff on the opposite side of the road—away from that same deep valley she had been viewing with such pleasure. The car slowed markedly before the left rear wheel dropped off the roadbed into a ditch at the foot of the bluff, bringing it to a stop.

Slumped over the steering wheel, Maria breathed deeply. She listened to the slight humming of the right front wheel as it slowly spun on its axle, lifted off the road by the angle of the car. When she felt in control of herself, she climbed out the passenger door. Walking across the road, she stood at the edge and stared down at the tops of the trees a hundred feet below. A red-tailed hawk, glinting faintly in the smoky blue light, sailed across the valley.

From down the road the tires-on-gravel sound Maria had come to regard as a kind of southern anthem brought her hurrying back to the rented coupe. A mud-splattered Model T clattered into sight from around the bend, pulled over on the narrow shoulder, and stopped behind her car.

The man getting out of the Model T had broad shoulders and a black mail-order suit with matching tie. He walked toward Maria's car, saying, "You're not hurt are you, miss?"

"No—no, I'm fine."

"Looks like you could use a friend." He smiled warmly, squatting down to take a look under the car.

"I think you're right." *He looks a lot like Henry Fonda.* Maria watched him inspect the underside of the car, balanced on his hands and the toes of his heavy-soled shoes.

"I don't think you hurt it too bad," he remarked, brushing the red grit from his hands.

Not quite as tall as Fonda, she thought, *and with a lot more muscles.* "Can you get it out of the ditch for me?"

"'Fraid not. We're gonna have to get a wrecker for that." He pointed to his homely little Model T, still clattering noisily at the side of the road. "That thing wouldn't pull a hat off your head."

Maria smiled at the unfamiliar expression. "Can you give me a lift to the closest mechanic shop?"

"Be glad to—after I preach the funeral. You're welcome to ride along with me."

"You're a minister?"

"There's some might disagree with you. Name's Jesse Boone." He offered her his hand and a warm smile.

"Jesse Boone," Maria echoed, taking his hand. "You're the man I came up here to find."

Boone observed the attractive young woman closely, trying to remember where he had met her. As a pastor, he had tried to train himself to remember names and latch them onto faces. "I'm sorry, but I can't seem to place you."

"Oh, we've never met," she explained. "J. T. Dickerson told me about you."

"J.T.? I haven't seen him in ages," he frowned. "Well, you'll have to explain all this to me on the way. Wouldn't do to have the preacher showin' up late."

"Is there—maybe some place you could drop me off where I could wait for you?" Maria asked awkwardly, following him back to his car. "I'm not much for funerals."

"Sorry. Nothin' but hills and creek bottoms between here and the church."

She sighed deeply and climbed into the sturdy-looking little car. On the way to the funeral, she explained the purpose of her visit to Liberty.

"Well, I still can't see why folks in New York City would want to read about me—Chance maybe, but not me. Anyhow, I'll do what I can to help you out."

"I sure appreciate it."

He gazed around him at the hills and valleys they were traveling through. "If you want to learn about the rural South, though, you're in the right place."

"What denomination are you?" Maria asked, trying to make polite conversation.

His eyes, dark and deep-set, came alive as he glanced over at her. "I'm not."

"You're not what?"

"Not in a denomination."

"What are you then?"

"I guess you'd call us a body of believers serving the Lord," he explained. "We're not affiliated with any of the mainline churches. Most of them call us holy rollers—when they're feeling especially benevolent, that is."

Maria felt uneasy, as though she were traveling through unfamiliar country without a guide or compass. "Well, I think people should be free to worship as they please—as long as they don't try to force their religion on someone else."

A short time later, they turned off the gravel road onto a narrow dirt lane rutted with wagon and automobile tracks. Passing through a stand of pines, the tires of the Model T whispered over the carpet their needles made as they angled down the side of a hill into a glade. A white-washed, clapboard church stood next to a clear creek that meandered through the woods. Several wagons and buggies, two ancient pickups, and a Model T very much like Boone's were parked near a sweet-gum thicket. Down by the creek, horses and mules, tied to trees with plow lines, grazed in a meadow lush with new growth.

One of the mules lifted its head and brayed at the sound of the Model T.

"He's aggravated at us for disturbing his meal," Boone smiled, parking next to one of the wagons.

59

"I never heard a horse make a sound like that," Maria frowned. "Is it safe to get out?"

Boone grabbed his brown leather Bible from the seat and got out of the car. "First of all, that's not a horse. It's a mule. And, yes, it's safe to get out."

She walked with him over to the tiny church, taking him by the arm before he reached the front steps. "Do I have to do anything special? I've only been to one funeral in my life."

"Try not to go to sleep during my sermon," he smiled, leading her up the steps. *The good sisters are gonna just love me bringing you in the church house wearing that short skirt.*

Maria followed Boone inside, thinking it irreverent of him to make jokes in the presence of death. *What kind of a minister can find humor at a funeral? He must not take his religion very seriously. Maybe he's only doing it until he can find something better.*

A dozen or so adults and three children were seated on the narrow, crudely built pews. The men wore khakis and work coats with no ties. Though they were plain in appearance, Maria thought them prettier than the women who had on long, drab dresses with long sleeves and high necks. They all wore their hair up in buns and were completely devoid of makeup and jewelry. She noticed too that all but one were as round as butterballs.

Maria took a seat on the back row next to the aisle as Boone made his way to the small raised pulpit at the front of the church. He greeted the people with handshakes and hugs, pausing to sit down next to a white-haired man on the front row. The man looked to be in his seventies. His overalls and red plaid shirt were neatly pressed. After speaking with the man a few minutes, Boone took his place at the pulpit.

A plain pine coffin in front of the pulpit rested on two sawhorses. Spattered with paint, they were covered with saw marks like old wounds that wouldn't heal.

Boone smiled out at his abbreviated congregation. "Sister Mattie Collins has just started to live forever in her brand new life. She's not looking through that glass darkly anymore—like we are. Now she sees Him face to face."

A few subdued amens sounded in the small building.

"Brother Collins, all her pain is gone," Boone continued, looking directly at the white-haired man on the front row. "And Jesus has wiped away her tears."

"That's right, Preacher," Collins responded, standing to his feet and lifting his left hand above his head. After a few seconds, he sat back down, his eyes toward the ceiling.

Boone motioned to a red-haired young woman on the front row. She walked across the bare pine floor to an old upright piano at the left of the pulpit. Maria noticed that she was the only one of the women under thirty years and 180 pounds. Lifting his hands, Boone began to sing in a rich, soft baritone. Although the piano was slightly off key, he held to the melody. The people rose and joined in.

> We are often destitute
> Of the things that life demands,
> Want of food and want of shelter
> Thirsty hills and barren lands,
> We are trusting in the Lord,
> And according to His word,
> We will understand it better by and by.
>
> By and by when the morning comes,
> When the saints of God are gathered home
> We'll tell the story how we've overcome
> For we'll understand it better by and by.

Maria stood with the others as she looked around for a hymnal. Seeing there were none, she tried to mouth the words until the second time they sang the chorus. After singing another hymn, which she also hadn't heard before, everyone sat down.

Leaning informally on the lectern, Boone spoke of the life of Mattie Collins. Of the love she had shared with her husband and the blessing she had been to her neighbors and friends. He told of how, not being able to have children of their own, they had taken so many into their home over the years and given them shelter and food and love. And finally he spoke of a faith that burned bright in the face of death.

Boone opened his big Bible and continued, glancing only once at the page. "'Let not your heart be troubled: ye believe in God, believe also in me. In my Father's house are many mansions: if it were not so, I would have told you. I go to prepare a place for you. And if I go and prepare a place for you, I will come again, and receive you unto myself; that where I am, there ye may be also.'"

Looking up, he appeared almost transformed—somehow taller with a kind of brightness different from the morning sun that streamed through the windows. "How many of you can truly say you are ready to follow Mattie Collins into a pine box like this one when the Death Angel passes your way? Follow her into that cold, dark ground and have somebody shovel the dirt in on top of you?"

Looking at the crude coffin, Maria shuddered.

Most of the congregation raised their hands.

"I pray that you all are. None of us knows the hour of his death, but we all know that somewhere out there—Death has each of our names written down in his appointment book."

Maria trembled on the hard bench in the back of the little church in the Georgia hills and felt a wall of darkness separate her from the rest of the world. She thought of the times she had sat on brass-trimmed pews of gleaming mahogany in the churches of New York with their massive stone spires and stained-glass windows—had remained emotionless and unaffected through so many services. Listening now to this simple and uneducated preacher, she found herself no longer unaffected.

"Beloved, there is another book. It's called the Lamb's Book of Life. And your name can be written there." Boone turned toward the back of his Bible, the pages rustling in the stillness of the church.

Maria noticed that the white-haired man on the front row was standing, both arms lifted toward the heavens.

"'And I saw the dead, small and great, stand before God; and the books were opened: and another book was opened, which is the book of life: and the dead were judged out of those things which were written in the books, according to their works. . . . And death and hell were cast into the lake of fire. This is the second death. And whosoever was not found written in the book of life was cast into the lake of fire.'"

"None of you has to die this second death. God's Word tells us that all of us have sinned and that 'the wages of sin is death; but the gift of God is eternal life through Jesus Christ our Lord.'"

Tears filled Maria's eyes. She bowed her head so no one would see, wiping them away with her handkerchief.

Boone closed his Bible, gazing at each person in turn. "There's no other path to eternal life. 'For there is none other name under heaven given among men, whereby we must be saved.' Jesus Christ was born the only begotten Son of God. He died, was buried, and rose again on the third day. If you believe this in your heart and confess Jesus as your Savior, you have eternal life."

Boone stepped away from the pulpit, his Bible clasped in his left hand. "Come to Jesus now. It may be the last chance you'll have." He began to pace slowly back and forth as the sound of the piano filled the church, bringing the people to their feet.

> Just as I am, without one plea,
> But that Thy blood was shed for me,
> And that Thou bid'st me come to Thee,
> Oh Lamb of God, I come! I come!

Maria stood to her feet, grasping the bench in front of her for support. She felt as though she would faint. Boone stopped his pacing and looked directly at her—for just a moment—then continued. *He knows*, she thought. *He knows.* She wanted to sing, but the words wouldn't come. She felt herself in a howling darkness with a sound like a great and terrible wind blowing.

> Fighting within and fears without,
> Oh Lamb of God, I come! I come!

While the people went down to take a last look at Mattie Collins and to comfort her husband, Maria slipped outside. The sunlight fell on her in a shower of brightness that held no warmth. A mile above her, a vulture rode the thermals, ever widening the circles in its search for the abandoned dead.

Maria walked over to Boone's car and sat on the running board, shivering with a sudden chill. *There must be an explanation for this. It must be the onset of some kind of depressive state. Guess I'll end up in analysis like most of my friends. Never thought it would happen to me. Can't think of that now. I've got a job to do.*

* * *

"Miss Vitrano, I'd like you to meet Cora Prentiss," Boone smiled as he walked over to where Maria sat on the couch.

"How do you do," Maria greeted her cordially, extending her hand toward the red-haired piano player from the church. She had met the others who had come to the home of Abner Collins after the funeral. Cora had gone out of her way to avoid Maria.

"I'm mighty pleased to meet you, Miss Victrola," Cora lied, staring deliberately at Maria's short dress, lipstick, and earrings. "I've got to help out in the kitchen, Jesse. Always work to be done and precious few to do it."

Jesse watched her go, then turned to Maria. "She's not much of a talker. Good woman though."

"You'll have to teach her to be more sociable when y'all get married, Preacher." Abner Collins sat next to Maria on the couch in his small living room. Several logs in the fireplace glowed brightly, warding off the morning chill that had lingered in the house.

"I reckon so, Brother Collins." Jesse smiled sheepishly at Maria, ambling off toward a table laden with baked goods and dishes of vegetables and meats.

"You enjoyin' your visit to the South, Miss Vitrano?" Collins's faded blue eyes held a gentle light.

Maria liked Abner Collins from the moment he first spoke to her. His genuine warmth was unmistakable. "Yes, I am, Mr. Collins. It's much different than what I expected."

"What *did* you expect?"

"Oh, I don't know. I thought it would be more—it's hard to put into words."

"Backward?" Collins smiled. "Most folks I've met from up north think there's only two kinds of southerners. A few rich ones like Rhett Butler, and the rest dirt farmers livin' in shacks or holler trees."

Maria laughed. "I didn't think it was exactly like that, but you're not too far off."

"Well, up here in these hills, I 'spect you'll find the people about as poor as any in this part of the state."

"I admire that love seat with the carved armrests," Maria remarked, glancing about the room at the dark, heavy antique furniture. "You look like you're living pretty comfortably."

"You might change yore tune after a few trips to the outhouse on them January mornings," Collins smiled, a twinkle coming to his wise old eyes.

"I expect you're right about that," Maria laughed. "You don't have electricity, do you?"

"Nope. And we use stove wood for cookin'. But I wouldn't trade livin' up here for anything."

Maria noticed that Collins hadn't spoken of his wife at all. "Mrs. Collins must have been a wonderful woman from the way Jes—from the way Reverend Boone spoke of her."

Collins looked over his shoulder to the table where Jesse was shoveling down black-eyed peas and ham hocks. "Preachers say ever'body's wonderful when they're dead. But that one preached the gospel about my wife today. He was one of the orphans she took in this house."

"You raised him?" Maria asked in surprise.

Collins shook his head. "No. Like most of the others, we kept him about six months before we found somebody to adopt him. I think he turned out pretty good."

Maria set the plate holding a piece of pound cake down on the end table and glanced at Jesse. "Seems to be a fine man. Where did he go to seminary?"

"In that little cabin of his I reckon," Collins answered with a grin. "Oh, he graduated from Liberty High School, but Jesse wasn't educated into the ministry—he was called to it."

"Called to it?" Maria saw the robed and collared men she had listened to in the churches of New York—back in the days when she went to church. She remembered their credentials in gilded frames hanging on the walls of their tastefully decorated studies. And she thought of one rainy afternoon in one of those offices when she was sixteen and believed what pastors spoke from the pulpit.

"Yes ma'am," Collins answered almost defensively. "A preacher don't 'mount to much if he ain't called by God—not spiritually anyway. He might make it big in the eyes of the world. And there's plenty that love the praise of men better than the praise of God."

* * *

"No wonder you don't want to live anywhere else." Maria gazed out over the purple haze of the evening hills and down into the deep valley directly below. She could see the quicksilver stream glinting through the trees now and then as it wandered along the valley floor.

Jesse sat down on the railing of his back porch, leaning back against a post. "Electricity and indoor plumbing ain't much to give up to have all this."

Maria squatted down and scratched the little brown-and-white beagle behind his floppy ears. "What's his name?"

"Mordecai," he smiled. "I call him that 'cause he's as stubborn as that old Jew in the Bible was."

The dog was moaning with pleasure now, his eyes closed. Maria patted him three times on the back and stood up. "I had a yellow cat named Daisy when I was in grade school. I was very special to her. She wouldn't scratch anyone but me."

He laughed. "I never did cotton much to cats. Never could figure out what they was thinkin'."

Maria found herself becoming quite comfortable with Jesse Boone and his primitive surroundings. "I really appreciate your taking the time to help me, Jesse."

"Nothin' to it." He caught himself staring at Maria and quickly looked away. "I remember when I first took over the church. I hadn't been out of high school but a couple of years. Scared! I didn't know where to turn."

"How did you handle it?"

"I didn't. Abner Collins did it for me."

"What did he do? Work some kind of miracle?" She hoisted herself up on the rail opposite his.

"No. He did a very simple thing."

Mordecai reared up on the rail, his front paws next to Maria. She began to scratch his ears again.

"We got in his old pickup and rode over to the church. That was before I bought the Model T." He gazed at the hawk that was climbing higher above the valley.

"I kind of like that old car, Jesse," Maria interjected. "It's got character."

"If you call character breakin' down every time I really need to be somewhere, I guess it does."

The ear scratching ended, and Mordecai ambled toward the back door and plopped down on a straw mat.

"Brother Collins and me got out at the church and walked around the grounds for a few minutes. The whole time I was telling him how scared I was and that I didn't have any business bein' a pastor. He never said a word.

"Then we went inside. By this time I just *knew* he thought the same thing I did. I was in the *wrong* business!

"Well, Brother Collins stood there lookin' down the aisle of that little church, his hands in the pockets of his overalls. He looked right at me and said, 'I'm glad we got us a new pastor. Sometimes it takes new blood to bring life back to a church.'

"I didn't know what to think after he said that. All I could say was, 'But, Brother Collins, what do I do now?' He looked back down the aisle. 'Well, Preacher, the first thing you gotta do is get yore benches straight.' Then he turned around and walked out the door."

Maria's eyes narrowed in thought. "I don't understand."

"I didn't either—at first. So I just started straightening the benches. When I was almost finished, a woman came in wantin' me to come pray for her sick husband."

Listening intently, Maria tried to figure out what straightening benches had to do with becoming a preacher.

"Well," Jesse continued, "Brother Collins took me to their house, and on the way back home a man flagged us down on the road. He said his wife had locked him out of the house and would I come see what I could do with her."

Maria finished the story for him. "And pretty soon you were so busy *being* a pastor you forgot you didn't *know* how to be a pastor."

"Exactly."

"I think your friend, Mr. Collins, is a wise man."

"Yes, he is." Jesse slipped off the rail and walked down to the end of the porch.

Maria followed him. "What do you think the draft board will do about your application as a chaplain?"

He turned around, his face dark in the growing gloom. "Probably deny it. They frown on independent churches like ours. You have to be ordained by one of the big denominations to have any real chance of being a chaplain."

"Will you fight if they draft you?"

"You cut right to the heart of it, don't you? I like that." He folded his arms across his chest. "I just don't know yet. I hope God gives me an answer soon. Some of the church folks think I oughta go to jail rather than fight."

"How do you feel about that?"

"It don't set right with me. These heathens have got to be stopped to make the world safe for God-fearin' people." He looked out over the valley again. The sun had dropped behind the hills leaving the sky bathed in shades of violet and rose.

Maria placed her hand on his shoulder, feeling the solid layer of muscle. "I'm sure you'll make the right decision."

6

THE PICTURE SHOW

*J*esse walked out of the Liberty Theater next to Maria, glancing about him, hoping he wouldn't see anyone he knew. "That feller, Humphrey—what's his name?"

"Hey there, Preacher. I didn't know you went to dens of iniquity like the Liberty Theater."

Jesse's face reddened as he turned to face Bonner Ridgeway, the high school football coach. "Well, I, uh—it's my first time. Miss Vitrano here asked me to go with her." He turned nervously toward Maria. "Maria Vitrano, this is Bonner Ridgeway. Maria is a newspaper reporter from New York."

"Hmm . . . I see," Ridgeway smirked, looking from Maria's pale yellow sweater down to her brown high heels. His bulk dwarfed her as he gazed down, his scalp showing whitely beneath the crew-cut blond hair in the marquee lights. "I heard about a reporter being in town, but I didn't know she was so pretty."

"Nice to meet you, Mr. Ridgeway." Maria held Ridgeway's stare until he looked away at Jesse.

"My friends just call me Coach, don't they, Preacher?" Ridgeway folded his massive arms across his chest. "By the way, how's Cora? Haven't seen her for a while."

"She's fine."

Maria saw Jesse's obvious discomfort. "Well, we have to be going now. Nice meeting you, Mr. Ridgeway." She turned her back on Ridgeway's frown, taking Jesse by the arm.

As they walked along the sidewalk in the thinning crowd, she said reassuringly, "Don't let him bother you. You haven't done anything to be ashamed of."

69

Jesse's eyes narrowed in thought. "I don't know. The Bible says to come out and be separate from the world. I was brought up to believe that the picture show wasn't good for nothing but to lead people down the wrong path."

"Well, did you see anything you thought was sinful in that movie?" she smiled, trying to ease the tension.

"Drinkin' and smokin' I reckon. But I see that ever' time I come to town. I'd have to stay up in the hills all the time to get away from that, and there's some that do it up there. Especially drinkin'—they'd make the people in that movie look like teetotalers the way they guzzle that corn liquor."

Maria laughed. "See, there wasn't anything you don't already see in real life."

"Bogart." Jesse snapped his fingers. "I remember his name now. He wasn't too bad—for a saloon owner anyway."

"How'd you like Ingrid Bergman? I think she's just about my favorite actress."

"Pretty," Jesse remarked. "But what I liked the most was the music. 'The fundamental things apply, as time goes by,'" he sang softly. "That's a pretty song."

He's got the nicest voice. With a little training, he might make it professionally. "I like your voice, Jesse. You never miss a note and you know how to handle the lyrics."

"You're just bein' nice, but it's good to hear anyway," he said awkwardly. "I never sang anything but hymns. I sure do like the song from that movie though, especially the words."

"Can we go somewhere and get something to drink? That salty popcorn's still got me thirsty."

"Sure thing. Ollie's drugstore is just around the corner. I 'spect he's still open."

They strolled along the sidewalk as the chill settled into the damp night air. Maria's heels clicked a slow staccato rhythm as he whistled the theme from *Casablanca*. The lights on the front porches of the houses were winking out, leaving in their absence a clearer view of the lights in the heavens. A dog barked in someone's backyard; a few bars of "Don't Sit under the Apple Tree" by the Andrews Sisters drifted from an open window.

Maria noticed Jesse's suit, exactly like the one he had worn at the funeral, except it was gray. *I wonder what he'd look like in different*

70

clothes. *He wears these cheap ones so well, I bet he'd be so handsome. He walks like he knows exactly where he's going. That little cleft in his chin is fascinating.*

"Well, this is Ollie's," he announced, opening the heavy glass door for Maria. "I bet he's in back filling prescriptions. Hey, anybody here?"

A man in black trousers, bow tie, and a white apron stepped through a door that opened into the soda fountain area. His short brown hair was almost the same color as his eyes. "Jesse Boone! Who drug you down out of them hills?"

"I guess you'd have to blame Maria here." He introduced her to Ollie Caston, explaining why she had come to Liberty.

"Well, we're proud to have you visit our little town, Miss Vitrano," Ollie greeted her cheerfully.

"I'm enjoying myself. Jesse—and Chance Rinehart too—have been a big help to me," Maria smiled.

"What can I get for you folks?" Ollie asked, wiping his hands on the apron.

"Fountain Coke for me," Maria replied, taking the place in from its gleaming black-and-white tile floor to its marble-topped tables and counter.

They took their Cokes to the last booth against the wall opposite the soda fountain. Maria stood before the jukebox, punching three songs in before she sat down. Harry James began to play "You Made Me Love You" as she slid into the booth across from Jesse.

"Ollie's nice," she observed, sipping her Coke.

"Yeah, we used to come in here after school. This was always the meetin' place for the high school crowd." Jesse cleared his throat. "I usually had to catch the bus back home, but I made it a few times. It was a real treat for me back then." He looked over at the soda fountain with its gleaming mirror. "Still is, I reckon. Ollie always keeps it so clean. Smells good all the time too."

"I kind of envy you—growing up in a small town like this," Maria said thoughtfully. "Seems like life wouldn't be as—complicated. People have more time for each other down here."

"Even Liberty's too crowded for me." Jesse found himself lost in the shimmering sweep of Maria's dark hair as it caught the light each time she turned her head.

Maria looked away into some unseen distance. "Wouldn't you just love to see some place exotic like—like Casablanca maybe? You know, Arabian nights, romance on the desert—things like that."

Jesse smiled. "Maybe so. If I was gonna travel though, I don't think my first choice would be Casablanca. All that sand and rock. Burn up in the daytime and freeze at night. No, I could come up with some place better than North Africa."

"Paris maybe? London?"

Jesse stirred the ice in his Coke with a straw, then looked into Maria's eyes. Their luminous depths sent a warmth into his chest, the long lashes distracting him. "Palestine! That's where I'd really like to go if I could pick anyplace I wanted!"

"Palestine? Whatever for?"

"To see where Jesus lived. Bethlehem. Jerusalem. Nazareth. I'd give anything to walk by the Sea of Galilee where He called Peter and James and John to be fishers of men. To see where He preached the Sermon on the Mount. See Gethsemane and Calvary."

Maria watched the transformation in Jesse's face as he spoke. It was as though he were actually seeing the places he spoke of. "You really take your religion seriously, don't you?"

"Religion?" His eyes held a light Maria found disturbing. "Religion is man trying to live good enough to make it to heaven. Christianity is man realizing he *can't* do this and trusting Jesus to do it for him."

"You don't believe a person has to do good deeds?"

"Not to be saved," Jesse smiled. "In the Book of Ephesians, Paul tells us, 'For by grace are ye saved through faith; and that not of yourselves: it is the gift of God: Not of works, lest any man should boast.'"

From the jukebox came the sound of Dinah Shore singing "The Nearness of You."

Maria shifted uncomfortably on her side of the booth, glancing toward the front of the drugstore. "How are things going with the draft board?"

Noticing that she had become uneasy, Jesse said earnestly. "I'm sorry. I didn't mean to start preachin' to you. Sometimes a man can overdo it. I've seen preachers that just about beat folks to death with the gospel. I hope I'm not like that."

"I don't think of you that way," she smiled. "I think it's refreshing to see passion in a man for something other than chasing money—or girls. Especially when it's something he's called to."

Jesse looked puzzled.

"Brother Collins taught me that," Maria smiled.

"You better look out, Maria. He's subject to turn you into one of them fanatical Southern Pentecostals."

Her voice took on a more serious tone. "I heard you and someone else call your church members 'holy rollers.' Do you really roll around on the floor during the services?"

"No, no!" Jesse replied gravely. "We've never done that. We swing from the light fixtures occasionally. Get a pretty good ride out of 'em too. But that's about it."

Maria's eyes grew wide in disbelief, until she noticed a mischievous light in his dark eyes. "You scoundrel," she said in a feigned attempt to scold him. "You'll have me putting false information in my articles for the newspaper. What kind of a preacher are you, anyway?"

Jesse smiled his big, warm smile—the one she remembered from the first day they met. "A pretty happy one most of the time. I get to tell people the Good News."

"I'm beginning to enjoy your company a great deal, Jesse Boone," Maria smiled.

"Good. Now if you're a real good girl, I just might let you go with me to run my set-hooks one night. That's something you'd never be able to do up in New York City."

"What in the world is a set-hook?"

"You'll find out when we go." Jesse finished his Coke. "If I told you now, it'd spoil the mystery. You 'bout ready to go? I've got a wedding in the next county tomorrow."

They slid out of the booth and left the drugstore, accompanied by the sounds of Artie Shaw's "Stardust."

*   *   *

Cora Prentiss stood on Jesse's back porch staring down the narrow path through the trees. It wound down to the stream at the bottom of the valley. Mordecai slouched over to her, brushing up against her leg and whining for some attention.

"Git! Git! You flea-bitten mongrel," Cora whined back at him, shoving him away with her foot. "Your days are numbered at this house. When I move in—you git out!"

The early-morning sun gleamed on Cora's red hair. Her face, fair-skinned and lightly freckled, held the promise of beauty, but chronic scowling held beauty captive. Jesse hadn't been to see her in several days, and the scowl threatened to do permanent damage to her smiling mechanisms.

A soft, white mist drifted across the valley floor. The songbirds flitted brightly among the trees, their songs a fitting symphony for the spring morning. Mordecai had slumped against the wall in his favorite spot near the back door where the smells of Jesse's cooking would waft to him through the door. He gazed sullenly up at Cora, the look in his eyes more eloquent than words.

"Well, it's about time," Cora trilled, seeing Jesse climbing the path up to the cabin.

"Time?" he replied, the weariness as apparent in his face as the new day breaking. "Time for what?"

"Time you were getting home," she scolded. "Where in the world have you been all night?"

"Settle down, Cora," Jesse said evenly.

Cora knew the look in his eyes. This wasn't one of the times when he would tolerate her pouting. She changed her disposition in the time it took him to climb the steps onto the porch.

"My goodness, you look tired. Come on in the kitchen and I'll fix us a pot of coffee."

"Thanks." Jesse sat down in a ladder-backed chair and began unlacing his hunting boots. Mordecai ambled over, reared up on the chair, and put his head in Jesse's lap. As he began to rub his head and scratch its ears, Mordecai rolled his eyes up in an attitude of unbounded affection.

"Jesse, don't do that. He smells so bad."

Jesse glanced up at her. "He's supposed to smell bad, Cora. He's a dog."

Cora pulled out one of her favorite frowns from her frown closet and tried it on. "Well, you just be sure to wash your hands before you come into my kitchen."

Your kitchen? Jesse listened to the sounds of Cora's coffee making as he ladled water from the bucket into a dishpan with a gourd.

After washing his face and hands, he bent over and petted Mordecai before he went into the kitchen.

Cora sat at the small table Jesse had made from some slabs he found at the sawmill. "Jesse, we need to have a talk."

"Seems like we always need to have a talk lately, Cora," he replied wearily.

She sat up rigidly, her hands folded on the wood he had sanded and varnished. "This is serious, Jesse."

You're tellin' me. "What's serious?"

Cora cleared her throat. "I know you told that—woman you'd help her with her newspaper stuff, for the war effort and all that, but this time you've gone too far."

"Cora, I'm too tired for guessing games. Will you get to the point?" He collapsed in a chair.

"The picture show, Jesse. That's what I'm talking about. You took her to the picture show."

Jesse leaned back in his chair and sighed.

Cora discarded her diaphanous frown for one more substantial. "You've never been to a picture show in your life. You, of all people, know they're good for nothing but to lead people into sin."

"Cora, I see things in everyday life a lot worse than I saw in that picture show. They're basically just a waste of time as far as I can see, but I don't think they're as bad as we were brought up to believe. The music was pretty."

Cora continued as if she didn't hear him. "And as if that wasn't bad enough, you go with a woman who paints her face and wears earrings—*and* short skirts!"

"Will you pour the coffee, Cora?"

"You've just got to stop this right now, Jesse Boone," she chided, pouring the coffee. "You tell that woman today you'll never see her again or . . ."

"Or what?"

Cora sat down, fiddling with her coffee cup. "Well, what if the board of deacons found about this?"

"How would they, Cora?"

"Well—I hope you don't think I would . . ."

"Doesn't matter."

"What do you mean, 'Doesn't matter'?" She leaned over the table toward him.

"The draft board turned down my application to be a chaplain. So it doesn't make much difference one way or the other. I won't be around whatever they decide to do."

"Well, you'll just have to tell them you won't go," Cora said adamantly. "You're a minister."

"I'm goin'," Jesse said flatly.

"But you . . ."

"Cora," he interrupted. "I've sought the Lord about this for weeks now. I didn't know which way to turn." He felt bone weary as he continued. "I didn't sleep much last night. Sometime before dawn I walked down to the valley to pray. God gave me an answer just as the sun was comin' up. It was almost like He planned it that way."

"But what about us?" Cora moaned.

"We'll just have to put things off like a million other men and women will. One thing I know for sure. I won't sit in a military jail somewhere while the other boys do my fightin' for me. I'm goin' in the army and be the best soldier I can."

* * *

"Help! Oh, Jesse, help me! He's too strong."

"Nope," Jesse said evenly. "You're a big girl. You'll have to do it yourself."

The three-pound catfish broke the surface of the creek in a mad twisting leap, showering Maria with cold water. She hung onto a sapling with her left hand to keep from sliding down the slippery bank into the water. With her right hand, she held the cane pole she had pulled from the bank to land the catfish.

It had been thrilling for her when she had seen the pole bobbing and weaving from the catfish's attempts to free itself. The line sliced through the water as it swam furiously back and forth. Now Maria thought the fish would pull her under.

"Well, I'd hate to see you end up as fish bait." Jesse grabbed Maria around the waist with both hands, pulling her back up the bank. "Take the pole with both hands. I've got you now."

Maria watched the fish break the water for the last time as she dragged it up the bank. Sitting breathlessly on the little path that ran along the water's edge, she tried to avoid the wildly flopping fish. Her blue jeans and saddle oxfords were muddy and the man's white shirt she wore was soaked. Tendrils of dark wet hair clung to her face and neck. And she was happier than she had been in a very long time.

"What do we do now?" Maria looked up at Jesse as she clung tightly to the pole.

He looked toward the ground. The battery-powered headlight he wore strapped to his forehead gleamed on the white underbelly of the catfish. "What do you mean *we*? It's your fish. You drug him out of his home—away from his family."

"You think I should put him back?" Maria's dark eyes were shining in the glow of his light.

Jesse laughed. "The only place he's going is in a frying pan and then on my kitchen table."

Maria took a deep breath and sat down, leaning back against a tree. "This is fun."

"I'm glad you're enjoying yourself. Wait'll you taste the fish though. That's the real fun part." Seeing that the fish had swallowed the hook, Jesse took a pocket knife from his jeans and cut it out. Then he strung it through the gills on a forked stick he had cut at the first set-hook. "You want to rest a minute before we check the others?"

"I think so. It's so nice down here listening to the sound of the stream." She watched Jesse rebait the hook with chicken entrails from a can. He stepped down to the water's edge and shoved the pole deeply into the bank so that the hook was about two feet underwater, the line moving about gently in the current.

"So, you like runnin' set-hooks, huh? Think maybe the people in New York will like to read about how we catch our supper down here?" He sat down against a tree near her.

"I think it'll be an interesting part of the whole story." Maria shivered slightly.

"Here, take this." Jesse took off his hunting jacket and handed it to her.

"No," she insisted. "You told me to bring a jacket. It's my own fault if I get cold."

He tossed the jacket to her. "Don't be stubborn. You'll get sick and then where'll your story be?"

Maria put the jacket on, her hands lost in the long sleeves. "Have you heard anything from the draft board?"

"Yep." He rested his arms on his bent knees.

"Well?"

He smiled. "They say I ain't fit to preach in their army, but they'd be mighty happy if I'd fight in it."

Maria frowned. "That's a shame, Jesse. If I ever saw anyone meant to preach it's you."

"No, it's not a shame, Maria. I think God would have me fight in this war. Maybe that seems strange for a preacher to say, but that's what I believe."

Maria moved over next to Jesse, rustling in the leaves that covered the ground. "What will the church do for a pastor?"

"Get somebody else, I guess. Or they might pass the preachin' around 'til I get back. Some of the members are pretty good preachers themselves." Jesse felt Maria's softness as she leaned against him, the scent of her perfume like spring flowers.

"I've grown fond of you in these last weeks, Jesse." She lay her pale hand on his, hard and brown from years on the farm and in the woods.

Jesse felt his heart quicken. He took a breath and let it out slowly. "You're on my mind a lot, Maria. Too much, I think. I thought my future was all arranged. Now I'm not so sure. I reckon this war's gonna change a lot of people's lives."

"How—how does Cora feel about your going in as a regular soldier—having to fight?"

"Upset. She'd rather I went to jail. Said she'd at least know I was safe then."

Maria caressed his hand softly. "I'm going to try to get permission from my editor to follow you and Chance through your military experiences. At least until you complete training—maybe even farther if they'll let me."

"Chance got drafted too?"

"Yes. I just found out. He's still trying to pull some strings, but I don't think it'll do any good." Maria sat up and looked into Jesse's face. "Do you two know each other very well?"

Jesse found himself holding Maria's hand, feeling the smooth softness of it. "Chance was two or three years behind me in school. He worked at the country club and I lived way out here in the country, so we didn't have much contact. I doubt we'd have a whole lot in common anyway."

Maria felt the strength of his hand in her own as if it somehow held the character of the man. "Do you know where the army will be sending you for training?"

"Camp Polk. It's in Louisiana, near a town called Leesville. I think it's over close to the Texas border."

"Sounds pretty desolate."

"I think that's the way they want military bases to be. Out in the middle of nowhere. Not much place for the men to get into trouble." Jesse tightened his grip on Maria's hand, standing up and bringing her with him.

Maria fell against him, her arms around his waist. She felt his hard stomach and chest pressing against her, felt his hand softly caressing her hair. Then they were walking away down the path by the creek with the night wind stirring in the trees.

*   *   *

Jesse walked down from his cabin through the woods to the glade where his little church stood. It glimmered whitely in the early-morning mist like it belonged in a city beneath the sea. A shotgun boomed faintly like the sound of distant cannon.

Going inside, he walked to the pulpit for the last time, placing both hands on the rough stand that had held his Bible. Surveying the empty pews, he saw them filled with the family and friends of a lifetime. "Lord, I want to thank You for letting me preach Your gospel. I won't be preaching from the pulpit for a while, but I ask that You'll give me the chance to tell others about Jesus wherever I might be. Watch over this little flock of Yours, Lord, and keep them safe. Bring a pastor here who'll minister to their needs."

Part 2

THE RAINCROW
SUMMER

7

INCIDENT ON HIGHWAY 117

*T*he pale yellow convertible hurtled through the evening beneath Saturn's pale gleam. Red Antares glowed faintly in the southern sky with light that began its journey toward earth long before the birth pangs of America began.

"Guess I better slow down this time," Chance grumbled, spotting the sign that warned him he would soon be entering the town of Winnfield.

Jesse looked up from the paperback he was trying to read by the amber glow of the dashboard light. "Wise move I'd say, seeing as how you already got two speeding tickets since we crossed into Louisiana. One thing you got to give 'em though. They sure don't dillydally around when they get you before the J.P."

"That's the gospel truth. They cleaned me out quicker than the casino did when I played that tournament in Monte Carlo. Didn't even give me a free drink either." Chance glanced over at Jesse, his hair starkly white in the gathering darkness. "Good thing I asked you to come along with me to buy the gas."

Jesse continued to pore over his book.

"You still readin' that travel book about Louisiana?" Chance fished a Chesterfield out of his shirt pocket, letting it dangle from the side of his mouth as he talked.

"Yeah. Figure as long as we're gonna be here awhile, I might as well learn something about the state."

"Like what?"

"Like Winnfield is where Huey Long was born," Jesse answered, holding the book closer to the faint light of the dashboard. "And, during the Civil War, it refused to secede from the Union. They established the 'Free State of Winn.'"

83

"That's real interesting, Jesse," Chance quipped. "Can't be much to 'em though if they wouldn't fight the Yankees."

Jesse thought of all the efforts Chance had made to get out of the draft. "You might be right."

A half-hour later, Chance slowed the Buick to a sedate twenty-five miles an hour as he drove along the banks of the Cane River in Natchitoches. They passed ancient homes with long galleries and wrought-iron ornamentation. The voices of mothers carried on the soft evening air, calling for their sons to come home for supper from their fishing spots on the grassy banks of the river.

"This kinda reminds me of pictures I've seen of New Orleans," Jesse remarked. "Same kind of architecture."

"Now that's a city I'd like to visit," Chance grinned. "They say that French Quarter is really something!"

They passed a two-story red brick house with wide stone steps, cast-iron grillwork, and massive white columns. A little girl with blue ribbons adorning her blonde ringlets stood at the railing on the upstairs gallery. Clutching her Raggedy Ann doll in her left arm, she waved shyly to the two men passing below in the big convertible.

Jesse noticed the child with yellow light shining from the hall behind bordering her face in brightness. He waved back to her just as she disappeared from his sight behind a live oak in her front yard.

"Who was that?" Chance asked, seeing him wave.

"Just a little girl." Jesse glanced down at his book. "Says here Natchitoches is the oldest town in the Louisiana Purchase. Goes back to 1714 when it was called Fort St. Jean Baptiste."

Chance scowled at him. "Give it a rest, will you? This ain't Mrs. Peabody's history class."

"You didn't like Mrs. Peabody?"

"Who did? If ol' Euliss hadn't got crippled when them logs fell on him, he'd have left her years ago." Chance grinned crookedly. "I kinda know how he feels. Trapped in this car, having to listen to your history lesson."

Jesse closed his book and dropped it on the seat. "You oughta be more interested in history, Chance."

"How's that?"

"You're helpin' make it right now."

Chance stared questioningly over at Jesse. "What are you talkin' about? Me, makin' history?"

"Not just you. All of us goin' off to fight this war." Jesse leaned his head back on the leather seat, staring up into the night sky as they hit the outskirts of town. "It's gonna change the shape of the whole world before it's over."

"To what—a square, a triangle?"

Jesse laughed. "You know what I'm talkin' about. If we don't win, democracy is finished."

"So, we'll have to goose-step and listen to Hitler scream like an idiot. Or maybe eat a lot of fish heads and rice," Chance shrugged. "What difference does it make who runs the show?"

"Chance," Jesse mused, his voice taking on a solemn tone, "when you turn pro, if you get the chance that is, how'd you like to turn over your prize money to the state?"

"What?" Chance barked, jerking his head toward Jesse. "What kind of insanity are you talkin' about now?"

"There's a good possibility that's just what will happen if we lose this war."

"You lost me."

"We've got democracy now—free enterprise. We pay some taxes for defense, police protection, things like that, but we spend most of our money pretty much like we want to." He paused to see if Chance was listening.

"Well, go ahead."

"If that fellow over in Berlin with the wild eyes and the silly little mustache gets his way, he'll run the whole show. He thinks the people don't have sense enough to handle their own lives, so he'll take all the money and spend it like he wants to. If we lose this one, say good-bye to your freedoms."

Chance glanced over at Jesse, his eyes narrowed in confusion. "Where'd you learn all this?"

"Well, they did teach us how to read at Liberty High, remember?" Jesse smiled. "And you can get books at the library for free. Even preachers get a break once in a while and there's not much to do up at that little cabin of mine but hunt, fish, and read."

"Yeah, I remember you at school," Chance remarked, kicking the speedometer back up to seventy. "Always haulin' a stack of books around with you."

"Did most of my readin' on that long bus ride back into the hills." He glanced over at the speedometer. "You better slow this thing down. I don't know if I've got enough money to pay off another one of them local J.P.'s."

Chance turned south onto Highway 117 that led to Leesville and Camp Polk, and was barreling through the Kisatchie National Forest. Tall pines lined the road on both sides, leaving a narrow strip of star-crowded sky above them. The headlights pierced the corridor of thick darkness ahead of them. Suddenly, a white-tailed deer leaped into the blinding glare.

As Chance stomped on the brakes, the Buick careened down the road to the screeching of tires on the blacktop and the smell of burning rubber. The deer almost made it. At the last instant before it cleared the road, the left front headlight of the heavy car slammed into its flank with a sickening thud.

Wrestling the car to a stop, Chance leaned on the steering wheel and took a deep breath. "Whew! I didn't think I could hold it in the road for a minute there."

Jesse looked back over his shoulder. "Let's go back there and check on her."

"Her?"

"It was a doe."

"Shoot!" Chance backed along the shoulder of the highway, the big tires crunching in the gravel.

"Watch out!" Jesse warned. "Don't back off that edge. Looks like it might be a long drop down there."

Seeing the crumpled bulk at the edge of the road, Chance hit the brake and turned to Jesse. "Go check her, will you? I don't think I'm up to it." Chance got out and looked at the front of the car, seeing that the bumper had taken most of the impact.

Jesse walked around to the back of the car. Kneeling next to the warm exhaust from the tailpipe, he ran his hand gently along the deer's ruined hindquarters and huge belly. She lifted her head weakly, her eyes wide with terror.

"How is she?"

"No hope," Jesse called over his shoulder. "She'll never last the night."

"Well, let's go then."

Jesse held a bone-handled pocketknife in his right hand, its blade casting a lethal glint in the red glow of the taillight. He could almost sense the night holding its breath as he plunged the blade quickly into the deer's neck, severing the jugular. A quick hot stream burst forth, flowing over his hand and wrist and down into the earth. When her breathing stopped, he rolled her down into the dark ravine.

"That blood on your hand?" Chance grimaced.

Wiping his hand and wrist with his handkerchief, Jesse got back into the car. "I couldn't let her lie there and suffer."

Chance shuddered. "I hate that kind of stuff. That's why I never would go huntin' much."

"She was pregnant."

"Poor little thing. He never even had the chance to be born. Never got to see what this old world looks like." Chance listened to the steady murmur of the engine, gazed ahead at the bright path the headlights lay before him, and roared off into the darkness.

*   *   *

"This is great stuff! You really made that little town come to life," Duncan Rourke growled, leaning back in his leather swivel chair until it appeared it would dump him over backward. "The readers love these human-interest stories, and the owner loves the sales figures."

"Thanks, Chief." Maria stood next to his massive desk, covered with enough scattered papers to print an edition of *Life* magazine. "But the story's just beginning."

"Just beginning?"

"Certainly," she declared confidently. "The next logical step is to follow the boys through training and then—wherever Uncle Sam decides to send them."

Rourke struck a kitchen match on his stubbly chin. At least it looked that way. No one could ever figure out how he did it—and no one ever asked him. "You haven't thought this thing through, Maria. What you're suggesting is a tricky business."

She pushed aside some crumpled papers and sat on the edge of his desk, her skirt sliding up her nylons above the knees. The clattering typewriters around them quieted for a moment, then continued. "First, I have to get approval from the State Department. They issue the passports."

Rourke squinted beneath his heavy gray eyebrows. "My apologies. You *have* given this some thought."

"Then the War Department has to accredit me as a correspondent," Maria continued. "With those two minor obstacles out of the way, I'm off to cover the war."

"Ow!" Rourke yelped as the match burned down to his finger. He flung the match across the room, struck another one, and lit his cigarette.

Maria giggled silently behind her hand.

"Minor obstacles," he scowled. "Is that what you call them? Do you know how many reporters in this country want to be war correspondents?"

"You mean besides me?" she smiled.

Rourke rubbed the back of his neck with his right hand. "I must admit it does have possibilities. If we could convince the stuffed shirts over at the War Department that it would help personalize the war for the American people—help mobilize the entire country in the war effort, we'd have a real good shot at it."

"Barney—I mean, Colonel Barney Oldfield—is the public relations officer. He's responsible for establishing the press camps." Maria smiled knowingly. "Isn't he a friend of yours, Chief?"

"You've given this more than thought haven't you?" Rourke observed, sitting forward and digging through a mountain of paper on the right side of his desk. "Fortunately for you, Oldfield supports the rights of women war correspondents. I'm not sure if he's ahead of his time or just distracted by a few pretty faces."

If I can just get into this war I know I can make my career take off. Maria tried to hide her excitement as she watched Rourke shuffling through the stacks of papers.

"Maybe you haven't thought of one thing, Maria, in your headlong rush to fame and fortune."

"What's that, chief?"

"Death!"

Maria felt a slight chill. "I know there's danger involved. I'm ready to take the risk."

"Getting wounded, maimed, captured, living under some pretty rough conditions." He glanced up at her. "And if it doesn't happen to you, it most assuredly will to a whole lot of others—people you've come to know as friends."

"I know I can take it," Maria said flatly.

"Well, you have somebody else going to bat for you too," Rourke went on. "General Eisenhower wants all correspondents to carry the rank of captain. Kind of quasi staff officers you might say. If you're captured, it'll give you the Geneva Convention privileges afforded to officers. Maybe you'll get a barracks with smaller rats."

"Eisenhower's got a soft spot for the press?" Maria shifted around on the desk, crossing her legs. The noise of typewriters and shuffling papers got a three-second moratorium.

"No, he's got a war to win. That doesn't leave much room for soft spots." Rourke responded absently, lifting a gray pamphlet out of the paper swamp on top of his desk. "But he's got sense enough to know the newspapers in this country have a big influence on public opinion, and he wants it leaning his way."

"Here we are," he mused, thumbing through the pamphlet. "If I can decipher this bureaucratic gobbledygook we might be able to get you accredited sometime before the war's over. I don't think the passport's gonna be a big problem. You haven't been involved in any subversive activities, have you?"

"Not a chance," Maria laughed. "I'm happy with this country just the way it is. Anything I can do to speed things up? The boys have already left for basic training. I'm wasting time up here when I could be down in Louisiana getting some good copy."

"Take a few days off. You deserve it. Spend some time with your father," Rourke mumbled, dragging his heavy black phone over to him. "He called me every day while you were away. Worries a lot about his little girl. Maybe it won't take very long to get you cleared for the stateside stuff. I'll let you know soon as I find out something."

"Thanks a lot, Chief," Maria said, sliding off the desk. "I'll do the best job you ever saw."

Rourke waved her off brusquely as he began dialing the phone.

Sal Como sat on Maria's desk, popping his chewing gum as she walked over and sat down. "Hey, Babe. How's things way down south in the land of cotton?"

"Peaceful, Sal, real peaceful." Maria began to sort through her mail, tossing most of it into the wastebasket at the side of her desk.

"How 'bout stepping out with me tonight?" he asked, dropping his wad of gum into the wastebasket.

Maria opened her mouth to send a resounding *no* at him, then felt a pang of guilt for the way she had treated him the last time he asked her out. "Maybe," she replied instead. "What did you have in mind?"

Como held up two tickets between his thumb and forefinger, dangling them in front of her face. "Know what these are?"

"Four dirty fingernails?"

"Aw, come on, Maria. Give me a break, will ya? I'm trying to be nice," he moaned.

"Sorry, Sal," she shrugged. "What wonders do you have displayed before my puerile eyes?"

"Hey, that's pretty, the way you said it! What I have here is two—count them, one-two—tickets for the greatest show this side of the Atlantic Ocean," he beamed.

"I didn't know Roy Rogers was in town," Maria sighed wistfully. "He's my favorite."

Como frowned, hopping down from the desk. "I'm about out of patience with you, Vitrano."

"Sorry, Sal. Sometimes I overdo it."

"Well, anyhow, what I have here are two tickets for tonight's performance at the Paramount Theater." He paused for effect. "Tickets for 'The Voice'—New Jersey's favorite son, Francis Albert Sinatra. By the way, did I tell you he's a cousin of mine?"

"I thought that was Perry Como?"

"Oh, yeah, him too. Well, what do you say? Are we on?"

"Why not, Sal? I've never heard Sinatra. I'd like to see for myself what all the excitement's about."

"Great!" he beamed. "I'll pick you up at seven."

"I'll be ready."

Sal swaggered back over to his desk and began engaging his neighbors in animated conversation.

I may live to regret this, but a little excitement might be a nice change after all that peace and quiet in Liberty.

* * *

"Give me Liberty or give me death." The words seemed to force themselves into Maria's thoughts. *What I wouldn't give for the peace and quiet of Liberty, Georgia, right now.* She stood with Como in a seemingly endless line of screaming, giggling bobbysoxers on the sidewalk outside the Paramount Theater. The line wound around the corner of the building and out of sight.

"I hope this is worth it, Sal," she grumbled as they inched toward the brightly lit marquee.

Sal was prancing with excitement. "Are you kidding? This man started the Age of Swoon. He does things with a song that makes Bing Crosby sound like Eddie Cantor."

Bedlam reigned inside the theater. The sound of a thousand conversations, the shuffling back and forth in the seats and constant movement up and down the aisles created an atmosphere that made Maria think of the Roman Coliseum.

"You know he left Dorsey," Sal screamed.

"What?" Maria leaned toward him.

"Dick Haymes took his place with Dorsey's Band. Sinatra's on his own now."

"Who's he gonna throw shot glasses at now that Buddy Rich isn't around?" Maria almost shouted, recalling one of the lapses of control Sinatra was becoming known for.

"With that temper of his, he won't have any trouble finding somebody," Sal laughed.

The house lights dimmed, the curtain went up, and the Benny Goodman Orchestra played "How High the Moon." Polite applause marked the end of the number. Peggy Lee walked to the microphone, accompanied by more applause, and sang "Why Don't You Do Right?" After two more numbers she was replaced by Dinah Shore, who did her two biggest hits, "The Nearness of You" and "Blues in the Night." The crowd responded with a few cheers and whistles.

"She's a beautiful girl, isn't she?" Sal asked, placing his lips close to Maria's ear.

"Dinah Shore? Oh, yes. There are a lot of pretty girls down south where she comes from. You'd love it."

Goodman stepped to the front of the stage and said simply, "And now, Frank Sinatra."

A thunderous roar greeted the skinny kid in the bow tie and

wide-shouldered sport coat. Walking out to the microphone, he was seemingly stunned by the mass female hysteria that greeted him. He smiled and looked around awkwardly at Goodman.

The deafening noise that followed Goodman's introduction caught him completely by surprise. He froze in his tracks, turning around and staring with wonder at this upstart in baggy pants. Sinatra appeared only as an "Extra Added Attraction" in the stage-show marquee.

When Sinatra was with the Dorsey Band, Dorsey had tended to keep the limelight for himself with such ploys as reducing Sinatra and the Pied Pipers to "with vocal refrain" on the label of his hit record, "Stardust." Although Sinatra was now on the Hit Parade with his recording of "There Are Such Things," Goodman seemed unaware of who he was.

When the pandemonium subsided somewhat, Sinatra burst forth with "For Me and My Gal." He continued with "This Love of Mine," and by the time he broke into "I'll Be Seeing You," the bobbysoxers had screamed and shouted until they were hoarse. They moaned and writhed, they jumped up on their seats, and some of them swooned dead away. The *New Yorker* later called him, "An American Phenomenon."

"He's the greatest singer ever," Sal shouted to Maria above the din.

She noticed that Sal dressed like the skinny kid on the stage and tried to comb his hair in the same manner. "He certainly has a way with a song," she admitted.

As Maria listened to the last song, she tried to figure out why this childlike, almost innocent-looking kid had such an effect on his audience. *Maybe he brings out the maternal instinct in them.* Then it hit her as she studied the rapt faces of the bobbysoxers: *He's got the ability to make every one of them feel that he's singing to her alone.*

* * *

"So, what do you think of the little Italian boy from Jersey?" Carmine Vitrano asked, sitting on his battered old wooden stool behind the counter. "He sings nice, don't he?"

"Very nice, Papa." Maria tried to summon up the courage to tell her father that she would be leaving him again to continue her war articles for the newspaper. She decided not to mention the fact that she could later be going overseas.

"All us Italians sing good," Vitrano affirmed by breaking into a few bars of "Oh Solo Mio."

Maria sat in the hard, ladder-backed chair that she always thought of as belonging to Avi Cohn, listening to the shouts of the stickball players out in the street. It seemed to her the same game had been going on ever since she could remember. The scent of onions and garlic and the huge cheeses on the meat counter brought back scenes of her childhood when she had helped her mother sweep and mop and stock the shelves of their little store.

The bell above the door jingled merrily. It never failed to make Maria think of reindeer. A tiny gray-haired woman in a flowered dress and black hat entered the store and walked daintily over to the counter. "Good day, Maria—Carmine."

"Hello, Mrs. Polito," Maria replied. "I sure appreciate your looking after Papa. He says you cook better than I do."

Carmine Vitrano smiled at his daughter. "You ain't had as much practice as Rose here."

Rose Polito lay her purse on the counter. "Raising nine children gave me plenty of practice all right."

"I don't know if my Maria here is ever gonna make me a grandfather, Rose. Twenty-two years old and she doesn't even have a steady boyfriend."

"Don't you worry, Maria," Rose Polito advised. "Getting married is easy. Anybody can do it. You just wait 'til the right one comes along. You'll know it in here." She touched her chest with a forefinger twisted by arthritis.

"I'm in no hurry, Mrs. Polito." Maria remembered how desire had swept over her when Chance Rinehart had taken her in his arms—thought of the warm, secure feeling that came to her when she was with Jesse Boone. *What will I know in here?*

"I want to pay on my bill, Carmine." Rose Polito opened her big felt bag and took out a black pop-open coin purse.

Vitrano reached under the counter for the Baby Ruth box he kept his accounts in.

As Maria watched the two people she had known all her life go through their weekly ritual, her thoughts wandered back to her childhood. She saw herself walking beside her mother down the

Sunday morning streets in her best dress with the pink lace, smelled again the dew-wet flowers of early spring. She listened to the sonorous chant of the priest echoing in the twilight realms of the huge church, experienced once more the austere beauty of the mass. After her mother's funeral, she never again went back to mass.

After church they always stopped at Lamonica's Bakery and sat in the wire-backed chairs at the little round table next to the window where they could watch the people in their fine clothes walk by on their way to the next mass. Maria tasted again the sweet hot doughnuts and the frothy-cold milk that was served in short fat glasses.

A thick darkness seemed to drift into her father's little store through the dusty front window. Maria could almost feel its clammy touch as the lines from Macbeth leaped before her mind's eye.

> Tomorrow, and tomorrow, and tomorrow,
> Creeps in this petty pace from day to day,
> To the last syllable of recorded time;
> And all our yesterdays have lighted fools
> The way to dusty death.

The face of her mother appeared before Maria, as she had seen it last—in the casket. It was painted with powder and rouge that her mother had never worn. She remembered the hair was all wrong. *Stop this!* Maria thought as she fought her way back to the present.

The bell jingled above the door as Mrs. Polito left.

"Papa, I have something to talk to you about." Maria slid her chair over closer to the counter.

Vitrano put his account box away. "I like that—our father-and-daughter talks. So many children today grow up and forget all about their parents. Not my Maria."

"Papa, I have to leave again." Maria still trembled slightly from the painful memories.

"But you just got back."

"Well, I don't know how long it will be before I leave again," she explained, hoping he would take the news well. "Maybe a week, maybe a month or two. Mr. Rourke is working on some clearances I'll need with the War Department."

Vitrano came around from behind the counter and took both of Maria's hands in his. "You got that same look in your eyes your mother used to have when she was worried about me. It makes an old man feel good to know somebody still loves him that much."

"Oh, Papa." She stood up, putting both arms around her father. "I do love you so very much."

Vitrano stepped back, taking her hands again. "I know I've been a burden on you these last years, but I want more than anything for you to have a good life. I'll be fine here. I've got Avi and Mrs. Polito and my other friends."

Maria let her father tell her the things that were on his heart—things she knew he needed to talk about.

"And you give me way too much money from your newspaper job. You need to save it for your future. Your mama and me wanted to do so much for you—I keep thinking of you as my little girl . . ."

Maria looked into her father's sad, kind eyes and thought briefly how much they looked like J. T. Dickerson's. "I had the best mama and papa any girl could ask for."

Vitrano squeezed Maria's hands.

"And, Papa," Maria said, putting her arms around him. "I'll always be your little girl."

8

ALL THE SHINING YOUNG MEN

Maria sat in the reviewing stand with the proud parents and girlfriends and wives who had come to watch the singularly most handsome and dashing soldier in the U.S. Army (their own Bill or Bob or Joe) graduate from basic training. Camp Polk was still under construction. The pine barrens had been ravaged by bulldozers, leaving the earth scarred by their passage. Here and there, a slender pine rose from the raw red clay as a token survivor.

Far across the parade ground, Maria could see the new barracks and administration buildings, freshly painted, stretching endlessly into the white distance. The sound of a marching band carried to her on the hot wind. *"Stars and Stripes Forever,"* she thought. *Almost makes me want to join up.*

Behind the band came the rigid phalanxes of troops, fitted out in their dress greens and still filing out of the dark woods at the far end of the parade ground. In front of each battalion marched the flag bearers, their banners flashing brightly in the sun, popping like spinnakers in the stiff breeze. The troops passed in review like a gigantic, green centipede, their left feet all striking the ground to the heavy beat of the drum. The band struck up "The Caisson Song," bringing the crowd to its feet.

"Eyeees—right!" Heads turned with a single swift movement at a forty-five-degree angle.

"Preseeent—arms!" Hands popped loudly on polished stocks as rifles snapped off shoulders.

Maria could not help being caught up in the fervor of the moment, seeing America's young men marching off to glory, putting themselves in harm's way for their country. Images flashed through her mind as she recalled fragments of a poem about golden horns singing warriors to rest. She looked for Chance and Jesse, but they were lost among all the shining young men.

*　*　*

"Jesse! Oh, Jesse!" Maria pushed her way through the crowd, trying to catch up to him as he strode toward the barracks with another soldier.

Hearing the familiar voice, Jesse turned to look for Maria. Finally he spotted her waving her white clutch purse wildly. Standing like a piling as the human current flowed around and past him, he shouted, "What're you doin' here? We thought you'd forgotten all about us—gone on to bigger and better things."

She had reached him by then. "Forget about you and Chance? Not on your life. You're my ticket to fame and fortune in the newspaper game."

"Well, I'd kinda hoped for a little higher callin', but I guess I'd rather be a ticket than nothin'." Jesse noticed the tiny beads of perspiration above the curve of Maria's red lips. He had an almost irresistible desire to touch them lightly with his fingertips, to brush them away.

"Good gracious! What happened to your pretty brown locks?" She ran her hand over his springy, close-cropped hair. "Feels like my mother's old hairbrush."

"Oh, this!" he replied, his hand following hers. "I asked the barber for a special styling. Told him I really wanted to stand out in a crowd."

Maria smiled, glancing at the hundreds of skinheads all around them. "It's certainly unique, Jesse. Don't know when I've ever seen anything quite like it."

He stepped back to take a better look at her, noticing all the G.I.s stumbling over each other as they gawked at her. "My, my! Don't you look pretty in that white dress."

She realized how glad she was to see him again. She somehow felt *safe*—that was the word that came to mind—when she was with him. "I bet you say that to all the journalists."

"Don't know but one—" He stopped himself in mid-sentence, turning to the slight, dark-haired man standing next to him. "I'm sorry! I've lost what little manners I had since Uncle Sam adopted me. Maria, this is Alcide Naquin. Al, Maria Vitrano."

"Glad to make your acquaintance, Miss Vitrano." Al took Maria's pale hand in his sunburned one, caressing it briefly. "Jesse talk about you a lot, him."

She turned to the man slightly behind Jesse. He held his brass-buttoned coat draped across one arm. Dark sweat stains ringed the armpits of his shirt. "Call me Maria, if that's all right with you, Al," she suggested, feeling somehow that his caress was an innocent display of affection endemic to a unique culture.

"Fine wid me," Al replied, his teeth white against the dark face with its thin, high-bridged nose and muscadine eyes. "We ain't formal where I come from, no."

Maria tried to place his accent but couldn't. *Sounds almost French, but not like any I ever heard before.*

"Al's a Cajun from the Louisiana swamps," Jesse offered, as if he had just read her thoughts. He began to unbutton his coat. "We've got a week's leave before we come back for specialized training. He's invited me for a visit."

Maria frowned slightly.

"What's wrong?" Jesse asked.

"That means I won't be able to continue my story unless I can catch up with Chance."

Al took her hand in both of his. "Oh, no, Sha! You come wid us. My family got plenty room, them. We all like people to come see us. Give us a chance to cook and eat plenty."

"What's that you called me?" Maria asked.

"Oh, you mean *sha,*" he explained. "That's what we call everybody we like. I t'ink it come from that Parisian French word, *cher.*"

Maria noticed that the word was pronounced like the first three letters of *shack*. "Sha," she said, emphasizing the softness of the word. "I like the sound of it."

"You gonna like a lot of t'ings about us, Sha," Al smiled. "You comin', yeah?"

"Yeah," Maria laughed. "I'm comin', me."

"I like this girl, Jesse," he grinned. "She talk kinda funny like them big-city people all do, but we could teach her right. I t'ink she learnin' already, her."

"When does your leave start?"

Al glanced at his watch. "Two hours. We takin' the Greyhound to Baton Rouge. Then we get a local bus on down into the basin."

"Basin?" Maria looked puzzled. "I thought that was a street in New Orleans where they played Dixieland Jazz."

"It is. That's where Jesse's friend Chance is goin'. To New Orleans. Not us. We goin' to the *real* basin." Al spread his hands before him. "The most beautiful place God created in this round world. When He takes a vacation—that where He goes. Straight to the Atchafalaya River Basin. Wait'll you see it."

Maria was enthralled by Al's enthusiasm. "My goodness! You make it sound like paradise."

He dropped his hands. His eyes glistened with moisture. "I talk about it so good, I got myself homesick, me. Let's get goin' to that bus depot, Jesse. I can smell them crawfish boilin' already."

"Oh, no." Maria blurted out.

"What you mean, 'Oh no?'" Al shrugged. "The bus leavin' in two hours."

"But you're not leaving on it. You're both going with me. The newspaper leased a car for me, so we'll be traveling in style." She took the car keys out of her purse and jingled them in front of Al.

He turned to Jesse. "I tole you I like this girl, Jesse. Let's go get our duffel bags."

Maria turned to Jesse, who had obviously been through this same kind of routine with Al before and was enjoying seeing her have her first experience with the Cajun culture. "You don't get a lot of chance to talk when Al's around, do you?"

"Not a whole lot," Jesse smiled. He found himself staring at Maria's shiny dark hair where it flowed softly around her slender neck and down to her shoulders.

"I need to see Chance before we leave though," Maria continued. "I've only got half a story without him."

Answering for Jesse, Al pointed toward the pale yellow convertible parked in front of a large, white two-story building. "He's in there with the company commander. That's who he's going to New Orleans with. Lives in the Garden District. Got more money than the basin's got catfish."

Maria felt a sharp rush of excitement through her breast when she looked at the car, remembering the time with Chance down by the river in Liberty. She glanced back at Jesse. "Where can I pick you up? This shouldn't take very long."

Jesse pointed across the open expanse of red clay, dotted with clumps of wild grass that were struggling to cover it. "The third barracks over there. We'll be waitin' on the stoop." He watched Maria walk briskly away across the hard-packed, dry ground, her hips swaying with a timeless motion that caused his throat to constrict. Looking away, he tried to remember what Cora Prentiss looked like, but couldn't.

"You ready, Sha?" Al asked.

"Let's . . . ," Jesse sounded like a frog trying to croak. He cleared his throat. "Let's go, Al."

* * *

Maria's eyes were drawn to him as soon as she stepped into the open foyer of the noisy administration building. Beyond the young men in their tan uniforms, typing at gray metal desks or clicking along the bare wooden floors with their hard heels, Chance sprawled in a chair in front of a large wooden desk. Caught in a glare of hard, white light from a single window at the side of the desk, he was even more deeply tanned than Maria remembered. His eyes were startlingly blue beneath the bright, sun-bleached crew cut. The jagged scar beneath his drooping left eyelid looked as white as bone.

Taking a few steps into the building, Maria's outfit caught Chance's eye. He sat up in his chair, said something to the man seated across from him, and strode across the room to her, flashing his best greeting. "If *you're* not the answer to a poor soldier's prayers, I don't know who is. Why didn't you let me know you were coming? The warden here still lets us have mail."

Maria was stunned when Chance took her by the shoulders and kissed her full on the lips. A tingling warmth spread through her cheeks and down her neck. "Well, I, ah—I left as soon as the clearances came through. Didn't have time to write."

He took her by the hand. "I missed you, Maria. Didn't think I would—but I did. Come on, there's someone I want you to meet. You'll like him."

"Captain Montgomery, this is Maria Vitrano. Best newspaper reporter in the country," Chance bragged, stopping in front of the desk.

Maria thought immediately of a swashbuckling Errol Flynn when she looked at the man. He was so tall, though, she couldn't imagine him jumping on tables and swinging from heavy drapes as she had seen in the movies. He wore thin, gold-rimmed glasses, and his voice was like honey and soft rain when he spoke. "Preston Montgomery, ma'am. Pleased to meet you."

Maria noticed an accent different from either Al's or the boys from Liberty. It had a touch of Brooklyn to it, but slower and without the harshness. She glanced at his big hand with its long slim fingers, offered almost as if he expected her to kiss his ring. She sensed that he was a man used to having everything his own way. His hand enveloped hers. "How do you do, Captain Montgomery."

"Please, call me Preston. All my friends do—to my face anyway," he laughed softly.

"You're running with some mighty fast company, Preston," Maria smiled, nodding toward Chance.

Montgomery smiled benignly. "I wouldn't know about his personal life, but Chance is fast on the tennis court where it counts." His liquid brown eyes never left Maria as he talked. "He's graciously consented to visit me at my home and give me some lessons."

Chance stepped back into the conversation. "Maria's doin' the story on Jesse and me for her paper."

"I surmised as much," Montgomery remarked, his eyes still on Maria's. "Chance will be gone a week on his visit to the 'City that Care Forgot.' That was my father's pet name for The City. Sounds rather old-fashioned now in this age of distress."

She noticed that Montgomery used 'The City' when referring to New Orleans, as if there were only *one* city in America. *I thought only New Yorkers were that conceited.* Maria turned to Chance. "When will I see you again? You're half of my story, you know."

Montgomery answered for him. "We're winging our way down in Chance's yellow chariot after lunch. Come with us. We have two guest cottages at our home. You can take your pick."

"Oh, I couldn't impose on you."

"Sure you can." Montgomery's voice took on an imperative tone. "Everyone else does."

Maria was taken aback, unable to decide what meaning his words held.

"Oh, come now, Maria," he chuckled. "This is the Deep South. It's the cradle of hospitality."

"Well, if you insist."

"I do indeed."

"I've made plans to spend some time with Jesse and his friend, Al, somewhere in the Atchaf . . ."

"Atchafalaya Basin," Montgomery finished the word for her. "I think you'll find it interesting. It's the largest wetlands wilderness in the country, to my knowledge."

"Ah-chaff-ah-lie-ah," Maria said slowly. "If I'm going there I should at least know how to pronounce it."

"When may we expect you?" Montgomery looked away from Maria toward a stack of papers on his desk.

"Jesse and I didn't decide on anything definite. Two or three days I suppose."

"Splendid. You'll have need of some creature comforts after three days in the wilderness." Montgomery's eyes crinkled when he smiled, and there was a cast to them that made Maria uncomfortable.

Chance shifted about uneasily in front of the desk. Maria half expected him to raise his hand like a schoolboy.

"Why don't you take your young lady to lunch, Chance?" Montgomery said without looking up from his paperwork. "It'll take longer than I thought to finish up here."

"Thanks, Captain." Chance took Maria by the arm. "I'll pick you up about one."

Montgomery remained bent over his work as they made their way across the crowded room among the silent typewriters and the loud stares. Outside, the glare of noon hit them with a heat that immediately began to wilt Maria's crisp white dress.

"Is there someplace cool we can go?" Maria took a handkerchief and blotted the perspiration on her face and neck.

Chance opened the door of the Buick for her. "Not on the base. There's a place in town though. Kinda reminds me of Ollie's. And it's always cool in there."

* * *

Maria sat with Chance at one of the little wooden ice-cream-parlor tables near the single front window of the drugstore. The building had sixteen-foot ceilings with three fans whirling softly high up in the gloom. The soda fountain curved around one wall. It was made of dark, elaborately carved wood and was softly lighted by four ornate globes above the mirror on the wall behind it. Malt, sundae, and Coca-Cola glasses sat on a shelf beneath the mirror. The finish on the pine floors had been mostly scuffed away by years of shoe leather.

Maria wondered how it could be so cool inside with no windows open for ventilation. It seemed that a crisp October day had somehow been trapped inside the building. The place carried an atmosphere of unreality about it, like a postcard mailed from the turn of the century.

A chunky seventeen-year-old with straight yellow hair, who wore a white apron over his overalls, walked around from behind the counter to the jukebox. He dropped two nickels in and punched the buttons. "Y'all need anything else?"

"No thanks," Chance called back. "We're fine."

"I'm gonna be cleanin' up in back if you do," the boy mumbled. The jukebox played "Little Brown Jug" by the Glenn Miller Orchestra as the boy disappeared through a curtain that hung over the doorway.

"So, how are things going for you in the army?" Maria sipped her tall, icy Coke directly from the glass.

Chance poked his ice with a straw. "Not quite as much fun as the summer tournaments on the Riveria, but not as bad as my ol' man's visits when I was a kid."

"Did he come to see you and your mother often?"

"Three times all total, best I can remember—maybe four." Chance looked out the window at a raggedy pickup sputtering by with a half-dozen children in the back. "Let's don't talk about this. I don't know why I brought it up. Better to keep the past buried. I don't like all them old bones poking up through the ground at me."

Maria was surprised at the touch of poetic imagery in his language. "Fine with me. Why don't you tell me about Captain Montgomery?"

"The captain," Chance smiled. "He's all right. Wants to impress his club friends by having a world-class tennis player hanging around with him. You know how the idle rich are? I expect you saw a lot of them in New York."

Maria nodded. "And what's the good captain going to do for the world-class player?" She had her suspicions, but wanted to hear the story from Chance.

His face grew cloudy for a moment, then he flashed his best smile. "You *almost* make me feel guilty, Maria. *Almost.* I'm just doin' things the army way. Making' friends. Exchangin' favors."

"Could you be a little more specific?"

"I don't think it'll help the reading public's morale to find out what really goes on in the army," Chance frowned.

"This isn't for the story," Maria went on. "This is strictly for my own information."

"Well, in that case, the good captain's moving up to battalion—headquarters company—and he's bringing me along as his driver. That's the way things get done in the army."

Maria stared directly into Chance's blue eyes. They seemed to have flecks of charcoal in the dim light. "What about Jesse? What job does he get?"

"Exactly what he asked for," Chance replied eagerly, glad to have someone else in Maria's sights. "Tanks."

"He *asked* for tanks?"

"Crazy ain't it? I talked to him about it. Thought I might could bring him along with me."

"What'd he say?"

Chance shook his head slowly. "Says he got some kind of word from God to be the best soldier he could. I'll tell you what I think. Ol' Jesse thinks a tank is just a big steel jawbone of an ass he can use to slay his enemies—only they're Germans, not Philistines. And the Germans got bigger jawbones than we do."

"Maybe he *can* do just that, Chance," Maria mused. "You may be right though. From what I've heard, the Germans are way ahead of us in the tank department."

"I don't think there's any doubt about that, but I've seen men like Jesse before. He'd take on the whole German army. I'm gonna stay as far away from him as I can."

From the jukebox, Walter Huston sang the haunting lyrics of "September Song."

"I wouldn't have thought he'd have picked that song," Maria remarked.

"You never can tell about people, can you?" Chance glanced at the door the boy had left through.

"Chance, don't you feel any responsibility at all to your country?" she asked solemnly.

"Sure. But we don't all have to be heroes. I worked hard all my life to get where I am." A knot of muscle at Chance's jawbone was working beneath the skin. "When this thing's over, I can turn pro and make some real money. Some of the best in the game told me I've got the talent to win a couple of Wimbledons. If I can do that, the racquet endorsements with Wilson or Dunlop, plus exhibition tournaments, will keep me in the chips for a long time. Then a teaching pro job at one of the big clubs in Miami or New York, and I'm set for life."

Maria remained silent, staring out the window at the heat shimmering in waves over the hot pavement.

"What's wrong with that?" Chance complained. "I don't want to spend the rest of my life at that crummy club in Liberty, teaching kids and rich women with too much time on their hands."

"I didn't say anything was wrong with it, Chance." She glanced over at him.

He looked puzzled. "You didn't? Well, in this ol' world a man's got to look out for himself."

"Why don't you give me Preston's address before I forget it?" Maria asked, still staring out the window.

"You're not mad at me are you?" Chance reached across the table, taking her small, slim hand in his.

Maria felt her hand, damp and cool from the Coke glass, warmed by Chance's. She looked at the lean brown hand covering hers, thinking it must have stored up sunshine from all those years on the tennis courts. "No, I'm not mad, Chance. You seem to think people only have two emotions—mad and everything's OK."

Walter Huston was singing the last notes of "September Song" on the jukebox. *And these few precious days I'll spend with you.*

"Things are getting a little confusing between us, Maria." Chance let his hand slip away from hers. "We've got a chance to

105

spend some time together at a beautiful home in a great city. See the sights, have a good time. Why complicate things?"

She felt a yearning to let herself flow into his arms—to feel his lean, hard body against hers. She fought against it. "Maybe you're right."

"Sure I am," he beamed across the table. "I thought about you all the time after you left. I'm so glad to see those big, brown eyes again. To hear that funny talk of yours. And to smell your perfume. I need to be a little closer for that though."

"You do make life seem simple." Maria struggled to keep her emotions in check.

"I missed you and I'm happy to see you again. And I think you feel the same way. That's the important thing right now, isn't it?" Chance stood up and took both of Maria's hands, bringing her to her feet.

Maria leaned against him, feeling the cold brass buckle against her stomach, his hard arms slipped around her, pressing her close. She felt she would become a part of him if she let herself go—would never be able to find her way back.

A nickel clunked into the jukebox.

"Chance," she gasped, pushing away from him.

The boy smiled, walked around behind the counter, and began washing dishes.

Maria looked at the big schoolhouse clock on the wall. "Oh, my goodness! I was supposed to pick up Jesse and Al an hour ago. They'll be waiting out in this heat. This is awful!" She hurried out of the drugstore ahead of Chance.

Outside, Chance opened the car door for Maria, then went around and got in behind the steering wheel. The car was parked in the shade of a sycamore growing in a vacant lot next to the drugstore. High in the leafy crown, a mockingbird's song told of how pretty the clouds looked raising their fleecy sails against the sky.

Maria turned to Chance. "Let's go. They're waiting for me in this dreadful heat."

"You really are comin' to New Orleans, aren't you?" Chance had both hands on the steering wheel, his face turned toward her.

Maria thought he looked like the boy he must have been, growing up in Liberty. She could almost hear his father making him a promise they both knew would be broken. "Of course," she said softly, placing her hand on his shoulder. "Why wouldn't I?"

He took her hand. "I don't know. Guess I just need to hear it again."

A warm breeze ruffled Maria's hair. "I'll be there, Chance. Don't worry about it."

Two reddish brown mules pulled an ancient wagon down the street. The driver was shiny black, wearing faded overalls and a wide-brimmed straw hat. He tipped his hat to the young soldier and his dark-haired girlfriend in the pale yellow convertible as he clattered and clanked by them.

9

ATCHAFALAYA

*T*he lake stands in the wild and forbidding southern end of the great Atchafalaya River Basin. Fifteen miles across and shallow, it has a reputation for swamping Cajuns foolhardy enough to try and cross it in their fragile pirogues when the summer storms come sweeping up out of the Gulf of Mexico.

During the hot months, fat water moccasins flatten out their charcoal-colored bodies along the cypress and willow limbs just above the dark waters of the swamp to soak up the sunshine. Beneath them swim the bluegills, black bass, crappie (called *sac-a-lait* by the swamp dwellers), goggle-eye, and redears or *chinquapin* that make up a large portion of the Cajun diet.

The swamps and countless bayous that meander through them are home to white-tailed deer and alligators. Snowy egrets wade the shallows along the shorelines stalking minnows. As the violet dusk settles over the basin, blue herons sail just above the open waters of the lake, their wings glinting like gunmetal in the sun's last rays.

A yearling white-tail, her white fawn markings slowly fading to the rich brown color she would wear for the rest of her life, stepped daintily out of the deep shadows of the swamp onto the open bank of a bayou. She had gotten separated from her mother and sniffed the familiar scent where the grown deer had entered the water to swim to the opposite bank.

She looked to the right where the bayou entered the bright open expanse of the lake. A rough log, almost submerged, floated heavily just offshore near the mouth of the bayou. Hearing a soft splash, she looked left and saw a beaver swimming upstream with a freshly cut willow limb in its mouth, a wide V spreading behind it from its passage through the dark water.

The yearling took one step into the edge of the bayou, sinking almost up to her shoulder in the black mud of the bottom. She jumped back, her leg making a sucking noise as it pulled loose. A slight rippling of the water at the mouth of the bayou startled her. Looking to her right, the yearling saw a snowy egret rise from its perch near the lakeshore, its wings spread in a white splendor of flight. Nothing else moved.

Summoning her courage, the yearling leaped into the bayou and began swimming furiously and clumsily toward the opposite bank. Her wide brown eyes mirrored a fear of the unknown at being in this alien place, these murky depths, without her mother. She gained the water's edge, struggling to free herself from the black ooze. Her forelegs reached solid ground, the right back leg pulled free.

The black surface of the water erupted in geysers of white as the alligator broke through, its jaws gaping whitely—then snapping shut like a steel trap on the very bottom of the left hind leg of the yearling. She jerked and struggled to pull free, slipping toward the edge of shock, but there was no hope of escaping the jaws once they clamped shut.

The alligator spun its huge armored body over and over in the water, ripping the hoof off and throwing the yearling down onto the muddy bank. The reptile righted itself and with a swipe of its ridged tail through the water, lunged again for the deer. Seizing her last chance for life, the yearling gained her feet. Summoning all her remaining strength, she leaped with her good right leg up the bank as the jaws of the alligator slammed shut inches from her hindquarters.

Through the thick underbrush, the yearling fled from the monster. She could hear it bellowing out its rage to the swamps, tearing at the dense trees that held it at bay. The deer would live to have her own young, but always she would carry the mark of the gator.

*   *   *

"What's that horrible noise?" Maria asked as she turned off the dirt road and parked under one of the huge live oaks that spread its limbs over the front yard of Al's home.

Al glanced down the lake where the noise was coming from. "That's a big bull gator. Something's got him mighty stirred up. You don't want to be around them when they get like that."

"One of my uncles saw some big gators down in the Okefenokee Swamp," Jesse chimed in. "Said they could outrun a man on a flat stretch of ground."

"Thanks, Jesse. That's just what I needed to hear," Maria muttered, staring down through the woods toward the lake where the sound was coming from. "I think I'll spend the next three days inside the house with Al's mother."

"Mama would like that," Al offered, handing Jesse the two cumbersome duffel bags they had stowed on the backseat. "She only had us two boys. Always wanted a daughter, her."

Maria watched Al struggle with the two heavy bags. "Why did you bring all that gear for just a week?"

"We've moved out of our basic training barracks," Jesse answered, handling one bag with each of his powerful arms. "We'll go to new ones for our advanced training, but for now we've got no place to store anything. So we pack it all around with us."

Al took Maria's keys and went around to get her luggage out of the trunk. She leaned against the hood of the car and took a good look at the house.

The home was an Acadian-style cottage with a staircase leading from the right side of the long front gallery directly up into the attic. It was constructed of heart cypress, using the board-and-batten method, and had weathered to a silver gray through a hundred years of summer sunshine and the torrential south Louisiana rains. Porch swings flanked either side of the wide front door, and ladder-backed chairs with cowhide seats were scattered at random over the wooden planking of the gallery. The high roof was made of tin, with gables at either end.

Maria saw a short round woman of about fifty walk out onto the front gallery. She wore a long, flowered dress and a white apron. Her black hair was streaked with gray and tied up in bun at the back of her head. "Alcide, you come give you mama a big hug, you," she beamed as Al walked around the car carrying Maria's two suitcases. She walked down the steps and into her son's arms.

Al stepped back from his mother and introduced her to Maria and Jesse.

"We so glad to have y'all wid us." Renée Naquin took Jesse by the shoulders and kissed him on both cheeks. "Alcide tell me in his letters you a good boy."

"How do you do, Mrs. Naquin." Maria greeted her formally, extending her hand.

Renée ignored the hand, gave her a big hug and kissed her lightly on the cheek. "My goodness, you a pretty little thing, Sha. I always wanted a little girl like you, but all I ever got was two big ol' ugly boys." She grinned at her son.

"I don't care what you say about me, Mama," Al started up the wide steps with Maria's suitcases, "long as you got plenty pots cookin' on the stove."

Leaving the bags on the front porch, the four of them walked down a dimly lit hall with several doors leading off of it. Renée pointed out the bedroom Maria would be using.

The huge kitchen was located at the rear of the house. Three coal-oil lanterns hung across the ceiling, casting a slightly flickering, smoky light about the place. A black wood stove sat against the far wall and held an assortment of heavy pots and pans. One large iron pot was full of bubbling gumbo, another of cooked rice. A long table and a dozen chairs made of rubbed cypress stood in the center of the floor. It was set with heavy white dishes and cutlery for four.

"Y'all set down," Renée ordered jovially, bustling about to serve the food. "I made us a little snack."

"Where's Daddy and Vernon?" Al asked, grabbing his spoon in preparation for the feast.

"They out in the swamps runnin' the nets." Renée took Maria's bowl over to the stove. "They'll be back sometime in the morning."

Maria watched her spoon out copious amounts of steaming rice and rich, dark-red gumbo into the large white bowl. "Oh, I'll never be able to eat all that."

Renée, ignoring her protest, kept spooning. "You too skinny, Sha. We gonna feed you real good. Then you be healthy like me." Renée laughed, patting her round belly.

Taking a spoonful of the rice, rich sauce, and plump, succulent shrimp, Maria thought she had never tasted anything so good. The spicy food had a special flavor that was different from anything she had eaten before. "Mrs. Naquin, this is the best food I've ever had. You'll have to give me the recipe."

"Recipe? I just trow it all in the pot and it come out like this, Sha," Renée smiled. "No recipe."

After the meal was over, Maria could barely get up from the table. She offered to help Renée clean up but was ushered politely out of the kitchen. She and Jesse followed Al out onto the large back porch. Maria was surprised to see that it extended over the lake itself. A set of steps led down four feet onto a dock that had a low wooden railing and stood about two feet above the water. Two pirogues and a wide flat-bottomed boat were tied to the railing.

Maria looked out over the dark expanse of the lake, shimmering in the moonlight. "This is different from any place I've ever seen. So vast and wild and beautiful."

"I wish I didn't have to go back," Al murmured, sitting down in a wicker chair.

"I see why you talked about it so much now," Jesse added, walking over to the porch railing.

"Leaving here is almost bad as dying. It seem like it anyway. I ain't never been dead, me," Al laughed.

"You'll be back one day," Maria encouraged. "This war can't last forever."

"You right, Sha," he agreed. "But I'm gonna enjoy this week like it was my last one on earth. I'm going up to bed now, Jesse. You come when you get ready. Right up them stairs out on the front porch."

"I won't be too long," Jesse replied. "Got to make up for some of that sleep we lost in basic."

Al turned to Maria. "I'll put your suitcases in your room, Sha. Y'all sleep good."

After he left, Maria moved over to the railing where Jesse stood. "Let's walk along the lake for a while."

"Sure."

They walked down a second set of steps that led to the hard-packed ground of the yard. Cattails and water lilies lined the edge of the lake that had been cleared of underbrush near the house. A few huge cypress and Tupelo gum trees remained, like towering sentinels against the night sky. Farther down the shore, where the sound of the bull gator's raging had come from, the trackless swamp began.

Maria listened to the soft lapping of the waves against the shoreline. She decided to get right to it. "Jesse, why did you choose tanks? That's the best way to get killed I know of. We've got nothing to match those German Tiger tanks."

"Sometimes I ask myself that, Maria. I wish there were a simple answer." He stopped and leaned against a huge cypress, its high-ridged roots extending darkly down into the lake. "I prayed a lot about this war, about how I could serve God—and my country—best. Sometimes the army lets you choose your field—most times they do it for you. I asked for tanks, and that's what I got. Maybe I missed it. Missed what God wanted me to do. It happens even when we try our best."

Maria gazed closely at him while he spoke, saw the intense light that came to his eyes, and felt his open, honest emotion. She suddenly realized that he considered himself irrelevant in the world, except as a means of serving his God. There was nothing contrived about the way he lived. It was as natural for him as selfishness is for other men.

"But I know this," Jesse continued. "God is faithful. That's what I'm countin' on to see me through this war."

As she started to speak, Maria found that she had no words to express what she had just found out about Jesse. A man who trusted completely in God, put Him first in his life, was beyond her comprehension. She moved closer to him, slipping her arms around his waist and laying her head against his chest. She felt his physical strength as he put his arms around her, pulling her close. But she knew the true strength of Jesse Boone had nothing at all to do with powerful muscles.

She stayed for a long time in Jesse's arms where she felt safe and warm and somehow like she had as a small child when her mother would sing to her at bedtime as she drifted off to sleep. She could almost hear her mother's song again in the sound of the night wind blowing across the lake.

* * *

Maria awakened to a deafening noise. Rising from the depths of sleep, she thought a terrible brawl was going on down the hall or that perhaps the house was on fire. Then she heard the music.

113

Nobody plays music for a fire—except Nero. From outside she heard the sound of children playing.

Dressing hurriedly, Maria stepped out into the hall. The first light of morning drifted through the open front door like a soft gray mist. She seemed to be dreaming still, caught in some kind of twilight world between sounds of children playing in the yard and the clamor coming from the kitchen.

"Co-mo-sah-vah?" a dark-eyed man wearing khakis and polished high-topped work shoes shouted to Maria as soon as she appeared at the kitchen door. He was playing an accordion and never missed a note while he spoke.

Maria knew the man was Al's father as soon as she saw him. They were almost identical, except for the man's gray hair.

Al came to her rescue. "This is my daddy, Jerome Naquin, Maria. Daddy, this is Maria Vitrano." Al turned to speak in Maria's ear so she could hear him better. "Tell him, 'sah van bien,' Maria."

Almost stunned by the noise and activity in the kitchen, Maria shouted back without thinking. "Sah van bien."

Naquin smiled broadly and continued his animated and athletic accordion playing.

Al ushered Maria about the large kitchen, introducing her to aunts, uncles, and cousins whose names she promptly forgot. His brother looked as much like their mother as Al did their father. An assortment of people, all with that unmistakable look of kinship, moved about the kitchen in various activities that tended to define their roles. The women tended toward work and the men toward crowding as much fun as possible into the shortest amount of time.

Al's mother led the work, and his father was the undisputed king of play. The women bustled about the stove and cabinets preparing food and drink. Jerome Naquin had assistance with the music making from two fiddle players. In the open area of the kitchen near three high, bright windows, a couple would occasionally break into the Cajun two-step, a dance that fascinated Maria. It appeared to her that those who stomped the floor the hardest were considered the best dancers.

Someone pushed a cup of coffee into Maria's hand and she made her way to the far end of the table where Jesse sat watching the show. The table held dishes of bacon, eggs, sausage, and other foods as well as clean plates and cups and those that had already been used.

"Sit down and enjoy yourself," Jesse smiled. "I doubt we'll ever see anything like this again."

Maria sat next to him, listening to the music and the laughter and the conversations in Cajun French. She watched the dancing and other activities in the room with the same fascination for people that had brought her to journalism. "I've never seen people enjoy themselves so much. I'll bet they have more fun in one day than a lot of people have their whole lifetimes."

"Try some of the sausage," Jesse urged.

"I've eaten southern sausage before," she replied, looking with wonder at the assortment of food on the table. "I want to try something different."

"*This* is different." Jesse forked a length of sausage from the platter and dropped it on her plate.

Taking a large bite, Maria's eyes grew round and began to water. She gasped and grabbed a glass of water from the table, drinking half of it. "What *is* that?"

"Boudin," he laughed. "Good, huh?"

"I think I'll have to get used to it." She drank more water. "Maybe smaller bites will help."

Renée Naquin appeared next to Maria holding a large black skillet. She spooned a brown mixture into a bowl.

"That's not hot is it?" Maria asked warily.

"No, Sha. You gonna like this, yeah." Unlike the sausage, Renée's smile had the perfect amount of warmth to it. "That boudin takes some gettin' used to."

"What *is* this?"

"Kush-kush. Corn meal browned in bacon grease." Renée spooned sugar onto the mixture, poured in some milk, and stood smiling down at her.

Maria took a small bite, chewing carefully. "This is wonderful." She ate the entire bowl as though she were famished, bringing a flush of pleasure to Renée's plump face.

"We make a Cajun girl outta you yet," she smiled, turning away toward her stove.

It was the fullest day Maria could ever remember. The music and dancing never ceased except for refreshments and a short nap in mid-afternoon. The men and boys raced pirogues on the lake and played softball on a makeshift diamond. Women and children cheered them on, and everyone ate crawfish and crabs boiled in large black pots under the shade trees.

"C'mon, Jesse," Al shouted, waving to him from an open area down by the lake. "We gonna show these Cajun swamp rats what two trained G.I.s can do."

Jesse sat next to Maria on the back porch, nursing his gorged stomach and enjoying the breeze off the lake. "I'm ready for anything, Al, long as I can do it lying down."

"C'mon! We gonna have two-man pirogue races."

"We've already done that."

"Not on dry land."

Puzzled, Jesse went down to join his friend.

Four pirogues sat side by side on the ground. A rope was attached to the bow of each of them. Two men stood next to each small boat trying to outbrag the other about how easily his team was going to win the race.

Al explained the contest to Jesse. "It's simple, simple. Even a ignorant Georgia cracker like you could understand it."

Jesse smiled at his friend and at the good-natured jests of the other contestants.

"First," Al continued, "you get in and I pull you to that big oak tree where Daddy's sitting in his chair.

"On the ground?" Jesse asked without thinking.

"You see any water between here and that tree?" Al smiled at the other men flexing their muscles for the women spectators. "Maybe he *ain't* smart enough to learn this."

Jesse grabbed him by his shirt collar, doubling up his fist in a feigned threat.

Maria sat on the porch, watching Jesse and the Cajuns at their games. She thought he looked handsome in his well-worn jeans and red-and-white striped pullover shirt that failed to conceal the whipcord muscles of his arms and shoulders.

Al chuckled as Jesse released him. "When you can touch the tree with your hand, you get out of the pirogue and pull me back across the finish line." He pointed where two young girls in bright print dresses held a plow line decorated with colorful strips of cloth.

"Sounds easy enough," Jesse smiled, stepping into the pirogue. "The first half, anyway."

The men lined up at the starting line, the ropes across their shoulders. Jerome Naquin fired his shotgun and the race was on. Grunting and puffing like steam engines, the men struggled across the open ground, towing the pirogues in the hot afternoon sunshine. Some used the strategy of saving the heavier man for last—others sought to build up a lead by putting the light man in the boat first. Two of the men paired up because they were of the same build, feeling that a balanced team would have the best chance.

Al was the smallest of the men in the race. He put every ounce of his strength into it, but the other three teams had reached the tree and were already on their way back toward the finish line when Jesse reached out and slapped the rough bark of the oak. Al collapsed into the pirogue like a dead man.

"You too far behind now, Sha," Jerome Naquin called out to Jesse from his chair in the shade.

Jesse threw the rope over his shoulder and leaned into it.

Al could already hear the humiliating remarks of the other men when they crossed the finish line last, but he was too tired to care. Suddenly the pirogue jerked forward like it had been hooked to a truck. He thought someone must have put wheels on it. Sitting up, he saw Jesse flying across the open ground after the other teams as though he were towing a balloon instead of a heavy wooden boat with a man in it.

Jesse passed the first man like he was tied to a post. The second man, struggling with all his might, had his eyes shut and didn't see him go by. His eyes wide in disbelief as he looked over his shoulder, the man in the lead doubled his efforts as Jesse drew nearer.

Al was sitting up in the pirogue now, cheering for Jesse in his native French, his arms flailing above his head.

Five yards from the finish, Jesse plunged past the lead team and broke through the bright splashes of color, dragging the plow line along with him. Al was out of the boat in a flash, still shouting in French. He jumped up and down, finally throwing himself on the exhausted Jesse until they both fell laughing to the ground. The other barefoot, sweating men trudged over to congratulate the victors.

* * *

The sun hung like a glowing red disk above the dark wall of cypress trees that stretched along the edge of the lake. It danced and sparkled on the wind-ruffled waters in a final display of brightness before the coming of the night.

Jesse sat on the back-porch steps with Al and all his family scattered about on the ground below. In the last light he could see the lily pads next to the shore blooming with purple blossoms. He smelled the dark, damp earth and the crimson and yellow four o'clocks in Renée's flower bed next to the house. And he gazed at the upturned, smiling faces of his newfound friends.

"Al asked me to say a few words to y'all," he began, "because I'm a preacher. And because, livin' way out here in the swamps, y'all hardly ever make it to church. He says I talk for a livin', so I had to do this for him. But I want to say them because I'm thankful I got to know all of you. Grateful that you've asked me into your home."

"We glad to have you wid us, Sha," someone in the crowd remarked for them all.

"In the fifteenth chapter of John, Jesus is talking to His disciples. He tells them, 'I have called you friends.' Next to giving your life to Jesus, there is no greater blessing on this earth than having true friends."

"Jesus called men like us His friends?" Al's father said in amazement. "I didn't know that, me."

Jesse smiled. "And He'll be a friend to any of us who accept Him into our hearts. He said that He would never leave us nor forsake us. If we believe in our hearts that Jesus Christ is the only begotten Son of God, that He died for us and rose from the dead on the third day, then we have eternal life in Him. And we have the best friend there ever could be."

Jesse paused and let the words sink in. "If any of you want to talk with me about this later, I'd be more than happy to. Right now I want to do something that was ordained of God in the sixth chapter of the Book of Numbers."

Holding his hands out over the people, Jesse began. "'The Lord bless thee, and keep thee: The Lord make his face shine upon thee, and be gracious unto thee.'"

By now every head was bowed.

"'The Lord lift up his countenance upon thee, and give thee peace.'"

Maria sat in the yard near the flower bed, watching the faces of the people as Jesse finished the words that God had spoken to Moses thousands of years before. Muted conversations ran through the crowd like soft breezes. Some of them gradually edged closer to Jesse. A little girl with a white ribbon in her long dark hair smiled shyly up at him. He bent over and took her up in his arms.

Renée Naquin asked Jesse a question, but his words were lost to Maria in the night wind blowing off the lake. She fell asleep under the tree to the sound of Jesse's voice. Others gathered around as Jesse sat on the back steps and spoke with them. The child begged her mother to stay with him and slept in his arms as he talked late into the night with all those who came.

10

THE IDLE RICH

Maria took Preston Montgomery's arm, which he had extended to her as though she were receiving a priceless gift. They strolled through the elegantly furnished rooms of the family mansion among the elite of Old New Orleans.

The home was furnished with English antiques, massive grandfather clocks, plush wine-colored divans and chairs with intricately carved rosewood frames, and Persian rugs with patterns that were centuries old. The waxed hardwood floors gleamed with muted light from crystal chandeliers and elaborate gold fixtures that looked like they had been rubbed daily with soft cotton cloths. Oil paintings of the family going back 150 years hung in gilded frames along the walls of the central hall that ran the width of the house.

The people whispering through the rooms in their silks and satins were from the oldest and wealthiest families in New Orleans. In their glittering gowns, white throats, and wrists dripping with jewelry, the women appeared as cool and remote as mountain laurel. The men wearing black tuxedo coats exuded power and robust good health.

Maria felt completely out of place, noticing that when Montgomery introduced her, the others gave her an oblique glance as though a direct look would somehow drop them a notch in the social register. She imagined that they could smell the onion and garlic taint of her from the years of working in her father's little grocery store. The black linen sheath she wore seemed like the rags of a street urchin amid such elegance.

As if to make up for her hasty judgment of his friends, Maria said, "Your friends are awfully nice, Preston."

"*Nice* being a synonym for pompous, I suppose," Montgomery replied as he nodded to a whippet-slim woman with silver-blonde hair who sipped a glass of champagne.

"But, I . . ."

"No, you're absolutely correct," Montgomery grinned ironically. "I knew you were an astute woman the moment we met." He patted her hand and continued. "We are, I'm afraid, a pampered and spoiled and—alas—a dying breed. The great cotton and sugar cane plantations vanished three-quarters of a century ago. Our way of life died with them. What you see here," he flicked his manicured hand gracefully about the crowded rooms, "are mere ghosts and shadows. Insubstantial relics of a way of life that has—please excuse the banality—'Gone with the Wind.'"

Maria laughed musically. "You're excused, Preston. But how can you go on about your friends like this?"

"Because I'm the worst of the lot," he replied, accepting two glasses of wine from a white-coated Negro waiter who balanced his heavy silver tray with the dexterity of a circus performer.

"I'm afraid I don't understand."

"I'm an insufferable bore, shamelessly narcissistic, and addicted to drinking myself into a stupor at after-hours clubs with friends who are as archaic and useless as myself." Montgomery gazed about him at the animated and glittering people he was speaking of. "We do little but engage in conversations that are fatuous beyond belief."

Maria gave him a puzzled frown. "If you're so dissatisfied with your life, why don't you do something about it?"

"Because," he whispered with a melancholy smile, "as my sainted grandmother was fond of saying, 'You have no gumption, boy.'"

She shook her head sadly.

Montgomery brightened unexpectedly. "No, Maria. Sing no sad songs for me. You see, I rather enjoy my dissolute lifestyle. Recognizing its shortcomings by no means diminishes the fact that it's the only one I'm suited for. Having briefly dabbled in the workaday world some years ago, I am now resolutely hedonistic."

"How are you getting along in the army?" After his discourse, Maria couldn't imagine his adapting to a spartan and rigorous life in the military.

"Surprisingly well, actually," he replied. "I've discovered that the essence of army life is politics and paper—not charging into the valley of death as is commonly believed. Don't take me wrong though. Wars are won by the Sergeant Yorks, but for every soldier on the front line, there's fifteen or so in support or administrative functions."

"And you've arranged to be one of the latter?" Maria stopped and stared directly at him.

"Precisely," Montgomery answered bluntly, as though he had no misgivings whatsoever about his actions. "And our tennis prodigy has graciously consented to accompany me."

They walked through an open set of French doors onto a flagstone terrace. At the opposite end another set of French doors stood open. A Negro with skin the color of damp sand played a baby grand that had been placed on the terrace just outside the doors.

Montgomery led Maria down wide stone steps, flanked on either side by flower beds, into a brick-walled garden area. Crepe myrtles were strung with Japanese lanterns, and the scent of gardenia and jasmine drifted on the damp evening air. Blue-green lights glowed smokily beneath the surface of a tiled swimming pool.

At the far end of the pool stood a newly constructed kiosk painted brightly with red-and-white stripes. Chance leaned casually on its counter, sipping from a champagne glass. In deference to his standing in the tennis world, he was dressed in a pale blue sport coat, light tan slacks, and an open-throated white shirt. Several women, ranging in age from the mid-twenties to more than fifty were gathered around him in modest adulation.

"Chance seems to be enjoying himself," Maria commented, trying to sound unconcerned.

"Indeed," Montgomery commented. "I think he'd like very much to become accustomed to the finer things in life."

Seeing Maria and Montgomery walking along the edge of the pool, Chance excused himself and went to meet them.

"You seem to be enjoying your admirers, Chance," Montgomery smiled, glancing at the gathering around the kiosk.

Chance looked sheepishly at Maria. "Just giving them a few tips on the fundamentals of the game. They're really lookin' forward to our match in the morning."

"No one is taking this exhibition seriously," Montgomery responded. "I'm not in your class. It's just to give these hopeless souls something different to talk about over cocktails."

"Preston's being modest, Maria. He played number-one singles for Tulane. Made the finals in the NCAA championships." Chance bent his right knee, hitting a backhand with an imaginary racquet. "Had the smoothest backhand in the country."

"You never said a word about that, Preston," Maria smiled. "Modesty is a quality I didn't expect from you."

"That's because it's one I don't possess, dear girl." That business at Tulane was eight years ago. "And I made the finals when my opponent defaulted because of illness."

Chance fell in beside Maria. "Maybe so, but you *played* your way into the semis."

Montgomery ignored the intended compliment. "Chance, be a good sport and fetch Maria and me some more wine, will you?"

Maria saw a shadow cross Chance's face, anger flickering briefly in the depths of his eyes. "Yassuh, Boss," he drawled, replacing an emotional response with contrived action. "I be happy as a little ol' June bug to fetch you some wine, suh."

Montgomery laughed condescendingly. "You'd never have made it in a minstrel show, Chance. The accent's not bad, but the blue eyes would give you away every time."

Chance turned away toward the kiosk where the waiters were serving drinks.

Maria watched Montgomery gloat over his small victory. "Chance is very accommodating tonight, isn't he?" she observed, beginning to feel uncomfortable in this social environment based on an economy of favors and the exercise of power.

"Most of my friends usually see the benefit of an occasional— accommodation," Montgomery remarked absently.

Chance returned with the drinks, but Montgomery had lost interest in the game.

"Here you are, Maria," Chance offered, handing her the wine. "Preston?"

Montgomery held his hand up, palm outward. "No thanks. I see some old friends who've come in from the country. Please excuse me, won't you?" He moved gracefully down a brick walkway toward a gray-haired couple in casual clothes.

"You having fun?" Chance grinned like a ten-year-old. He was trying hard to let nothing spoil the visit.

"Not especially," she replied. *I'd much rather be in those lovely swamps watching Jesse and Al in the pirogue race.*

Chance frowned like someone had told him there really *was* no Santa Claus. He led her over to a cast-iron bench and slouched down on it. "How could you not enjoy all this?"

Maria sat next to him. "I just feel uncomfortable. I've got nothing at all in common with these people. Most of the men never did an honest day's work in their lives, and the women have been pampered like royalty."

"I think they're nice," Chance protested. "How do you know so much about them anyway?"

"Preston told me a lot. But even if he hadn't, I think it's pretty obvious. I saw the same types when I was covering the society beat for the newspaper."

Chance felt himself losing the sense of elation the party had given him. "Let's get something to eat."

Maria followed him to a brick barbecue pit where four waiters in white jackets were serving plates from a pig impaled on a roasting spit. They both chose plates of pork, barbecue beans, and fresh corn on the cob, as well as glasses of red wine. Returning to their bench, they balanced the plates on their laps and ate the spicy food.

A breeze from the river rustled the banana plants next to the brick wall. Food smells blended with those from the flower beds in a richly textured aroma that was slightly intoxicating. Conversation hummed through the enclosed garden area like a distant swarm of bees, punctuated by the rich bass voices of the men and the tinkling laughter of the women.

Maria sipped her wine. "Are you and Preston really playing a match in the morning?"

"I think that's the real reason he invited me. Not to give him lessons." Chance sliced a chunk of pork and forked it into his mouth, chewing it with contentment.

"He's not in your league, Chance. He may have been an excellent college player, but even I know there's light-years of distance between college and world-class players."

Chance gulped his wine. "Preston knows that. I told you. It's just a lark for him. What he really wants is a shot at the man who beat Fred Perry and Don Budge on the same day."

"Did you really do that? Isaac Paul mentioned that to me the day I saw him at the club."

"Those were just exhibition matches," Chance smiled. "Anything can happen in them. It'll be something to talk about, though, when I'm rocking my way through old age by somebody's fire."

They finished their food and sat sipping tiny glasses of crème de menthe brought to them by one of the waiters. The man at the piano began playing "As Time Goes By." Maria thought of walking down the streets of Liberty with Jesse after he had seen his first movie ever and of how he had sung the lyrics to the song. She turned toward Chance, who was nodding sleepily on the bench. He reminded her of a playful puppy she once had as a child who always got drowsy when his belly was full. *He's not quite as cute though.*

Maria stayed next to him on the bench, removed from the ebb and flow of the party now. She thought of what lay ahead for the two of them—and for Jesse. *This is not the time to get romantically involved with any man, Maria. Especially one going off to war.* The lonesome sound of a boat whistle came from the river like the cry of a lost soul wandering aimlessly in the night mist.

* * *

In the tennis match the next morning, Chance played to the crowd, such as it was. A dozen or so people left over from the party sat at white wrought-iron tables scattered along the edge of the court drinking Bloody Marys and nursing extravagant headaches.

The court was located beyond the garden on property that extended all the way through to the next street. Bordered by crepe myrtle and oleander, it was freshly clipped and lined. Chance thought its playing surface was as good as the courts at Wimbledon.

Montgomery was a surprisingly accomplished player with classic strokes. And he did have a flawless backhand. Chance ran down his best shots, floating the returns back like a ball machine so that Montgomery would be perfectly set up for his next shot.

Just to make it interesting, Chance would occasionally blast a ground stroke past Montgomery as he hit an approach shot and attempted to finish the point with a volley. Several times he would rocket a serve in for an ace. But to Maria and the others who had played the game, the match was more theater than tennis.

After the match, they all returned to the walled garden for a jazz brunch of café au lait, beignets, and fresh fruit. The piano player from the night before serenaded them with a repertoire ranging from Chopin to Fats Waller. The food was good, the coffee hot, and the music cool. All in all it proved to be a pleasant morning for the idle rich, except for the throbbing in their heads that beat out a metronomic and exasperating reminder of their mortality.

11

IN THE LAND OF
DREAMY DREAMS

W hy don't we go to the French Quarter?" Chance suggested as the three of them sat in rockers on the spacious front gallery overlooking St. Charles Avenue. He was stylishly casual in his tan slacks, white tennis shirt, and scuffed brown loafers, worn without socks.

After their naps, the remainder of the guests had bidden their farewells, leaving Maria, Chance, Montgomery, and the household staff in the sudden hush of the massive stone home.

"Capital idea," Montgomery agreed.

"Can we ride on one of those?" Maria chimed in, pointing to a green streetcar rocking along the grassy esplanade that divided St. Charles Avenue.

Montgomery smiled benignly at Maria, as though he was being tolerant of a child's request. "Of course. It goes all the way to Canal Street. The Quarter's just on the other side. I haven't taken the streetcar there in years."

Maria had heard about the French Quarter since she entered college. It held for her the same sense of mystery and forbidden desires as the Kasbah or Paris's Left Bank. The pictures she had seen of it looked more European than American. "What should I wear?"

"To the Quarter?" Montgomery laughed. "Anything's acceptable—from evening wear to au naturel."

Maria's face colored slightly. "How about some sloppy jeans and saddle oxfords?" It was the closest thing to a bohemian outfit she had with her.

"Perfect. You'll be the Betty Co-Ed of the Jackson Square ne'er-do-wells." Montgomery rose from his chair and waved for Maria

127

and Chance to follow him into the house. "Come, let us gird our loins to venture among the citizens of the netherworld."

Twenty minutes later they sat on the scarred wooden benches of the streetcar with the late afternoon breeze blowing through the open windows. The iron wheels clicking along the tracks made a pleasant, rhythmic sound as the car rocked gently back and forth. Working-class people and college students, as well as men in business suits carrying briefcases, waited next to palm trees or in the shade of oaks at the frequent stops along the avenue.

"This is just perfect," Maria sighed, gazing out at the hundred-year-old homes passing by in the flickering shade and sunlight. They were white-columned with wide galleries painted marine gray. Many had second-story porches and intricate latticework wreathed with ivy. Some had been built with widow's walks so that wives could look out across the roofs of the smaller houses near the river for the ships of their seafaring husbands.

Chance turned around from his seat in front of Maria and Montgomery. "Sure beats Liberty, Georgia."

"It's the loveliest part of New Orleans, in my estimation," Montgomery remarked.

The streetcar rattled to a stop at one of the cross streets. A wizened old Negro in a tattered sport coat and straw hat sat on a nail keg next to a makeshift snow-cone stand. Standing up, he walked over to the side of the streetcar and squinted up at the passengers. "Sweetest snowballs on the streetcar line."

"Three please," Montgomery said, handing him a dollar bill.

The man quickly made the snow cones with hand-ground ice and strawberry syrup, hurrying back with them just as the door of the streetcar creaked shut.

Maria took a small bite of the bright red snow cone, letting it melt in her mouth. "Absolutely delicious! I feel like a little girl again when my daddy used to take me to the zoo."

Montgomery, his arm resting on the back of the seat, let his fingers trail along Maria's arm. "You're about to have a similar experience, my dear. The Quarter resembles nothing more than a human zoo where the creatures voluntarily cage themselves."

Maria shivered slightly under his touch, glad when he returned his hand to the back of the bench. She gazed at the passing homes beyond sidewalks that were cracked and tilted upward by the roots of the huge spreading oaks. The lawns were clipped and bright with the colors of blooming flowers. Through the iron gates of the brick-walled gardens, she could see splashing fountains flanked by iron benches set among the banana plants and palm fronds.

They got off the streetcar at Canal and St. Charles. Canal Street looked tremendous under the wide evening sky, dwarfing the people and even the automobiles humming along the pavement that stretched from City Park to the Mississippi River.

"I've never seen a street so wide," Maria remarked.

"Widest in the world," Montgomery informed them, brushing streetcar dust from his pleated gabardines. "Or so I'm told."

"There's one in Paris that'd give it a run for its money," Chance added. "I saw it when I played the French championships."

"I would imagine your traveling *has* been educational, Chance," Montgomery muttered, as though offended by the threat of another street rivaling his hometown's.

"Not unless you call locker rooms, tennis stadiums, and hotels educational," Chance laughed. "That's about all we have time for on the circuit."

"This way," Montgomery ordered and began walking down St. Charles away from Canal Street.

Maria pointed in the opposite direction. "I thought the French Quarter was over there."

"It is," he agreed. "But right now I have a taste for some oysters on the half-shell."

A half-block down they turned into The Pearl, a plate-glass-fronted restaurant with black-and-white inlaid tile on the floor and a long metal-topped counter on the left. Ceiling fans turned slowly twenty feet up. The place was airy and spacious and smelled of the sea.

"Give us three dozen on the half-shell, DeJean," Montgomery demanded, seating himself at the counter on one of the chrome cushion-topped stools. "They are fresh, aren't they?"

Curet DeJean was born in Barataria, in the swamps across the Mississippi River and below New Orleans. He came from a family of fishermen and trappers who plied the same waters as the pirate Jean Lafitte. City life suited the dark-skinned, wiry little man much better than the stifling summers and damp, cold winters of the bayous. "Fresh? Does the bishop wear a funny hat?"

Montgomery frowned at Maria and Chance. "I've known this swamp rat for twelve years, and I've yet to have him answer a question—except with another question. Don't know why I keep bothering to come to this disreputable establishment."

"'Cause we got the best oysters in New Orleans," DeJean grinned, turning toward the ice bins behind him. He raked the oysters out of the bins, shucking them open with a short, thick-bladed knife and dropping them on metal trays with surprising speed. In a few minutes he set three trays of oysters on the counter.

Maria stared at the fleshy pink-and-gray oysters still resting in their shells. "Do we cook them ourselves?"

"And ruin the flavor? I think not." Montgomery took a slice of lemon from a saucer and squeezed it onto one of the oysters and added a few drops of Tabasco from the green-labeled bottle. Then he brought the oyster up to his mouth, letting it slide out of its shell, into his mouth, and down his throat in one motion.

Maria winced slightly. "I've eaten them fried. But never like this before."

Montgomery washed the oyster down with a hefty swallow of draft beer from a mug DeJean had set before him. "Try one. You'll never eat them cooked again."

Maria and Chance found the oysters weren't bad after the first two or three. As they ate, the restaurant gradually began to fill up. Office workers and longshoremen sat side by side on the stools along the counter, while couples and families occupied the tables scattered about the tiled floor.

When the trays were empty, Montgomery waved DeJean over and handed him a twenty from a wad of bills in a gold money clip. "You were right for once. The oysters were fresh."

"I been right a hundred times now, at least," the Cajun smirked, stuffing the twenty into his right front trouser pocket. "You wouldn't keep bringing all your friends in here if I wasn't."

"You ready to see the Quarter now, Maria?" Montgomery asked, sliding off the stool.

She followed him. "Oh, yes! I can't wait to see all the old buildings and Jackson Square."

As they left The Pearl, Montgomery turned back toward the counter, the hint of a smile on his face. "DeJean! Do you still have your night job tending bar at The Arsenal?"

DeJean looked up from wiping a beer mug with a large white cloth. "Do people get stupid on Mardi Gras Day?"

"He never disappoints me," Montgomery grinned, walking out the door.

When they left the broad expanse of Canal Street behind and walked down the sidewalks of Royal, Maria felt that she had crossed into another country. The streets of The Quarter were narrow and dark with the atmosphere and architecture of Paris or Budapest. She stopped in front of a small, dimly lit grocery store that reminded her of her father's. Through the screen door, she could smell the coffee beans, bananas, cheeses, and fruit. She thought of her mother briefly, but feeling the sadness lingering at the back of her memories, she pushed them aside and caught up to Chance and Preston.

"See something interesting back there?" Chance asked, gawking at a rouged and painted woman wearing spiked heels, black net stockings, and a bright red dress.

"No, just being a tourist," Maria answered.

They continued down Royal, past the antique shops and the jewelry stores, with tiny show windows glittering dimly in the settling dusk. Turning right on Toulouse, they went a block before taking a left on Chartres.

Gazing down Chartres, Maria saw the towering twin spires of the St. Louis Cathedral glinting in the last rays of sunlight. "How beautiful!" she exclaimed.

"Built in 1794," Montgomery commented. "The frescoes are spectacular."

"What?" Chance asked, watching an organ grinder's monkey snatching coins from bypassers.

Maria pointed upward toward the building two blocks away.

Chance stared for a moment as the light suddenly vanished from the facade of the ancient church. Maria noticed that a light seemed to come on in his eyes. "It is nice," he said softly as if he were inside the church.

Montgomery led them under a wooden colonnade and through a glass door into a quiet, dark club. A mahogany bar trimmed with gleaming brass occupied one wall. They sat at a corner table, listening to a jazz ensemble and drinking. Chance nursed a glass of beer while Maria sipped a glass of white wine. Montgomery had several Scotches with water on the side.

After visiting two more bars, Maria asked Montgomery, "Couldn't we see some of the old buildings?"

"You are seeing them, my dear—the interiors—and they're all old in the Quarter."

Later they walked down Pirate's Alley that led them alongside the cathedral and into Jackson Square.

"William Faulkner lived here in Pirate's Alley during his New Orleans sojourn," Montgomery commented. "Wrote a series of articles for the *Times-Picayune*."

"I think he also wrote *Soldier's Pay* while he was here," Maria added. "I believe that was his first novel, but I'm not sure. As a lit major, I'm supposed to remember these things."

"We'll finish the evening in grand tourist fashion," Montgomery suggested, moving to another topic of conversation. Maria had noticed that he did that often when someone knew more than he about the subject at hand.

"How do you mean, Preston?" Chance asked as they left the alley, entering into Jackson Square.

"Café au lait and beignets at the Café du Monde."

Maria noticed that Montgomery spoke with a thick tongue. *All that Scotch is catching up to him.*

"Boy, that's a mouthful of French!" Chance responded, looking through the tall, piked iron fence at the statue of Andrew Jackson astride his spirited horse.

"A mouthful of heaven," Montgomery added happily. "Wait'll you taste them, Maria."

"Didn't we have some of those for breakfast this morning?" she asked.

"Yes, but not like the ones you're about to sample. I really don't know what gives them such a special flavor. Maybe it's just the atmosphere."

They turned right on St. Ann, walking along next to the square in front of the Pontalba Apartments, the oldest in the United States. Adorned with iron columns and delicate wrought-iron balustrades, they extended all the way to the Café du Monde, located next to the levee bordering the Mississippi.

The threesome took a table on the patio next to Decatur Street where horse-drawn carriages clattered along the pavement, giving the tourists a chance to step back into the nineteenth century. The smell of fresh coffee and pastry from the café blended with those of the watermelons, cantaloupes, and strawberries displayed on long tables under the arched colonnades of the French Market next door.

A gangly black waiter in an even blacker uniform served them milk-rich coffee in heavy white mugs, along with the square-shaped beignets. The beignets were flaky brown, dusted with white powdered sugar, and so hot they had to be held with napkins.

Maria tasted the warm, sugary lightness of the flaky beignet. "You're right, Preston. There is something special about these. They almost melt in your mouth."

Sipping the rich tan coffee, Chance declared, "This has really been a great day, Preston. You folks down here really know how to treat your guests."

"Just an ordinary day among the obscenely wealthy," Montgomery smiled, slurring his words slightly. He leaned toward Maria, covering her hand with his. "And how about you, lovely lady? Did you have a good time today?"

She eased her hand away. "It was just wonderful, Preston. You're the perfect host."

Afterward they followed Decatur Street past Jackson Square to Tchoupitoulas and turned left on Iberville to The Arsenal. It stood close by the wharfs on the river and was a favorite watering hole of the longshoremen as well as foreign seamen.

Curet DeJean spotted them as soon as they stepped through the door. "Over here, Mr. Preston," he called out, coming around from behind the bar. "I saved your booth."

"You're a prince, DeJean," Montgomery remarked, ushering Maria into the velvet-cushioned booth.

"What y'all havin'?" DeJean asked, glancing from Maria to Chance and back again.

"Coffee," Chance replied with a suppressed yawn.

"Noth—"

"Nonsense," Montgomery cut Maria off. "The young lady will have a touch of your famous absinthe."

Maria gazed at several couples seated at tables and at several roughly dressed and crude-talking men strung out along the bar. There seemed to be an unwritten law that the working men couldn't sit at the tables and booths.

133

When DeJean returned with the drinks, Chance was nodding off, his head gently bumping the back of the booth. Maria thought of all the years he must have gone to bed early and gotten up even earlier, training himself for the rigors of the tennis world.

Montgomery knocked back his double shot of Scotch, following it with a swallow of water. "You haven't tried the absinthe."

Maria took a small sip and shuddered. "Oh, it's awful! It tastes worse than medicine."

"Like all the finer things in life, it takes some getting used to." Montgomery ran his fingertips along the back of Maria's arm, causing her to shudder again.

"If you'll excuse me, I have to go to the ladies room," she insisted, rather than asked.

"Of course." Montgomery got up to let her out.

When Maria stepped back out of the ladies room, she ran headlong into a hawk-faced, dark-skinned man with a shiny bald pate. Several missing teeth gave him the appearance of an off-color jack-o'-lantern. He wore a dirty T-shirt and green work pants stained with grease.

"Oh, I'm sorry!" she gasped, trying to get by him.

"Not to worry, Sweetheart. You can bump me anytime." He stepped in front of her, blocking her path.

Maria almost gagged at the stench of his body and his fetid breath. "Please, let me by."

"One little kiss, Baby." He took her by the shoulders with both hands and began pulling her toward him.

In the dim light of the bar, she saw the tall shadowy form of Montgomery moving quickly up behind the man. He lifted a magnum of champagne from a table and in one swift motion brought it crashing down on the man's head with a sickening thud. His eyes went dull instantly and rolled back in his head as he hit the floor like a corpse. Blood streamed from his split scalp, down his neck, and onto the floor, forming a slowly widening pool.

"DeJean. Would you come clean up this mess, please?" Montgomery called out, as if he had merely knocked over a drink.

"On my way, Mr. Preston."

Montgomery took Maria by the arm and escorted her back to the booth without a second look at the bleeding man.

"But—you hit him so hard. He—he may be dead," she cried out, glancing back over her shoulder.

"That riffraff has precious little to live for anyway," Montgomery admonished. "He'd be better off dead. Unfortunately he'll live to inflict himself on decent people again."

"Where's Chance?" Maria asked, staring at the empty booth.

"Said he was going to step outside for a breath of air. It's time we were going anyway."

Thirty minutes later the three of them stood in front of a darkened store at the corner of Canal and St. Charles listening to the rain beat on the metal awning. The dark green streetcar glistened wetly as it stopped to let them board.

As the streetcar hummed along the burnished tracks in the steady downpour, Maria thought of the man lying on the floor in the bar. She saw again the malevolent gleam in Montgomery's eyes when he crashed the bottle down on the man's skull as if he were a mad dog rather than a human being. And she remembered his callous remark, demeaning the importance of the man's life. Chance had wanted to go back and check on the man, but Montgomery had assured him that DeJean would tend to everything.

Maria stared out the streaming windows at the blurry streetlights and neons along the avenue. The gentle rocking of the streetcar made her drowsy as the misty trees and houses passed by her window like scenes out of a dream.

*   *   *

"Maria . . . Maria." The whispered words seemed to be coming from a great distance as she struggled up from a deep sleep.

Maria and Chance had gone directly to the tile-roofed, stucco guesthouses located beyond the main garden wall and separated from the tennis court by a stand of bamboo. Forcing herself to make her end-of-the-day notes that she wrote her articles from, Maria was exhausted when she stepped into the shower. The hot water relaxed her, driving her deeper into weariness, so that she fell asleep almost as soon as her head touched the pillow.

Now this unwelcomed, disembodied voice was pulling her from the misty dream world where she wanted to stay. She slowly opened her eyes to the murky darkness of the room. Light filtered in dim bars through the slats of the partially opened venetian blinds.

"Maria." Montgomery, sitting in the chair next to her bed, switched on the tiny lamp. He wore a burgundy smoking jacket and an insidious expression. An almost full bottle of Scotch and a moisture-beaded bottle of white wine sat next to him on the night table. He extended his left arm toward her. "Thought you might like a little nightcap." His speech was thick and slow.

Maria blinked at the glass of wine in his hand, then glanced at the clock on the nightstand. "Preston, it's three-thirty in the morning. I was sound asleep."

"Com' on, take it," he mumbled impatiently. "One little drink won't hurt."

Realizing all she had on was a silk nightgown, Maria pulled the sheet and bedspread up around her shoulders. "Preston, would you please leave now?"

Downing the half-glass of Scotch he was holding, Montgomery banged it down on the nightstand. "Leave! Unless I've suddenly fallen victim to hallucinations, this is *my* home!"

Seeing that Montgomery was irrational, Maria decided to humor him. "All right, Preston, one drink. But then I have to go to sleep. I'm a working girl, remember?" She took the wine from his hand and sipped it.

"Sure you are. Right out of the common working class of New York City. Second generation. Old man probably came over on a tramp steamer," Montgomery muttered sarcastically. "Protect me from the pious, simpering slobs who think they're bloody saints because they have the misfortune to work for a living."

"We can't all be born to wealth." Maria wished she hadn't said it before her words died away in the hush of the room. She felt a chill of fear creep over her when she saw the look in his eyes. It was too similar to the one she had seen just before he struck the man in The Arsenal bar.

Montgomery poured another glass of Scotch and gulped it down. The heavy glass made a dull thud as he dropped it on the rug. "I know one thing you working-class girls are good for."

Maria felt her heart pounding in her chest as she set the glass of wine down gently and slid back against the headboard. "I didn't mean to offend you," she gasped softly.

"Well, I certainly know how you can make it up to me, working girl." Montgomery sat on the bed and grabbed Maria by her shoulders, pulling her roughly to him.

Maria screamed once before she felt his lips pressing against hers. His breath smelled of mouthwash and raw Scotch. She felt his drunken movements, slow and sluggish as he tried to hold on to her. His mouth moved down to her neck, his left arm reaching up for the strap of her nightgown. She screamed again, twisting her head around and clamping her teeth down on his ear as hard as she could.

Montgomery cried out hoarsely, grabbing his ear with his hand. Maria struggled free and tried to stand up, feeling part of her gown rip loose in his other hand. With a murderous glint in his dark eyes, he leaned across the bed toward her.

The door slammed open and they both jerked around toward the noise. Chance stood there wearing only a pair of tan trousers. His lean, hard frame looked sculpted in the shadowy room. Disbelief on his face, he stared at the scene before him—Maria holding her ripped gown up with one hand and Montgomery reaching out for her. He noticed the liquor and wine bottles, the empty glass on the floor and the partially drunk glass of white wine on Maria's nightstand.

"Get out of here, you uncouth sycophant," Montgomery growled, his face twisted with rage.

Maria stood up from the bed, glancing over at her wine glass. "No, Chance! Don't go! It's not what you think."

Chance walked deliberately across the room toward Montgomery with an effortless, flowing motion, his knees slightly flexed and arms hanging loosely at his sides.

Montgomery stood up, trembling with anger and drink. He picked up the bottle of Scotch from the nightstand. "I told you to get out! You sniveling white trash!"

At the sound of the words, Chance was flooded with memories of his childhood. *White trash.* The words echoed down through the years from a thousand recesses on the school playgrounds of Liberty. From Montgomery's extensive verbal arsenal, he had chosen the wrong weapon to fling against Chance Rinehart.

Montgomery saw something deadly appear in Chance's face, like an apparition slithering toward him out of the dark. A cold fear touched his heart. He bared his teeth like a tormented wolf and swung the bottle at Chance's head.

Chance rocked back away from the bottle, already moving forward as it hissed past his face. As though he were standing casually aside, watching actors run through their parts in a play, he saw his right fist slam against Montgomery's left temple as the tall man's momentum carried him around with the heavy bottle.

Montgomery grunted and went to his knees, releasing his grip on the bottle. It rolled across the floor and banged into the wall. Pulling himself up, he sat on the side of the bed, his head resting in both hands.

Chance stood perfectly still, fists doubled at his sides, trembling slightly with anger.

Maria stood against a tall antique chiffonier with her arms crossed over her breasts.

Montgomery got to his feet and walked shakily across the room. Leaning against the door frame, he glanced at Maria, then turned his puffy, red eyes on Chance. "I suppose you know this has put something of a damper on my hospitality. I expect to find you both gone in the morning."

Maria and Chance glanced at each other in the heavy silence of the room.

Stepping out into the dark, Montgomery turned back as though he had to retrieve something. He remembered that Jesse Boone was the most aggressive man in their company, the most likely to be in the thick of the fighting. A malignant smile lit his face. "I do have a parting word for you, Chance."

Chance remained expressionless, refusing to enter into the game.

"Tanks!" Montgomery said with contempt and vanished into the dead hours of early morning.

Chance smiled weakly at Maria. "Well, that was some ending for our visit to the City That Care Forgot, wasn't it?"

"Chance, he came in here while I was asleep." She glanced over at the wine glass next to her bed and the bottle standing next to it. "I thought if I humored him, he'd leave after a drink."

"It's your business, Maria. I'm just glad I got here before things got real nasty."

She sat on the edge of the bed, hugging herself. Silent tears coursed down her pale cheeks.

Chance took her robe from the bedpost and draped it gently across her shoulders. He sat down next to her and took a deep breath. "I know it wasn't your fault."

Maria turned and saw a gentle light that she had never seen before shining in his eyes.

"Why would you want that poor slob," Chance smiled, "when you could have a classy fellow like me?"

"He was so drunk he'd probably have passed out in another minute, even if you hadn't shown up." Taking Chance's hand in hers, Maria said contritely, "I'm so sorry I messed up your plans. I know Preston will give you the worst possible assignment now."

"Kind of like what David did with Uriah the Hittite," he laughed bitterly.

"Who?" Maria asked with a puzzled frown.

"Uriah. Bathsheba's husband. David put him at the forefront of the battle to get killed because he wanted Bathsheba."

"I didn't know you were religious, Chance." She felt there was a complexity to Chance that she was just beginning to see.

"Every kid in Liberty goes to Sunday school. I'm not a total heathen, you know."

"Chance, you and Jesse will both be in such danger now. The Germans are so much better at this than we are."

"Nah. You don't have to worry about me." He tried to dismiss the subject.

"What do you mean?"

"I'll be all right as long as they keep puttin' reverse gears on our tanks."

12

TANKS

Soo-weeeee! Pig! Pig! Pig!" Chance stood in the turret of the M3 Stuart light tank, barreling along the narrow trail through the piny woods. Ahead of him was a domestic pig gone wild, running as fast as his stubby legs would carry him and squealing loudly every time the tank got close to his curly little tail on one of the straightaways.

Below and in front of Chance, Jesse had a tight grip on the twin levers that were used to steer the tank. "You're gonna kill us, Chance!" he shouted back over his shoulder, trying to make himself heard over the roar of the engine. "Let that fool pig go!"

Chance was having the time of his life with the tank the army had so generously provided for him to chase pigs. His hair flattened by the wind and his face alive with the thrill of the chase, he yelled down into the turret. "You'll be proud of me tonight, Jesse, when you smell that pig roasting over the fire."

Alcide Naquin, seated to the left of Chance next to the ammunition racks, yelled over the grinding, clanking noise of the tank, "He's right, Jess. We'll have us a 'coushon de lait' around the ol' campfire. I wish I had my fiddle, me."

Jesse fought the levers to keep the tank under control. "You'll have to explain that to me later, Al."

Suddenly the pig cut off the trail into the underbrush. Chance tapped Jesse smartly on his right shoulder with the heavy sole of his combat boot. Jesse worked the levers, and the tank spun right, careening and bouncing off through the underbrush and scratch pines after the squealing pig.

"Give it the gas, Jesse," Chance bellowed, jolting against the steel sides of the turret, "he's gettin' away."

The red clay hills of Camp Polk were covered with scrub oak and cut-over pine. Scattered throughout these woods were small shacks that the owners had abandoned when the government bought them out to build the military base. Chance's tank plunged wildly out of the woods into one of the clearings, bucking and snarling as though it had a personal grudge against the terrified pig that shot into the woods on the other side. The weathered clapboard shack lay dead ahead.

"Hang on, boys!" Chance shouted, ducking his head below the turret. "We're gonna make some kindling."

The tank picked up speed when it hit the hard-packed ground of the yard, exploding into the side of the shack with a cracking and popping of boards splitting apart and the sound of glass shattering. A shrieking of metal followed as the tin roof buckled and collapsed. The tank slowed momentarily, its tracks slipping and grinding for purchase in the debris. Then it broke free, bucking over the wreckage of the house and back into the woods in pursuit of the pig.

Al squeezed by Jesse, tapping Chance on the legs to get his attention. "Let me get up there."

Chance glanced downward briefly. "Whatta you want? You're gonna make me wreck this thing."

"I want to finish that pig off, me," Al shouted. "We'll never catch him in these woods."

Chance waited for a clear stretch of woods and ducked down quickly, letting Al slip past him and out onto the tank. Standing back up in the turret, he saw Al pull his army .45 out of its holster. "You got live ammo in that thing?"

"What you 'tink I'm gonna did, you? Trow it at him?" Al gripped the stowage rack tightly with his left hand. Leveling the Colt at the exhausted pig, he squeezed off three rounds, the heavy pistol rocking back in his hand with each shot. Two of them kicked up dust in front of the pig and the third clipped off the top of a tiny sapling.

"That's great shootin', Hopalong," Chance taunted. "I can see right now this pig's gonna die of old age."

At that moment, the pig vanished, like it had dropped off the edge of the world. Jesse slowed the tank, easing it forward until the tracks hung over the edge of the steep ravine the pig had disappeared into. Al stood up and saw the bristly back of the pig bumping down into the ravine where a stream flowed muddily through the red clay and gravel at the bottom.

"I got him now," Al whispered, holding the pistol out in front of him with both hands. *Wham! Wham! Wham!* The heavy slugs clunked into the gravel sides of the ravine as the pig began climbing, the last round sending a rock whining off into the woods. The pig continued to plod along up the slope.

Chance sat on top of the tank now, watching the show with an unlit Chesterfield dangling from his lip. "Like I said, Al. That pig'll live to see his grandbabies."

Al glared at Chance, taking his time to line up his final shot at the pig. *Wham!* The slug clunked into a tree four feet above the pig's head as it disappeared into the underbrush at the top of the ravine.

Jesse climbed up out of the turret and sat next to Chance, shaking his head disgustedly. "Three trained killers in a tank, and we can't handle one pig. What's gonna happen when we run up against the Germans? They shoot back."

"If we can get 'em inside some tin-roofed shacks," Chance grinned around his Chesterfield, "they're in big trouble."

Al jammed the empty pistol back into its holster. "I gotta get some practice with dis t'ing. I couldn't climb up a tree and hit the ground with it."

"Where'd you get live ammo?" Jesse asked, lying back against the warm steel of the turret. He watched a vulture circling against the high blue sky. "We're not supposed to have live ammo."

"This is the army, Jesse," Al replied, seriously. "Shootin' is real important when you a soldier. I'm surprised you didn't know that. I figure anything that belongs to the army is just as much mine as anybody else's. So I took a few of my army bullets."

Jesse had learned the fallacy of trying to reason with Al's logic. What worried him was, after a few months in the army, it was starting to make sense. He let the subject drop.

"How come you don't light them cigarette, Chance?" Al asked, staring dejectedly across the ravine to the spot where the pig had disappeared into the brush.

"Got to stay in shape, Al. When this little fracas is over, my life starts back up again and that means the tennis circuit."

"This is life too, Chance," Jesse offered, waving his hand at the sunlit woods all about them. "You look like you're havin' a pretty good time to me."

Chance shrugged, tossing the cigarette into the brush. "I just ain't gonna take it too seriously, Jesse. It ain't my idea of life."

"Paul said that he'd learned to be content no matter what circumstances he found himself in," Jesse added. "I think that's a good way to live. We're not promised tomorrow."

"Save the sermon, will you, Jesse?" Chance shot back. "I'll come up to that little church of yours when we get back home, if I get the urge to hear some preachin'."

"I'll look forward to it," Jesse smiled quickly. Then the smile vanished. He sat up straight, staring directly at Chance. "This playin' around is OK for now, but the time's comin' to take all this real seriously, Chance. If you don't, somebody could get killed."

"Not in my tank, Jesse," Chance scowled back. "I ain't plannin' to be a hero for anybody."

"Nobody's askin' you to." Jesse's face had gone dark with an intensity in his eyes that made Chance uneasy. "But the three of us are in this together, and we're gonna do our part in this war whatever that turns out to be."

Chance stood up quickly on the tank. "Don't you start givin' me orders, Jesse. I'm the tank commander. This is my show, and I'll run it the way I want to."

"Fine with me." Jesse never let his eyes wander from Chance's. "As long as you follow your orders. As long as you don't back off when things start to heat up."

Doubling up his right fist, Chance took a tentative step toward Jesse. Then he noticed, as if for the first time, the bulk of Jesse's chest and shoulders and the corded muscles of his forearms shining with perspiration beneath the rolled-up sleeves of his tanker's coveralls. He took a deep breath and relaxed, deciding that he wasn't as mad as he had first thought he was.

Al felt things getting out of control, and it grated on his easygoing Cajun disposition. "All right, boys. Chance is the boss, him." He stood up next to Chance and pointed to the chevrons on the sleeve of his green fatigues. "One, two, three."

Chance smiled at the wiry little Cajun from the swamps of South Louisiana.

"Now, Jesse," Al continued, grinning, "we all know Chance got them third stripe 'cause he big buddies wid Montgomery." He turned back to Chance. "Guess he found out how sorry you really are, else he wouldn't a dumped you back on us."

Chance found he couldn't work up any anger for Al, no matter what the little man said about him. "I guess that's pretty much the size of it," he chuckled.

Al continued, pointing at Jesse's sleeve. "I see you only got two of them stripe. So you got to shut up and do what the big boss say, you. Me, too, cause I only got one of them stripe."

"You make it all sound so simple, Al," Jesse remarked, glancing over at Chance.

"It is simple," Al said flatly, hoping that he was right. "Now we all friends. Just one more t'ing I wanna say. Y'all got to agreed with me before I say it though."

Chance and Jesse looked at each other and shrugged.

Al lay back on the tank, putting his hands behind his head. "Whoever shoot Hitler first—he get to be the boss, him."

Chance grinned and glanced at Al, lying comfortably on the tank, humming a Cajun song. Then he leaned toward Jesse. "I don't think he's kiddin'."

"He's not," Jesse replied under his breath.

*   *   *

"How'd you find this place?" Jesse asked, gazing up at the ceiling fans whirling high above them.

Maria said, almost apologetically, "Chance brought me here the day of the graduation ceremonies."

Jesse remembered that he and Al had waited two hours for her in the hot sun. "Well, it sure is nice and cool."

Maria saw the same boy in his overalls and white apron step behind the soda fountain from the door to the back. His straw-colored hair hung in his face, and she wanted to brush it aside for him. "He'p you folks?" he drawled.

"Coke," Maria smiled.

Jesse was staring at the colorful ads stuck to the mirror behind the counter. He pointed to a banana split piled high with whipped cream. "That looks good to me."

They went to sit at a table while the boy went to work on their orders. After he served them, he walked over to the jukebox. *Maybe he plays music for all his customers,* Maria thought.

Jesse attacked the banana split. After swallowing his first mouthful of ice cream, chocolate syrup, strawberries, and the heavy whipped cream sprinkled liberally with chopped pecans, he closed his eyes. "Ummmm. Last one of these I had, Ollie fixed it for me back in Liberty. Think I'll have one at the Marriage Supper of the Lamb."

Maria decided not to ask what his last remark had reference to. "How's the training, Jesse? The army teaching you boys anything?"

On the jukebox Harry James began his soulful, trumpet version of "You Made Me Love You."

Jesse swallowed another huge bite, grabbing a napkin from the shiny holder on the table to wipe chocolate syrup from his chin. "Discipline and physical conditioning."

Maria sipped her Coke. "Sounds like basic training."

"We're learning' about tank warfare now. Mostly classroom stuff so far, but we've started a few maneuvers."

Listening to the music, Maria gazed out the dusty window at a flop-eared hound sleeping in the shade next to a bench in front of a grocery store. "Where do you think they'll send you, Jesse?"

Jesse's dark brown eyes gazed inward, as though he were searching for something, found it—but quickly discarded it. He smiled, holding a big spoonful of the banana split in front of his face. "Wherever the army needs tanks the most, I reckon."

"I think it's going to be North Africa."

Taking another bite, Jesse savored the ice cream. "What makes you think that?"

"I stay in touch with the wire services. Part of the job." Maria felt that he understood a lot more than he let on. "Rommel took Tobruk back in June."

Jesse assumed a noble posture in profile. "'Gentlemen, for you the war is over. You have fought like lions and been led by donkeys.'"

"What are you babbling about?"

"That's what Rommel told the British soldiers at Tobruk after he captured the city."

"How would you know something like that?"

"I don't for a fact, but the ol' army grapevine's always at work. We never know what's gonna happen to *us*. All we hear are rumors. But our information about the enemy is usually better."

"Well, Rommel may be a great tactician, but the Germans will never be able to match us in production. Lend-lease has sent a pretty good number of tanks to the British—with more on the way. They just might help spoil his little African chess game against the British." Maria sipped her Coke thoughtfully, pleased that she had the opportunity to cover a part of the war even if it were only from stateside for now.

Jesse shrugged. "Maybe so. But when *we* get there with those new Shermans, that's when the ol' Desert Fox is gonna start lookin' for a desert den to hide in."

Maria was finding this talk of warfare exciting in a way that was almost glamorous. She could picture all the brave young soldiers in their formidable tanks, the big guns blazing away at the enemy, as they roared across the desert toward glorious victory. But she kept her dreams to herself. "The Germans have three years of combat behind them, Jesse. They're battle-hardened. They know what they're doing."

"They haven't seen anything yet. Wait'll the Americans get there," he smiled.

Don't sit under the apple tree with anyone else but me. The boy had dropped two nickels into the jukebox, and the Andrews Sisters were filling the drugstore with their energetic version of the song.

"Tell me about the new Shermans, Jesse." Maria sat eagerly forward in her chair.

A shadow crossed Jesse's face. He poked at the ice cream melting in the bowl, then dropped the spoon. "Don't you have enough for your story? Can't we talk about something else?"

"I'm sorry. I get carried away by the job sometimes." Maria ran her fingertips across the top of his brown hand, tracing a vein that ran from the knuckle of his ring finger to a spot above his wrist. "I noticed that you and Al never mentioned the war while you were on leave. Neither did Chance for that matter."

"We'll get more than enough war before this thing's over. No need to talk about it on our free time." Jesse noticed her dark hair flowing softly about her face as she talked, shimmering as it caught the light from the single window. He tried to think of Cora and of the little white church by the stream.

"I've grown very fond of you and Chance," Maria smiled. "I'm afraid I'm losing that sense of detachment that a journalist needs to remain objective."

He felt the warmth of her soft hand resting on his. It seemed to flow into him, to become a part of him. *Something I can keep with me for the cold times. What's wrong with me? I've got to stop thinking like this!*

"Jesse, are you all right?"

"Oh—sure! You 'bout ready to go? Big day tomorrow. Montgomery's coming down from headquarters company to bless us with a lecture. Then maneuvers in the afternoon." He rose from the table and dropped a dollar bill next to his soupy banana split. He tried not to look at Maria's full, wet lips.

She sat gazing up at him in the pale gold sunlight streaming into the dusky drugstore. "Did I say something to upset you? You seem uncomfortable."

"No. I'm fine. I just need to go."

Maria took his arm in both her hands as they left the drugstore. "Are you sure you're OK, Jesse? It feels like you're trembling. Maybe you're catching a virus."

* * *

"Battle tanks have a threefold mission. It's based on Fuller's Plan of 1919, the underlying employment of armor, and it's still relevant to today's combat. I'll go over it a final time for those of you who've forgotten." Preston Montgomery paced back and forth in front of the blackboard on the bare pine planks, so fresh from the mill that sap still oozed from them. The razor-sharp creases of his trousers bent stiffly with his movement and the brand new silver oak leaves shouted from his epaulets of his promotion to major.

On the back row, Chance leaned over close to Al and whispered, "I'll bet they have to use a block and tackle to lift him in and out of those britches."

Al sat up straight-faced, biting his lip to keep from laughing.

Preston scowled at the minor disturbance, but continued. "A—to breach the front. B—to drive deep to flank and rear. C—to disrupt the enemy's will to fight."

Chance whispered out of the side of his mouth, "Preston's disrupting my will to fight."

"And the operative word for the battle tank *is* and always will be—what?" Preston stood stiffly erect, his hands behind his back.

Jesse raised his hand.

"Yes, Corporal."

"Mobility," Jesse answered flatly, standing to attention.

"Precisely! To remain immobile is an invitation to disaster." Preston resumed his pacing. "You may be seated, Corporal."

"This afternoon's exercises will be critical as far as your future assignments are concerned. We'll undoubtedly switch from light to medium tanks when we reach our theater of operations and the best crews get the best tanks—Stuarts, Lees, or Shermans in order of ascending firepower and armament. One more thing—don't pass up your targets of opportunity. Orders can't cover everything."

"Lee's the best general of that bunch," Chance remarked to no one in particular.

Preston pointed to a master sergeant on the front row. "Dismiss the troops, Sergeant." Then he turned sharply on his heels and walked out a side door.

"Tennn—hut!"

The men scrambled to their feet in a scraping of chairs on the wooden floor.

"Dismissed!"

Two hours later, Chance and Jesse sat on their tank in a small grove of pines watching an intersection twenty yards away. Beyond the main road, the land dropped off into a long sweeping field of tall grass. Al lay asleep on a bed of pine needles beneath a tree where a blue jay was squawking.

Awakened by the bird, he sat up and yawned. "I'm gonna shoot that bird, me."

"You couldn't hit the tree, Al," Chance jibed, a Chesterfield dangling from his lip.

"I think we ought to be ready to fight," Jesse said, rebuking Chance's laid-back attitude. "We don't even have the engine runnin'."

Chance continued to stare down the long slope toward the distant tree line where he knew a river ran clear and cool. "Nobody's comin' this way. We're so far out of the action, they'll have to mail us the casualty report."

"You sure took care of that for us, you." Al stood up, staring at Chance. "Every time we play this war game, the report say we not suggestive enough."

"That's *aggressive*," Jesse corrected with a grin. "We're not *aggressive* enough."

"That's what I said. Anyhow, I'm tired of being made fun of because of you," Al said flatly, still staring at Chance. "The men been calling us 'Chance's Chickens' since we started playin' war. And now they callin' our tank the 'Rinehart Reverse,' 'cause you always backin' away from the fightin', you. That make me hot, yeah."

"It's only games, boys. Don't take it too serious," Chance grinned, thinking about the shady river gurgling over the rocks in the distant woods.

Jesse spoke in an even voice, controlling the anger behind it. "It'll only get worse when we're in battle, Chance. You'll get us or somebody else killed. Now's the time to change things."

Before Chance could reply, the sound of men shouting hoarsely was carried to them on the hot wind. From over a rise to their left, what appeared to be an entire company came running and stumbling through the high grass. They had started down the long slope toward the distant tree line when the three men in the shade heard the sound of tanks. The men in the field looked back quickly and sprinted ahead, their equipment jangling and bouncing as they ran.

"Those are our boys," Al shouted. "Where's all their support? The tanks, the APCs, artillery?"

Jesse was on his feet. "Must've been knocked out. Com' on, let's give 'em a hand."

"Our orders are to guard this intersection," Chance said flatly, making no move to get up.

"Don't be stupid, Chance," Jesse barked, throwing Al the fire extinguisher as he climbed inside the turret.

"I hate these gasoline engines, me," Al said, pulling the cover on the exhaust in case the engine caught fire when Jesse started it. "I be glad when we get a diesel tank."

The engine roared to life without catching fire, and Al slipped down the turret and into the tank.

Three enemy tanks topped the ridge to the left and made

straight for the fleeing company, cutting through the tall grass like scythes. The men would never make it to the tree line.

"Com' on, Chance!" Jesse shouted above the growl of the engine. "We can hit 'em from the flank. Get at least two—maybe all three!"

"Count me out," Chance yelled back, knowing Jesse needed him to guide the tank.

"We'll fight blind then!" Jesse gunned the engine, and the tank leaped forward, almost throwing Chance off.

"You're nuts!" Chance yelled, scrambling to get into the turret.

Jesse was flying down the slope now, the engine at full throttle, when he felt Chance guiding him into the battle. They made a pass at the tank closest to them, knocking it out. The other two, caught by surprise, tried to turn on the intruder, but Chance had flanked them on the opposite side and nailed the second one.

Chance felt all the classroom lectures coming back to him. He somehow remembered the strategies and ploys from the classes that he had been half-dozing through. A kind of exhilaration swept through him as though he were squaring off against one of the massive Tiger tanks in the deserts of Morocco or Tunisia.

The men down the slope were cheering their rescuers on, too caught up in the fever of battle to seek the shelter of the woods. They watched the two tanks locked in an all-too-real show of combat. Like plunging steel beasts, they wheeled and roared through the tall grass, tearing out great chunks of earth. The element of surprise gone now, "Chance's Chickens" fought the third tank to a draw.

The men in the doomed company came charging back up the hill toward their rescuers. The lieutenant in charge yelled at Chance as he climbed down from the turret. "Great work, Sergeant. The scoring teams will get a full report about this."

"Hey, boys, it's 'Chance's Chickens,'" one of the soldiers yelled out to the laughter of his comrades.

The lieutenant smiled at Chance and at Jesse and Al, who had climbed out of the tank, then turned and yelled to his men. "Looked more like 'Rinehart's Revenge' to me."

Laughing and joking, the men walked off down the slope, heading for the road that would take them back to the barracks.

"You did real good, Chance," Jesse said with a big smile on his face. "I knew you had it in you all the time."

Chance slid off the tank to the ground. "Tank battles are just tactics, Jesse. I grew up on tactics around the tennis courts. Same rules apply, except in war there's no *love* and in tennis there's no *death*. Timing and coordination are important, too, just like tennis."

"Makes sense to me," Al chimed in.

"Both of you should know." Chance stared at Jesse and Al, stretched out on the tank. "I still feel the same way about this war. I don't plan to take risks, and I don't care what anybody says about me. I'm getting out of this thing in one piece."

Jesse leaned forward, his arms hanging limply off his knees. "But you just ran those guys into the ground a few minutes ago. No one in the battalion could have fought better."

"I was protecting my own skin, you dumb preacher," Chance snapped. "You would've killed us all tearing down that hillside blind as a bat."

Jesse held Chance's gaze. "You could just as easily have directed me away from the battle."

"Too late for that," Chance snorted.

Jesse laughed softly and lay back on the tank, staring at a single fleecy cloud drifting by overhead. "I think there's more to you than you let on, Chance."

"Don't count on it."

Al saw it was time for him to take on his role as peacemaker. "Hey, y'all, we need to celebrate our victory."

"How?" Jesse mumbled.

Al thought about it for a while, looking about him at the field and the woods. He snapped his fingers. "I've got it. There's a little river down in those woods at the bottom of the hill. Let's go swimmin'."

"Now there's a man after my own heart," Chance smiled, leaping onto the tank.

"Wait a minute," Jesse protested. "We've got to get back for the debriefing. It'll be starting in an hour or so."

Al looked up at Chance, pointing his finger in Jesse's face. "This boy could learn a few things from you. He don't know how to have a good time, him."

"Well, let's start the lessons," Chance laughed. He pointed to the three chevrons on his sleeve. "I'm the big boss, me. I say we goin' swimmin' right now."

"Maybe I *could* learn something from you, Chance." Jesse slipped down the turret and rammed the tank into gear. It lurched forward, almost spilling Chance and Al onto the ground.

"You dumb preacher, you'll kill us yet," Chance yelled, hanging onto the bouncing tank.

Jesse revved the engine up to top speed and did a blind figure eight on the open hillside. "I think I'm havin' a good time now, Chance. Are you proud of me?"

Chance was laughing too hard to talk as he took his place in the turret and guided them safely down to the river.

13

HOME FRONT

Maria pulled over to the curb in her rented Ford coupe. *Looks like J.T.'s caught the real spirit of the home front.*

The children of Liberty were at work for America. Boys and girls from six to sixteen were straggling in and out of the side door set into the brick wall that surrounded the garden area behind J.T.'s office. The younger girls wore cotton dresses and shoes that buckled over their colored socks, while the older ones wore baggy jeans rolled up to their knees and wrinkled men's shirts with the tails hanging out. The boys wore an assortment of jeans, khakis, and overalls with black tennis shoes, saddle oxfords, or brown loafers. Some even wore army boots with jeans rolled up to show off their prized possessions. One proudly sported a white sailor's cap.

A red-white-and-blue sign read "Official Salvage Depot" and was tacked to the side wall of the office. Two other signs hung on either side of it. The one to the left depicted a young soldier in dress uniform sitting on a park bench talking with his blonde girlfriend. A Hitler look-alike sat next to them reading a newspaper, his oversized ear trained on the soldier. "Loose Talk Can Cost Lives" was printed in bold letters below the trio. The sign on the right pictured a young sailor staring through the porthole of a ship. It admonished, "If you talk too much—THIS MAN MAY DIE!"

Maria noticed a girl of about eight struggling along the sidewalk with a red wagon loaded with newspapers, a few pots and pans, and two automobile tires. She wore blue overalls and had a bright red ribbon in her shiny blonde hair. "Let me help," Maria offered, climbing out of her car. "That wagon looks much too heavy for you."

"My brother was pulling it, but we got too much stuff," the girl replied, pointing to a boy of about sixteen dragging a tub of rusty scrap iron through the gate.

"Well, you've worked hard enough. Let me pull awhile." Maria took the handle of the wagon and headed toward the gate.

"My name's Sally. What's yours?"

"Maria."

"That's pretty. Do you know Mr. J.T.?" Sally brushed her hair back from her soft brown eyes, smiling up at Maria.

"Yes, I do."

"He's a nice man. He gives us lemonade and cookies when we bring in a load of this stuff."

Entering the garden area, Maria was astonished at the amount of scrap that had been collected. In the far left corner, piled in a jumbled heap, were old tires and tubes of every size and description. Next to them, stacks and stacks of newspapers leaned precariously against the brick wall. In the opposite corner, pots, pans, bedsprings, tin cans, ancient shovels and hoes, and scrap metal of every kind imaginable clanged and jangled as more scrap was thrown on by the children eager to collect the reward for their hard work.

Maria helped Sally unload her wagon. "You're certainly doing a good job for your country."

Lifting a battered galvanized bucket from the wagon, the child turned toward Maria, her eyes bright with emotion. "Mama says it'll help Daddy get home safe. He's a sergeant in the army."

"I'm sure it will, Sally." Maria took the bucket and flung it on the growing pile of scrap metal. She knelt and took the child's grimy hands in her own. "You're helping a lot of our boys come home safely."

"Oh, I don't worry about Daddy too much," Sally said brightly. "We pray for him every night. I know God's angels will watch over him and keep him from gettin' hurt."

Maria pulled Sally to her, embracing her gently. "I know they will too, baby. This old war will be over before you know it."

"I'm thirsty! Let's get some lemonade!" The child pulled free. "You want some?"

"Sure," Maria replied, following after her as she skipped across the grassy area of the garden.

"Hello, pretty girl. How's the newspaper business?" J.T. walked down the back steps carrying a huge brown crock by the handles on its sides. He wore a gray Harvard sweatshirt with the sleeves cut off, neat khakis, and brown loafers.

"Well, you certainly have gotten industrious since I saw you last," Maria smiled, hands on the swell of her hips.

J.T.'s face now had some color to it and had lost much of its puffiness. "Just my piddling effort against the dreaded Hun. I'd hate to have to goose-step down to the liquor store every day."

Maria laughed. "Same ol' J.T." She noticed a spark of youth in his brown eyes and in the way he carried himself, even burdened with the heavy crock of lemonade. *I'll bet you had the girls from Wellesley and Radcliffe and Vassar crying to their mamas in your Harvard days, J. T. Dickerson.*

Walking over to a table made from rough planks laid across two sawhorses, J.T. set the lemonade down and began ladling it into paper cups for the children waiting patiently in line. "Make yourself handy, girl," he smiled over at Maria. "We've got to feed the troops, keep 'em working. Like Bing Crosby says in that song, *Junk ain't junk no more, 'cause junk can win the war.*"

Hurrying behind the table, Maria opened several large white boxes tied with string and began handing out cookies. "Don't you have any napkins, J.T.?"

"We're not much on etiquette here . . . Hold on, Sally!" J.T. held up the little girl's hands. "If your mama saw me serving you with hands like that she'd have my hide. You go on over there to the faucet and wash up now like the others are doing."

"Aw, Mr. J.T.!"

"Go on now. Hurry up."

"You do this very often?" Maria was beginning to be caught up in the enthusiasm of the children.

"Every Saturday." J.T. glanced at Maria's trim figure in her wraparound green skirt and white blouse. He watched the play of light in her dark hair and the graceful way her hands moved when she handed out the cookies. And he remembered another dark-haired girl of thirty years past as she pressed against him in a convertible with her hair blowing silkily against his face—spinning along Memorial Drive in the achingly crisp October air, with the sailboats skimming over the choppy surface of the Basin. They crossed the Cottage Farm Bridge with the Harvard towers, Gothic and lovely against the blue sky, slid past the club mansions along Mount Auburn and later to Soldier's Field for the game against Dartmouth. Afterward, they finished the last of a flask under a blanket in the backseat, parked in some dark corner next to the Yard with the sound of the house parties drifting on the chill night . . .

"J.T., are you all right?"

"Huh? Oh, yeah. I'm fine. Just fine."

Pardon me, boy, is that the Chattanooga Choo-Choo? The radio in the open kitchen window spilled the sounds of the Glenn Miller Band out into the garden. Some of the older boys and girls set their lemonade and cookies down and started jitter-bugging.

"May I have this dance, ma'am?" J.T. dropped the ladle and extended his hand to Maria.

"You certainly may. I don't know if I can keep up with a youngster like you, but let's give it a whirl." Maria was pleasantly surprised by J.T.'s dancing. He was graceful, with some funny steps of his own that he added to the dance, and he spun and twirled her without missing a step or losing his balance.

After the song was over, J.T. sprawled breathlessly in a lawn chair near the almost-dry fountain. "Most exercise I had since the last time I said, 'Oh, yeah—you and whose army?'"

Maria gave him a puzzled look and sat down next to him. "What's that got to do with exercise?"

"Well," he replied with a wry smile, "it was intended as verbal parry only. But I said it to a Georgia State Trooper after he pulled me over for speeding outside of Atlanta. The ol' boy failed to see any merit in the nuances of my caustic wit."

"What happened?"

He rubbed his jaw slowly with his left hand. "It's kind of foggy now, but as I recall he gave me some rather memorable and painful lessons in the manly arts."

"Maybe you needed some lessons," Maria smiled.

"I expect I did," J.T. agreed. "He probably improved my manners. I certainly deleted that particular phrase from my dialogue."

Maria was distracted by a commotion around the makeshift lemonade stand.

"Hold on a minute!" J.T. called out. "Tommy, you get behind there and serve up the last of the lemonade and cookies. It's about time to wind things up here."

"Yes sir, Mr. J.T." A chubby boy of fifteen with a brown crew cut stepped behind the planks and served the other children until the refreshments were gone.

"Where'd you get all the cookies?" Maria enjoyed watching the children as they cleaned up the last of the scrap, putting it in the proper piles, kidding and joking with each other, saying their good-byes as they headed for home.

"Bakery sends them over every Saturday morning. Their part of the war effort, I guess." J.T. leaned back in his chair, gazing upward at a fleecy cloud that caught the last of the sunlight, looking as though it were shot with silver against the darkening sky. "Would you do a kindness for an old man, Maria?"

"No, I wouldn't," she said flatly. Then added, "But I just might for you."

J.T. smiled. "You just did, didn't you? Well, let's make it two then. Would you have dinner with me?"

"I'd be delighted." Maria caught the quick joy that flickered in his sad eyes and wondered how long ago he quit keeping the company of women.

"Great. We'll eat at the hotel. Best food in town, and all you have to do is walk down the stairs."

"You want me to come by and pick you up?"

J.T. rose from his chair, holding his hand out to her. "No, I'll walk. I enjoy it. 'I have outwalked the furthest city light.'"

"That's a lovely poem, isn't it?" Maria reflected. "Sad, but so very lovely."

* * *

"Chicken and dumplings?" Maria gazed at the huge white dish on the even whiter tablecloth in front of her. "Just when I thought I'd sampled most of your southern fare, up pops a new dish."

They were seated at a corner table of the hotel dining room next to a long window that looked out on the street. Maria had pinned her hair up and had on the simple black linen sheath she had worn to Preston Montgomery's party. J.T.'s face was shiny from soap and razor, and he wore a red tie and a dark suit that hardly showed any wrinkles. It was seven-thirty, late by Liberty's dining standards, and there was only one other table occupied in the dimly lighted room. J.T. had waved at them as they came in.

"Well, go ahead and try it." J.T. forked up a large dumpling and shoved it into his mouth. "Mmmm . . . that's good."

Maria looked at the rich gravy with its white dumplings and large pieces of chicken that had been cooked off the bones. Cutting off a piece of dumpling with her fork, she placed it carefully into her mouth. It was tender and chewy enough to keep it from being mushy, spicy, but not too hot, and with a richness of flavor that spoke of hours of slow, deliberate cooking.

"Well, what do you think?"

For a reply, Maria smiled contentedly, cut a piece of the plump succulent chicken and ate it along with a whole dumpling, chewing with obvious pleasure.

J.T. returned her smile and went back to his food.

As they ate, Maria found herself drawn to the other couple seated next to another window three tables down. The boy was about six feet, slim, and had raven-black hair and gray eyes that looked almost like dark silver in the muted light of the room. He wore neatly pressed khakis and a blue plaid shirt. The girl was small and well formed with soft, curly brown hair and skin that glowed with good health. Wearing a simple pink cotton dress, she reminded Maria of a grown-up Shirley Temple. *They look so very young—and vulnerable.* "Who are they?" she asked, nodding toward the pair.

"Oh, that's Ben Logan and his girlfriend, Rachel Shaw."

Maria was caught off guard. *"That's* Ben Logan?"

J.T. chuckled softly. "Maria, your mouth's open."

"Oh, sorry. But he looks so—so small!"

"What'd you expect? John Wayne with a Thompson submachine gun in each hand?"

Maria smiled. "I—I guess so. That *Life* magazine cover was pretty spectacular."

"That Hollywood Special Services bunch staged it!" J.T. snorted, then seemed to reconsider. "There's some good ones out there like Jimmy Stewart, Clark Gable—some others who joined up to fight. Carole Lombard was on a tour selling war bonds when she got killed."

"Glitter's just part of the big picture, J.T.," Maria remarked off-handedly.

J.T. laid his fork on the table and stared at his transparent reflection in the window. "I think they tend to glorify war too much." He remembered crouching in a trench near the Ardennes Forest under rainy skies, artillery thundering in the distance and a hail of shrapnel singing like hornets overhead. He held his closest friend in his arms as his intestines spilled out into the muddy water. And that last mortal scream for life echoed down through the years, from another continent, another time, another war.

"J.T.?"

J.T. stared through the man in the glass. Beyond the window, another man, old and insubstantial in his threadbare jacket and tattered straw hat, shambled along the sidewalk.

Maria touched his arm.

"Hmmm . . . must've slipped away for a moment there," he mumbled, turning toward her.

"J.T., don't you feel well? We could leave now if you'd like." Her brow furrowed in concern for this man she had become so fond of in such a short time.

"No. I'm fine now. I tend to drift off now and again." He cupped his hands, rubbing his eyes with the tips of his fingers. Then he smiled broadly. "How could I not be ecstatic with such a lovely and personable dinner companion?"

The look of concern left Maria's face. She leaned across the table. "Do you suppose we could go over and meet Ben Logan? I've read so much about him. He's the country's biggest hero right now."

J.T. glanced over his shoulder. "I think not, Maria. He's traveling around the country promoting war bonds most of the time. I expect he and Rachel have precious little time to themselves. Ben was always one to keep his own counsel anyway. Let's respect his privacy."

"I understand."

"By the way, how're your two heroes doing? I heard they finished their tank training over at Camp Polk." He leaned back in his chair, sipping his iced tea.

"Well, Chance went over to Atlanta for his final leave before shipping out. Seemed it was a town more—*suitable* for his *needs* than Liberty," Maria sneered. "Jesse's up in the hills doing whatever preachers do when they don't have a church anymore."

"Jesse Boone doesn't need a church to be a preacher. Got the calling on him. He'll be telling somebody about Jesus wherever he is. I've seen men like that before. That girl's daddy is cut from the same cloth." J.T. pointed over to Rachel.

Maria's dark eyes narrowed in thought. "You're absolutely right about Jesse. I've been around him enough to know that. People seem to sense there's something—special about him, even when he isn't quoting from that Bible of his. Sometimes I think he's got the whole thing memorized."

"What do you think about the scourge of the tennis circuit, our boy Chance?"

"Wouldn't hurt him to be a little more like Jesse," Maria shrugged almost cynically.

"And maybe Jesse could take a few lessons from Chance," J.T. quipped. "Like not trying to take the problems of the whole world on his own shoulders."

"You've got a crystal ball tucked away in one of those junk piles at your office, haven't you? Jesse is a little . . . intense at times, but it always seems to involve doing something for other people. And it's never for show—couldn't care less if anybody knows about it or not. He thinks about *himself* less than any man I've ever known." Maria watched Ben and Rachel get up from the table and walk across the dining room.

J.T. waved at them. "You watch out for Ben now, Rachel. Don't let him get to running with those Hollywood starlets when he goes on the war bond tours."

"I won't, Mr. J.T.," Rachel smiled shyly, taking Ben by the hand.

"That crowd's too fast for a country boy like you, Ben," J.T. added with a smile.

Ben laughed and kissed Rachel on the cheek.

Watching them leave, Maria observed, "I just expected him to be so much bigger."

J.T. glanced over at Ben as he paid the bill at the hotel desk. "I reckon those Jap pilots thought he was about a thousand feet tall the way he was battin' them out of the skies over Pearl Harbor."

"Well, he certainly is a nice-looking boy," Maria remarked, "and there's something else about him that reminds me of Jesse. Something I can't quite pin down."

Someone in the hotel bar dropped a nickel in the jukebox and the relaxed sounds of Dooley Wilson singing "As Time Goes By" drifted into the dining room.

"Such a beautiful song," Maria sighed. "Jesse sang it the night we saw *Casablanca*. He could probably sing professionally if he had the right training."

J.T. turned his deep brown eyes on Maria. "The only thing Jesse Boone's gonna do is preach the gospel."

"That's his one passion," she agreed.

"Which one's it gonna be, Maria?"

Maria was caught off guard. "What do mean?"

"You know precisely what I mean, young lady. Don't think you can fool ol' uncle J.T."

"Oh, you just hush." Maria blushed slightly. "This is the wrong time for anything like that."

"Don't I know it," J.T. whistled under his breath. "Trouble is, that's when it always happens."

"This is just part of my job, J.T.," she protested weakly, feeling the emptiness of her words.

He didn't press the issue. "Things are gonna get a lot worse before they get better. A lot of our boys won't be coming back. Or they'll be coming back a whole lot different than they were when they went away. I guess what I'm trying to say is . . . maybe I'd better just keep my mouth shut."

Maria reached across the table and took his hand. "I know what you're trying to say. It's awfully sweet of you, but I'll have to work this out for myself. I'm sure I'll get to know a lot of nice boys before this thing's over."

"Did you get your approval as a war correspondent?"

"It's real close. I talked to Duncan last night. He said a couple of more clearance checks and I'm in."

"That's real fine, Maria," J.T. smiled. "I'm proud for you. Guess maybe I'll start a victory garden. Peas ain't peas no more, 'cause peas can win the war."

Maria laughed at the parody on the Crosby number. "We've all got to do our part, don't we?"

"Ol' FDR's got four sons on the front lines. I think that sets a pretty good example for the rest of us to make sacrifices," J.T. added somberly. "Didn't like him very much in peace. Eleanor and he think they're everybody's mama and daddy. If they have their way, they'll turn us all into a bunch of crybabies, lying around waitin' for a government handout. Maybe he'll do better as a wartime president."

Squeezing J.T.'s hand, Maria said softly, "Think about me once in a while when I'm away, will you?"

J.T. was drawn to her dark brown eyes, luminous in the pale yellow light from the room. "How could I not think of you, Maria? How could I not?"

*   *   *

The tires of the rented Ford whispered over the bed of pine needles and out into the glade where the tiny whitewashed church stood in a dazzle of sunlight. Maria parked in the shade of a sweet gum and sat listening to the wind rustling through the trees and the tinkling, musical sound the creek made as it flowed over the rocks. On the opposite bank, where the woods grew almost down to the water's edge, a red fox appeared magically out of the underbrush. He sniffed the air, looked cautiously about, and drank from the clear blue water. With another quick look around, he vanished like smoke.

Leaving the car, Maria walked over to the church and peered in the front door. Jesse stood at the pulpit, his hands raised toward the heavens. He wore his scuffed hunting boots, threadbare khakis, and a green army T-shirt, but in Maria's eyes it somehow appeared to be the garb of a warrior arrayed for battle. His mouth moved in prayer, but she couldn't make out the words. She waited a few minutes, seeing him drop to his knees as though he were in agony. In the light that poured through the high, narrow windows, she could see drops of sweat beaded on his face, although the inside of the church was shadowy and cool.

Maria felt a sudden chill as though something slimy and cold had brushed against her. Inside the building a storm seemed to be raging out of a howling void. Her breath began to come in short gasps. Sitting down on the last pew, she tried to remember the prayers of her youth, but they were lost in a moaning wind and thick, smothering darkness.

Sometime later, Jesse rose almost painfully to his feet as though he had been in a terrible struggle. He sat on the first pew, his head resting in both hands.

Maria felt a calm fill the church. Walking softly down the aisle, she sat next to him and placed her hand on his shoulder. She could think of nothing to say.

Jesse turned his head slowly toward her. He smiled weakly, rubbed his eyes with both hands, and wiped his face with his handkerchief. "How long you been here?"

"Not long."

"Well, I'm glad to see you."

Maria looked around the small church: its hard benches, pine floor, and the single rough cross on the wall behind the pulpit. She noticed the flowered curtains, pushed back against the walls now, that could be pulled out to divide the building into several rooms. "You come here often to pray?"

Jesse shrugged and put his handkerchief in his back pocket. "Silly, ain't it? I could just as easy stay up at the cabin. God don't live down here in this old church building."

"I don't think it's silly at all." Maria stared at his eyes. They burned with an intense light.

Jesse stood and walked over to the pulpit. "Guess it's 'cause I got saved in this ol' church house. Felt the Spirit of God move mightily many a time when I was growin' up."

Maria didn't understand what he meant. She wanted to ask him, but surprisingly couldn't seem to find the right words.

Jesse turned back toward her. "Let's take a walk outside. Get a breath of air."

His face was shining. Maria started to mention it, then thought, *It's only the perspiration and the angle of the light.* "I'd like that. It's a lovely afternoon."

They walked down to the creek. The surface of the water, ruffled by the wind, caught the sunlight in a shimmering radiance. Far across the valley floor, they could hear the high, lonesome sound of a truck whining along the highway.

Sitting on the cool grass in the shade of a willow, she reached out and took his strong, brown hand. "Jesse, I'm afraid."

He turned to her, a look of concern on his face. "Afraid of what? Nothing's going to hurt you."

Maria thought of the feeling she had had inside the church, of how she felt herself being dragged down into that awful howling blackness, but she fought to push it out of her mind. "Of this war, I guess. I'm afraid for all of us."

"But you'll be back in New York. At home."

"No, I won't. I've qualified as an official war correspondent," she murmured, forcing a smile.

"You mean you're going with us?"

"That's right."

"But we'll probably end up in North Africa. That's where they need the tank outfits most. You can't go into those heathen countries. What would happen if you got captured?"

"I just won't let it happen," she laughed nervously. "You're probably right about where we're going though. That's exactly what my editor thinks. He tells me that the British need all the help they can get against Rommel's Afrika Korps."

Jesse took a deep breath. "Well, I reckon it's better than having to deal with the Japs. Look how many of our men they killed on the Bataan death march. Those poor boys didn't have a chance." He thought of trying to talk Maria out of going overseas but knew how hard she had fought for the assignment and that she wouldn't be swayed.

Shuddering at the thought of getting captured, Maria declared with little conviction, "I'll be all right. They won't let us get too close to the front lines."

Jesse saw the shadow of fear cross her face. "Here, let me pray for you," he said, placing both hands gently on the sides of her head. "May God grant you His mercy and grace from everlasting to everlasting. May He set His angels over you to protect you and keep you in all your ways. And may His peace and loving kindness fill your days." He smiled and kissed her on the forehead.

Maria felt something like warm oil flow from his hands as he touched her. She wanted to remain like that forever. Wanted him to never take his hands from her. "Thank you so much," she murmured.

Jesse lay back on the soft grass, staring at the hard blue sky. After enduring the struggle inside the church he felt physically weak and spiritually drained, but an ineffable peace had come to him that he didn't question. He accepted it as he did all gifts from God, with gratitude and the humility of a man who never has to think of the word *humble.*

"Aren't you afraid at all, Jesse?"

"Sure I'm afraid." Turning on his side, he spoke with a calm assurance. "We all are. The only way I've found to handle fear is to stand up to whatever comes in His strength, not my own. I think that's how we're gonna win this war. Go out to battle in the name of the Lord of hosts like David did."

"You really believe that?"

"Yep." Jesse smiled, lying on his back again. "'Course a few million bullets might help get the message across to the other side—just in case they haven't read that particular passage of Scripture."

Maria laughed and stretched out next to him, staring at the play of light on the pale willow leaves as they stirred in the breeze. "Cora still feel the same way about your being a soldier?"

"I don't know."

Intrigued, she went on. "I don't understand. Didn't she mention it?"

"We didn't get around to it."

Deciding she had gone far enough, Maria chewed on a blade of grass, hoping Jesse would continue on his own.

"It's over between us." He spoke conversationally with little emotion, as though there had never been much there to begin with. "I guess people just sort of expected us to get married, growing up together the way we did. We were always together. Not a whole lot of choice for either of us in that little church. It was pretty much our whole world."

With a casual motion, Maria let the back of her hand slide against his arm.

"I realized finally there was no . . . passion between us. We were almost like brother and sister." Jesse cleared his throat. "Anyhow, I couldn't ask her to wait for me. This war could go on for years. I might end up in a shallow grave in the desert somewhere."

Maria felt a sudden chill touch her at the sound of his words. She turned toward him, resting her head against his shoulder, sliding her arm around his lean waist. He reached for her, his fingertips tracing the flawless curve of her cheek down to her neck. Maria leaned closer as her lips brushed against his, then sought his mouth with an unexpected urgency. She desperately needed the kind of strength and assurance that Jesse Boone possessed—desired it to become a part of her as she clung to him on the cool grass beneath the willow in the flickering September shadows.

Part 3

NORTH AFRICA

14

AFTER THE FOX

West of El Alamein, the stony landscape stretches flat and unbroken to the distant purple hills. Only ugly little clumps of camel's thorn and scattered patches of sand break the monotony. To the north is the Mediterranean, but inland from its blue and shimmering beauty there is nothing but dry desert.

It was here in September and October of 1942 that the Afrika Korps dug in to meet the British. The Germans were outnumbered two-to-one in men, guns, and tanks, but more importantly they had precious little fuel. Rommel, for the first time in his career, was on sick leave in Germany. With their commander away, the battle-hardened troops sat behind their elaborate minefields (Rommel called them "Devil's Gardens") and waited.

On the night of October 23, under a bright moon, their waiting ended. The heavy silence of the desert night was shattered by a thousand-gun artillery barrage. Harbinger of the most massive British attack of the desert war, it proved to be the beginning of the end for the Axis powers in North Africa.

General Bernard L. Montgomery, commander of the British Eighth Army, had been quietly building vast supply dumps along his northern front while staging a sham buildup to the south. The deceptive tactics worked. His major drive against the northern line caught the Germans completely by surprise.

Adding to their plight, Montgomery also had the German army hemmed into a forty-mile corridor between the sea and the impassable Qattara Depression. Back at the front by the twenty-fifth, Rommel saw immediately that he must either go forward or backward. His army was bombed day and night. Swarms of tanks, including the new American Shermans, along with a seemingly inexhaustible array of artillery and infantry, hit him relentlessly.

Montgomery had outfoxed the Desert Fox. After nine days Rommel realized he had no alternative but to retreat. His already desperate situation, however, was compounded when Hitler sent him a victory-or-death order, which kept him fighting at El Alamein twenty-four hours longer than he should have, costing him unnecessary losses in infantry and motorized troops.

Rommel ordered a complete withdrawal on November 4. His destination was the Sollum and Halfaya passes on the coast near the Libyan frontier some 270 miles west of El Alamein. Montgomery sent his armor sweeping around behind Rommel, and two days later the German escape route was blocked. Rommel now faced the annihilation of the sad remnant of his forces; 90 percent of his five hundred tanks had already been lost.

But the Desert Fox had a trick or two left in him and somehow slipped through the British blocking force. He abandoned every nonessential, including his Italian infantry. His escape route was littered with burned-out vehicles and other debris of war.

Heading west along the coastal road, the defeated Panzer Army Africa stretched forty miles long. They not only succeeded in making it to the vital passes, but they fled fourteen hundred miles across Libya where they linked up with other German forces in Tunisia. There they would make their final stand in North Africa against the British, still pursuing from the east, and the Americans, moving inexorably toward them from the west. The United States joined the fighting against the Axis powers in North Africa on November 8 in the invasion of Algeria, named Operation Torch by Winston Churchill.

* * *

Just after midnight on November 8, Major General Charles W. Ryder, in charge of the Operation Torch Eastern Task Force off Algiers, offered a somewhat dubious encouragement to his men: "Some of you will not make the beaches—but you will be immortal!" In the throng of troops, a regular army corporal bent over and made a gagging sound to the great pleasure of his comrades.

Nine hundred miles to the west, Sergeant Melvin J. Havard lay on his bunk aboard the cruiser USS *Augusta* listening to a short-wave broadcast of the Army-Notre Dame football game. Two decks above him, Major General George S. Patton, Jr., sat in his quarters reading a paperback mystery, *The Cairo Garter Murders.* As commander of the Western Task Force, however, his objective—Casablanca—lay on the Atlantic coast, some two thousand miles west of Cairo.

"I wish I had some crawfish bisque, me." Alcide Naquin stood on the deck of a Liberty ship swinging quietly at anchor six miles off the coast of French North Africa. "I gar-roan-tee you, the cow this hamburger came from died of old age, her."

In the ship's dim red lighting, designed to adjust the men's eyes to night vision, Chance appeared ghostly with his sunbleached hair as he slouched against the rail. "You think if something don't creep, crawl, or swim it ain't fit to eat. Everybody's food don't have to come out of the swamps."

"It ought to." Al continued to chew with obvious distaste. "You take them Nazis." He pointed with the hamburger out into the night toward the distant coast. "The poor boys don't know how to eat, no. All that sauerkraut! Bleh! I'd be mean too."

Chance looked over at Jesse and shrugged.

Jesse swallowed the last of his fried Spam sandwich. "Maybe you're right, Al. I doubt anyone's ever thought of it that way before. I can see your name in print now. *Sauerkraut—The True Culprit Behind the Rise of Fascism in Postwar Germany,* by Alcide Naquin, Ph.D. Sounds real good, don't it?"

"My mama would be so proud." Unexpectedly, Al's bravado began to fail him. He fell silent, trying to comfort himself with thoughts of home—a still morning in October with a fine white mist hovering above the bayou as he glided along in his pirogue. The sound of songbirds celebrating another dawn high in the cypress and tupelo gum.

Al was not alone in clinging to his memories. Along a nine-hundred-mile stretch of Atlantic and Mediterranean coastline, more than 107,000 men waited aboard the 500 ships of the American and British armada. Each carried with him his own thoughts of home like talismans. Most had never seen battle. Few realized what awaited them in the deserts and mountains of North Africa.

Aboard the transports, riding the dark waters beneath a new moon, only muffled sounds could be heard: the muted whine of winches as boats were lowered over the sides, the muffled curses of the foot soldiers burdened with their sixty-pound packs as they climbed down rope ladders into the landing craft, rising and falling with the waves.

"Over the side!"

Jesse stood against the cold steel of a bulkhead in the second wave of assault craft gliding shoreward. Glancing behind him at the silvery wakes churned up by the propellers, he leaned toward Chance. "I hope the French got the message that we're coming here as their allies. The Germans are gonna give us all we can handle without having to fight them too."

Chance sat on the deck, staring down between his legs. He didn't understand Jesse's words over the roar of the powerful engines and didn't bother to respond. In his mind, he raced across the manicured grass of Center Court Wimbledon. Fred Perry was a blur of white in his peripheral vision as he whipped a forehand past him for match point. The stadium thundered with applause for their new champion.

Ne tirez pas. Ne tirez pas. Nous sommes vos amis. Nous sommes Americains. The loudspeakers on the landing craft repeatedly boomed the message toward the unseen coast.

"What're they sayin', Al? That's your language ain't it?" Chance looked up at Al, who stood next to Jesse.

The Cajun came back from his reverie in the swamps. "They're sayin', 'Don't shoot. Don't shoot. We are your friends. We are Americans.'"

As if in reply to Al's translation, the dark horizon they were racing toward flashed randomly like sheet lightning. The French crews were opening up with their seventy-five-millimeter coastal guns. Word spread rapidly among the men in the landing craft. "They're fighting. The French are gonna fight us." Geysers of white water rose as the shells landed in the choppy waters around them.

A thunderous explosion rocked the boat, throwing Jesse and Al to the deck. They struggled up and peered over the side to see a landing craft next to them shattered by a direct hit from a seventy-five-millimeter shell. Bodies were strewn about where the sides had been gutted, and men were scrambling over into the sea to escape the fires that would set off further explosions in the stores of ammunition.

Overhead, the rising sun glinted dully on the wings of the American dive bombers and fighters as they streaked in from the west toward shore. Wave after wave flew over to the cheers of the men in the landing craft. Jesse could see the yellow and orange blossoms of light far ahead as their bombs hit the shore batteries. Soon the French guns were silenced and another round of cheers broke out among the ranks of men as the landing craft droned steadily toward the dark coastline.

No sooner had the coastal batteries been silenced than Jesse saw lights winking on the southern horizon, followed by the muffled roar of naval guns. Looking behind him, he saw geysers of white water exploding near the cruiser *Augusta*. The American warships, their big guns roaring in reply, began their slow turning arcs and zigzags toward the horizon to engage the French ships coming out of Casablanca harbor.

When they hit the beachhead, Jesse leaped off the ramp into chest-deep water. Struggling toward shore, he saw the first of the French fighters zooming low over the beach, strafing the unloading landing craft. Unseasoned troops were cowering behind huge stacks of supplies, piling up on the beach because there were no transport vehicles available to carry them inland.

Gasping for breath after his struggle through the high water, Jesse heard the high, dopplered whine of an engine as a fighter bore down on him. "Look out!" he yelled, grabbing Al by his shoulders and dragging him behind a pile of crates. Chance dove almost on top of them as the heavy fifty-caliber slugs stitched a jagged line across the beach.

Al lay white-faced and sodden on the damp sand. "Whooo-wheee! That was close, yeah!"

Chance rolled over and stared at Al, noticing a thin line of blood trickling down his neck and onto the collar of his green utilities. "Al, you've been hit!"

"Where? I don't feel nothing, me."

Jesse bent Al's head to the side. A pale splinter from a crate shattered by one of the heavy slugs protruded from his neck three inches below his earlobe. "Hold still just a second." Jesse grasped the splinter at its base, jerking it free before Al could protest.

"Owww! I didn't feel nothin' till you did that!" Al touched the side of his neck where the flow of blood continued.

Chance crouched on the sand, peering at the fighters whining low over the beach, strafing the men hiding behind stacks of supplies. "Don't gripe too much, Al. You'll get a Purple Heart for this."

"I will?"

"Sure. Think how it'll impress the girls." Like most of the men, Chance had never been under fire and was numbed by fear into inaction. Somehow, his kidding with Al gave him a sense of security, as though they were still lying around the barracks in basic training. Several heavy slugs thudded into a crate next to him, sending more splinters flying. *This is not basic training!*

"Give me your sulfanilamide packet, Al," Jesse demanded, staring at the naval battle far out at sea.

"Snuffalide?"

"The sulfur packet. For the wound."

Al dug into his pack and brought out the packet. After cleaning the wound, Jesse sprinkled the sulfanilamide on it. "Here. Take two of these." He handed Al two tablets. "That ought to take care of any infection from that splinter."

Vehicles and supplies were now piling up rapidly on the beach. The pounding Atlantic surf had swamped or stranded many of the landing craft. Inexplicably, the engineers, who should have been among the first ashore to organize exits from the beaches, had been held up. Rather than evacuating to safer ground, men began to dig foxholes to escape the hail of bullets from the fighters.

Still crouching with Chance and Al by the pile of crates, Jesse knew they should get off the beach, but in all the confusion and noise he had no idea how that should be accomplished. As he watched the bedlam around him, a brutal stream of profanity rose above the din of voices, gunfire, and engine roar.

A man in battle dress appeared out of nowhere, his trousers tucked into his high boots. With a face broad and beefy under the helmet, he strode among the confusion of men, his voice snapping like a whip.

Chance saw the two stars on the man's shoulders, recognized the twin, pearl-handled revolvers. "That's Patton! He'll make something happen."

Patton had no tolerance for men under fire for the first time. He stalked among them, cursing and bellowing orders. He shamed them into unloading supplies rather than hiding from the enemy's firestorm of lead. They seemed more afraid of his bark than of the deadly bite of the bullets. He waded waist deep into the surf guiding in landing craft, dragged men from their foxholes, and kicked the backsides of any man he found cowering in fear.

At 6:45 on the morning of November 11, the French forces in Morocco capitulated after a half-hearted, sporadic resistance. Later that day, Patton's fifty-seventh birthday, the commanders of the French naval, air, and ground forces arrived at the Miramar Hotel in Fedala, Patton's headquarters fourteen miles outside of Casablanca. He commended them on the defense they had mustered and read them the armistice terms. Then he added a condition of his own: They had to drink with him to the liberation of France by their combined efforts.

*   *   *

Chance sat in the turret of the lightweight M3 Stuart tank, admiring the beauty of the countryside. He reached down and patted the word *Maria* stenciled in white on the side of the turret. The three of them had agreed on the name for their tank. They were traveling with their company of seventeen tanks through a winding valley in the eastern end of the great Atlas Mountains. The cork forests were dressed in their late-autumn foliage of scarlet and gold. Vineyards lined the hillsides. Towering above them, the red rock ranges shone like glowing embers in the slanting afternoon light. "This is the life, boy," he announced, breathing the crisp air deeply. "Haven't seen a German in three days."

Al sat near the rear of the tank, leaning against the storage bin. His tanker's coveralls were open to his waist and the dark goggles were pulled up on his leather helmet. "What difference it make to you if we see any Germans? You keep us so far away from the fighting we might as well stayed at Camp Polk."

Chance scowled over his shoulder at the wiry little man, then forced a smile. "Just being prudent, Al. Somebody's got to hang back in support. That's the way it's done."

"You stay right on the edge, Chance. Get in just close enough, fire just enough rounds to keep the colonel off your back." Al didn't try to hide his contempt for Chance. They were gaining the same reputation they had carried in training.

"Get below, Private," Chance growled. "You're supposed to be at your battle station when we're on the move." *What does he expect from me? Can't he see he's better off than if I was some nitwit out to make a reputation for himself?*

"You manage to go by the book when you feel like it don't hurt you, Chance," Al laughed bitterly, easing down through the turret as Chance stepped out of his way.

Al had spoiled the afternoon for Chance. He knew what his reputation was in the company, in the whole battalion for that matter. *What difference does it make? When I get through this war, I'll never see these guys again. I'm not a coward. I just know how to play it safe. Jesse and Al oughta thank me for takin' care of them.*

Gradually letting the anger flow out of him, Chance lost himself in the dusty clanking, grinding progress of the column of tanks. Suddenly the company commander's tank stopped just this side of the crest of a hill. The captain waved the column to a halt as his signal was passed back. Chance grabbed the microphone off its hook just inside the turret. "Hold it, Jesse! Something's happening up ahead."

Jesse ground the Stuart to a halt and climbed up the turret. "What's going on?"

At that moment the commander's voice crackled over the radio. "German airfield ahead. No activity. Full frontal assault at my command. Flanks out now."

Jesse dropped back into the driver's seat. "German airfield," he barked to Al, who had heard the radio and was already in a loading position for the thirty-seven-millimeter cannon.

Chance pulled his goggles down over his eyes as the tank moved slowly forward and toward the right of the column. "Straighten her out. Hold it steady." *Those planes oughta be ducks in a barrel if we can hit 'em before they get airborne.* Seeing a chance to redeem himself in the eyes of his fellow tankers, Chance positioned the M3 up front rather than in his usual support position.

"What's it look like?" Jesse's voice startled him over the radio.

"Can't tell yet." Chance knew things would go quickly now. Soon they would be above the barrier of the hill that muted the sound of the tank column from the airfield. He gave the halt order over the radio when he could see over the top of the rise. The bulk of the tank remained hidden on the downslope.

Below, thirteen Messerschmitt fighters sat along the runway like sparrows on a power line. On each wing and on the fuselages of the aircraft, black crosses outlined in silver stood out like the cross hairs of a gun sight. Swastikas decorated each stabilizer, calling to mind the frenzied marches shown in the newsreels of the thirties when America rested beyond the reach of tyranny.

"Fire at will!" The order snapped through the radio, and the cannons on all seventeen tanks roared almost simultaneously. The closest planes caught the brunt of the barrage. Wings collapsed, engines were blown open, and gas tanks exploded. After two more volleys, the column began the assault.

On the right flank, Chance rumbled down the hill in the bouncing, clanking Stuart, lost in the roar of engines and the rattle of machine-gun fire. Dust clouds rose in the light wind as he fired his thirty-caliber machine gun at the nearest fighter, watching the canopy shatter.

A German pilot raced across the tarmac toward a plane in a desperate attempt to get airborne before the tanks could blow it apart. As he leaped onto the wing, Chance let go a three-second burst from the machine gun. The pilot crumpled, rolled over slowly, and dropped to the ground.

Chance barked an order to Jesse, sighted the thirty-seven, and sent a round through the plane's engine, putting the fighter out of commission. He raced down the line, riddling the aircraft with the light machine gun, firing at men who were now running from the buildings. More gas tanks exploded; all the planes were on fire or heavily damaged.

Cannon rounds riddled the frame buildings used as control tower and barracks for the airfield, blowing out windows and collapsing entire walls. A few German airmen tried to resist with small-arms fire, but they were immediately cut down. The rest fled into the low hills beyond the base.

"Move out! Move out!" The order jerked Chance away from the destruction around him. Amid the fire and billowing smoke, he directed Jesse back toward the hill from which they had come. Glancing toward the ridge, he froze in the turret. Fear gripped his chest like an iron claw, numbing him. His breath grew labored.

Stretched out along the crest of the hill, six German tanks stood in massive dark silhouette as the orange sun dropped behind them. The dreaded Panzer IVs crouched on the hilltop like great iron beasts bent on revenge.

Chance knew his company of light tanks would be torn apart under the withering fire of the panzers. He had seen their destructive force in action, remembered the burned-out hulks of the American tanks that had the misfortune to encounter them in their passage through the desert. One thought raced through his mind. *Escape!*

Suddenly the world around him blew up as the seventy-five-millimeter canons of the panzers unleashed their awesome power. The rounds came screaming in like banshees. A tank twenty feet away took a direct hit, the shell buckling the Stuart's front like a tin can. Jagged shards of metal whined through the air. The commander's helmet, its goggles still intact, rolled along the side of the tank, dropping to the ground. Chance stared with disbelief. The head was still inside it! He looked up at the lifeless body draped backward over the turret. Blood poured from it. A bizarre thought occurred to him. *Now I know why the British use "bloody" as an obscenity.* He forced his eyes away from the body—from the crimson infinity of blood flowing down the steel plate of the tank.

The night before Chance had won eight dollars from the man in a poker game. His name was Henry. He had spoken of his family back in Pittsburgh, showed him a picture of his six-year-old daughter, two teeth missing in front and bangs hanging in her eyes.

Chance noticed a shallow gully to the left, cutting its way through the floor of the small valley. *If I could make that, I'd be out of sight.* "Hard left!" he screamed into the mike.

Jesse knew they were already on the left flank. "Take over!" he yelled to Al, climbing out of his seat and up the turret. He saw at once the panzers grinding down the hillside and his company's M3s banging away at them like children with peashooters. Then he saw that Chance was guiding them toward the depression and away from the battleground. "Get down there and take over for Al," Jesse growled.

"I'm the commander here . . ." Chance started to object, but saw the cold, dark rage burning in Jesse's eyes. He knew he could never stand up to him. Dropping below, he took up his position and rammed a shell into the breech of the thirty-seven.

Jesse launched three rounds at the closest panzer, seeing the armor-piercing shells bounce uselessly off its fifty-millimeter-thick steel plate. "Ahead full!" he yelled into the mike. *This isn't going to work. Got to hit them where they're weakest.* Chance had positioned them on the fringe of the action where they hadn't been noticed yet.

"Ahead full!" Al repeated, gunning the engine until he received the order to turn hard right and stop.

Jesse carefully lined up his scope on the track of a panzer that had stopped to fire its turret gun. Firing his canon, he watched the shell hit squarely, knocking the track off and disabling the enemy tank. "Hallelujah! That's one out of commission."

The battle raged fiercely on all sides now. Eight Stuarts had been disabled, three of them wrecked and burning. Jesse directed Al in a flanking movement that took him behind the five remaining enemy tanks. In the heat of battle, his tank had still remained undetected so far. Quickly, he lined up his canon on the engine doors of a panzer moving directly away from him. Loosing his round, he saw it spang off the steel plate above the engine. The next two hit the doors squarely, blowing them loose as the engine spouted flames. The huge machine lumbered about, a wounded beast trying to retreat from the Stuarts snapping around it like a pack of dogs. But in seconds the remaining panzers rallied to its aid, cutting through the M3s like scythes through ripe wheat.

And Jesse had drawn attention to himself. The nearest panzer pulled away from the others, driving full speed at *Maria.* Jesse fired six times at it, watching the shells bounce off like hail on a tin roof. "All ahead! Left turn! Left turn!" he bellowed into the mike.

The panzer stopped and fired its seventy-five, but the angle of Jesse's left turn kept it from destroying the tank. The shell struck the front plane, buckling it, but not crushing it completely. The panzer loosed another round, blowing a track off. A third round sent smoke billowing from the engine.

Chance lost his hearing when the first round hit. The sound was like a thousand huge bells clanging inside his head. The tank ground to a halt. He knew he had to get out before it caught fire. The second round hit, rocking the Stuart almost on its side. After the third hit, he saw smoke from the engine and crawled for the turret.

"Give me a hand!" Al, knocked out of his seat, held his hand out to Chance.

Without thinking, Chance pulled him free and pushed him up the turret, following close behind.

The concussion of the first round had blown Jesse out of the turret. He felt himself sucked down into a whirling maelstrom of darkness and unbearable screeching noise. Around and around he went, lights of red, white, and orange seeming to slash at him like sabers, burning him with their touch. Then the thundering darkness dropped on him. He felt himself sinking into a sea of darkness. Down, down into the endless dark.

15

ERNIE

Maria sat on the flat roof of the white stucco villa that the battalion had taken over for headquarters. She wore combat boots with two buckles on the sides, tankers' coveralls against the desert chill, and dark sunglasses. Below her, the treeless prairie reached out toward a distant range of smoky blue hills. *They're almost the same color as Chance's eyes. I wonder where he, Jesse, and Al are now. Somewhere out in this godforsaken desert freezing at night, burning up in the daytime, choking in the dust storms.*

The prairie around the villa looked like a vast Gypsy camp. Men in various stages of dress and undress were washing mess kits and clothes in five-gallon gasoline cans that sat over open fires made from pieces of packing crates. Their low two-man pup tents stretched almost out of sight. Some had floors made from scrap lumber and sideboards to keep out the wind and sand.

Violin music drifted up to the roof. *Mendelssohn: Violin Concerto in E Minor,* Maria thought, remembering her Music 101 class. *That was Dr. French's favorite piece. Where in the world is the music coming from?* She stood up and looked down from the roof. Seated on the "front stoop" of his pup tent, a young soldier with short dark hair, wearing only green utility trousers, played a violin. His eyes were closed and his hand moved the bow across the strings with relaxed precision. *"The Artist Goes to War." Might be an interesting idea for a story.*

"I want you to meet someone, Maria."

Startled by the intrusion, she spun to face the battalion commander. He was a small man with a jutting chin and bristly gray hair, cropped short. "Hello, Colonel Walker," she replied.

Walker gestured toward his companion. The man standing next to him was of average height, his gray hair thinning in front. He wore the clothes of an army infantryman with the casualness of long acquaintance. "Maria Vitrano, I'd like you to meet a colleague of yours. This is Ernie Pyle."

Speechless for a moment, Maria merely stared at him. With his craggy face, he looked to be in his mid-fifties, although she knew he was ten years younger. Here was the man who made the war real for the average American back home. They saw their sons, daughters, and husbands in all his dispatches. He was a legend among journalists. "How do you do, Mr. Pyle?"

"I'll do just fine if you call me Ernie," he smiled, extending his sunburned hand.

"Maria, then, Ernie," she laughed, taking his hand.

"How do you like North Africa so far?" he gestured about him.

Maria gazed out over the prairie. "It's a rough place to adapt to. I live for mornings and sunsets. They're beautiful."

"Absolutely," he agreed. "Everything in between is just dolor or darkness."

"That's a good way to put it."

"I thought so. That's why I stole it. It's a loose translation of an old Bedouin proverb. Makes people think I'm a whole lot smarter than I really am."

Maria laughed. For some reason, she didn't expect a legend like Ernie Pyle to have much of a sense of humor. "I love your work."

"I'm flattered. How's yours going?"

She tried to think of something creative and incisive to say, but decided to be frank instead. "Pretty routine I'm afraid. Mostly secondhand information."

Pyle glanced at the colonel, knowing that he and his men had just been ordered to stand down for a rest after months of hard fighting. "Well, you want to hang around here with these rear-echelon paper-pushers, or do you want to go up to the front and see the real war with me?"

Again, Maria was caught off guard. "But I—I'm a woman," she stammered.

Pyle's eyes crinkled as he grinned. "Are you now? I know I'm getting on in years and I've been in the company of fighting men far too long now, but I'm not that old or out of touch."

"What I mean is—can I do that?"

"Why not?" he shrugged. "Pin your hair up, keep your helmet on, and no lipstick, please! Once we get out there," he pointed toward the open desert, "who's to tell? Nobody much bothers with me anyway. I hitch rides, occasionally get my own jeep. What do you think?"

"You really mean it?"

"I hear you've got talent, but you'll never amount to anything getting your copy from briefings given by the likes of Walker here. What do you think about it, Colonel? A woman going up front?"

"I think you're gonna do pretty much what you want to, Ernie—and get away with it too. Like you've always done." Walker turned away, looking down at the camp below him. In an open space between the rows of tents, bare-chested soldiers played a noisy game of softball. "I don't want to know anything about this."

Ernie grinned at Maria and shrugged. "See? No problem."

This was better than anything she could have imagined. "When do we leave?"

"Pack some warm clothes. I'll pick you up in half an hour." He turned and left with Walker.

* * *

"Where're we heading?" Maria sat next to Ernie in his jeep spinning down the long narrow road that ran south and into the vastness of the desert.

He kept his eyes on the road, his arms hooked loosely over the steering wheel. "We'll spend tomorrow night at an airfield up near the front. Then we'll join up with an armored outfit."

"Why didn't we wait until morning to leave?" Maria asked, staring ahead at the road that was little more than a dirt trail. "We always traveled in the daytime where I've been so far. Isn't it awfully dangerous driving at night?"

Smiling wryly, Pyle glanced over at her. "Not nearly as dangerous as traveling in the daytime."

"But what if we have a wreck?" she complained. "You can't possibly see the road very well."

"Can't *be* seen either—by Stukas or Messerschmitts. Nobody travels much in the daytime." He spoke gravely. "Out here you've got to get used to a different way of thinking. Take a lesson from the front-line soldiers. Your survival may depend on it."

They traveled in silence for a while. The sun slipped down the sky, flaring brightly as it hung momentarily on the western rim of the earth. Maria gazed at the open, empty landscape about her. "The desert reminds me so much of the sea," she remarked.

"They're very much alike. The Arabs call their camels *ships of the desert*," Ernie commented, his eyes trained on the road. "The battles out here are fought more like naval battles than land. There's no way to hold a front. With so much open space, the enemy can always go around you."

Maria listened, taking mental notes.

"This desert war's gonna be won through attrition. Fortunately for us, we've got more men and equipment than the Germans. With the British Navy sinking so many Italian transport and supply ships now, it's an even greater advantage." Ernie glanced over at her. "I do tend to rattle on, don't I? Must be creeping senility."

"Oh, no! Please go on," she encouraged him. "I've got so much to learn."

"Well, you won't learn it from me, young Maria. Watch the fighting men, listen to them. That's where the lessons are."

Maria felt comfortable already with this friend of the common soldier—this hero of the folks back home. In their open jeep, they moved on through the desert. Gazing upward, she imagined they were drifting, beneath the pale winter moon, like mariners across an arid sea.

* * *

Clang! Clang! Clang! The incessant bell dredged Maria up from a deep, dreamless sleep. She and Ernie had arrived at the airfield at four in the morning and been shown the pup tents where they would spend the rest of the night. Squinting out into the dark, she could barely make out the silhouette of a man ringing a dinner bell that hung from a date palm tree. The noise was deafening.

Then she saw them! Focke-Wulf 190's flying low out of the rising sun. There was no time to hide. Maria flattened under her army blanket and prayed. This was her first taste of the *real war*. No more trying to imagine what being under fire felt like from some dry briefing in a stuffy tent. The sounds of war terrified her: the high-dopplered whine of the fighter engines, the clattering of machine guns, the ground-jarring explosions of the bombs, the smothering rush of air and pressure on her lungs as the concussion hit.

The heavy slugs from the fighters tore along the runways, riddling two B-25 Mitchells. They came back for a second pass, but this time a fireworks show awaited them as the antiaircraft batteries tore loose at the German fighters. Immediately after the second pass of the fighters, the Stukas came screaming down out of the lightening skies. Their bombs tore massive craters in the runways, but the murderous fire from the American batteries spoiled their aim and no aircraft were hit. In a matter of minutes it was over.

Maria lay breathless in her darkened tent. The silence seemed more of a threat than an ending. A rooster crowed in the distance. Above her the sun's early rays were changed into jagged beams of light as they passed through the shrapnel holes in the canvas walls of the tent. A wet warmth soaked her left calf, but she felt no pain. Trembling, she sat up. She saw to her great relief that it was only tepid water leaking from her canteen.

"You all right?"

She twisted around at the sound of Ernie's voice. "I think so. How about you?"

"Fine. Let's get some breakfast."

Still trembling, she tried to control the panic in her voice. "Be right with you." *How can he think of eating after what we just went through?* Then it occurred to her. *This is a war zone. Things like this happen all the time.*

After breakfast, they wandered around the base together. It was located on a flat endless desert in the middle of a two-mile-long date palm oasis. Sand was everywhere. In the distance, hazy purple mountains broke the flatness.

The German air raids had spawned a zeal for labor among the men. Trenches were scattered all about the base. Some were just square holes. Some were L-shaped. A few were the regulation zig-zag. Most were shallow, but some were so deep steps had been dug at each end for easier access. All were for the purpose of hiding in when the fighters and dive bombers came screaming out of the bright and deadly skies. Nowhere on the huge base did a man have to run more than fifty yards to dive into a trench when he heard the bell.

"It certainly does warm up quickly." After the sharp, dry chill of the night, Maria was amazed at the sun's warmth here in the interior.

Ernie grinned at a group of Arab children as they approached a sunbaked adobe village at the edge of the base. "The desert's a place of extremes. You have to learn to respect it if you want to live in it for any length of time."

Taking off his helmet, he squatted down about twenty yards from the children who were playing under a tall date palm. Their clothes were threadbare, loose robes belted at the waist with twine. Dirty and barefoot, their smiles brightened the shade they played in, and they laughed in the same language as children on a playground in Brooklyn.

Maria watched a little girl of about five smile shyly at the rumpled American soldier. She eased away from the other children. Ernie took a Hershey bar from his pocket and carefully unfolded the wrapper. The child came closer. He broke a square off, put it into his mouth, and chewed slowly. Then he extended the candy bar toward the little girl.

Rubbing her right foot back and forth in the sand, the girl looked up and smiled again at him. As she came closer, Maria saw a mass of scar tissue beneath her matted hair where her left ear had once been. The child reached out with both hands for the candy bar; the left one was missing the thumb and forefinger.

"She looks enough like you to be your little girl." Ernie grinned up at Maria, and she thought she could see in his eyes why his writing had captured the imagination of the American people.

Maria looked again at the child, at the thin face, the big dark eyes full of wonder and innocence. A photograph glowed in the back of her mind like an old Linotype—her mother as a child in Sicily. She felt that she had been thrown back in time and was staring at her own mother when she was five years old. A pain of regret (for what?) stabbed at her breast. "She looks more like my mother."

"You said your family came from Sicily, didn't you? It's not that far away." Ernie stood up, looking at the other children. "This is a seafaring part of the world. You two might have the same blood flowing in your veins."

Maria had nothing to give the child, so she knelt down and held out her arms. "How about a hug?" she said softly. More comfortable now with these strange intruders, the girl put her arms around her. As she took the damaged hand in her own, for the first time since her arrival in North Africa, Maria felt the true sadness and horror of war.

Stepping back, the child broke a piece of the candy bar off and held it out. She had yet to take a piece for herself.

"Thank you," Maria whispered, her eyes growing bright with tears as she took the candy.

The child ran to join her friends. Ernie was already among them handing out Hershey bars. They flocked to him like chicks around a mother hen. Maria sat down under a date palm and felt the mild desert breeze on her face. She gazed up at the cloudless sky, so blue it almost hurt her eyes. Taking her pad out, she scribbled a few notes, but mostly she just watched Ernie and the children.

"Well, you ready to get to work?" He walked back toward her palm tree, his pockets empty and his heart full.

Maria got up, dusting the fine sand from her clothes. "That's what I came for. What did you have in mind?"

Ernie stroked the stubble on his chin, a thoughtful look on his face. "How'd you like to meet the leading American ace in North Africa? Think that'd be worth a column?"

Trying to contain her excitement, she walked along with him back toward the main part of the base. "I think so. I hope he flies one of those fighters the Germans call the 'two-tailed devil.' The readers back home would love that."

"You're in luck then. That's exactly what he flies. Except we call it the P-38 Lightning."

As they approached the rickety-looking control tower, its paint already splotchy from the sandstorms, Ernie pointed to a hastily constructed barracks at the edge of a palm grove just beyond it. "I think he flies this afternoon. He should be in there now. Name's Lieutenant Wayne Rayburn. From Flagstaff, Arizona."

Maria stared at the unpainted barracks, sand piling up around the plank steps. "Aren't you going to introduce me?"

"Got my own work to do," Pyle explained. "Then I've got to make arrangements for us to be in the convoy that's leaving tonight. Besides, it's time you got weaned. Struck out on your own."

"Well, if you think it's all right."

"One way to find out," he grinned. "I think you'll find most of the fighter pilots are pretty easy to get along with out here. They're not cocky like they are back in the States." He seemed to look inside himself. "The work they do is so—lethal, and they've seen so many of their friends shot down, it seems to have a humbling effect on them. Oh, they get excited and brag about what hotshots they are when they score a German fighter or blow up a convoy, but living so close to death all the time makes them pretty nice guys. You'll do fine, Maria." He walked off toward the administration building.

Standing in the hot wind, Maria squinted up at the sun, blazing now in the desert skies, a sky incessantly and noisily full of airplanes. Constant takeoffs and landings had overlain the base with the roaring of engines since the dawn attack. It reminded her of a trip to LaGuardia in New York, except these aircraft had that unmistakable malevolent look of war.

She took her jacket off and lay it across her arm, trudging through the yellow sand toward the barracks near the date palms. As she climbed the three creaky steps, she heard a guitar and someone singing in a clear, soft baritone, "I'd give all I own if I could but atone to that silver-haired daddy of mine."

Standing on the steps, she listened to the song. It was a sentimental tale of someone's father aging alone in a cabin and the son who had gone wrong. A sense of unreality swept over her like the desert wind. Listening to this Gene Autry song in a landscape right out of a Hollywood western, she had to struggle with her sense of being thousands of miles away from America where there were no soda fountains, no movies, no clean sheets—and where death came screaming out of the skies.

When the song was finished, Maria knocked on the door.

"It's open."

She stepped into a long, open room with two rows of bunk beds running its length. On the second-to-the-last bunk on the right, a chunky man with straight black hair, unusually long for a soldier or airman, lounged with his back against the wall. He wore brown cowboy boots that looked ten years old, fatigue trousers, and a tan, sweat-stained Stetson. "I'm looking for Lieutenant Wayne Rayburn."

"My name's Rayburn," he smiled, showing perfect white teeth against his dark skin, "but I'm a lieutenant only when I'm on duty. Right now, I'm Wayne."

"Hello, Wayne. I'm Maria Vitrano. I'm a war correspondent, and I'd like to interview you," she informed him, proud of her title.

Rayburn laid the guitar aside. "I didn't think you'd be a *peace* correspondent—not over here."

"Well, I—I guess it was a little redundant," Maria stammered, shifting about uneasily.

"Don't take it so seriously," Rayburn insisted. "We try to keep things kind of informal around here. It gets serious in a hurry up there." He pointed toward the skies. "Why don't you sit down?"

She sat down gingerly on the edge of the bed. "Thank you. Guess I'm a little nervous."

"Shows good sense to be a little nervous out here." Rayburn crossed his arms over his beefy chest. "Never saw a female reporter this close to the front before."

Glancing around nervously, Maria murmured, "I came up with Ernie Pyle. No one's supposed to know."

Rayburn smiled at her uneasiness. "Well, if you made it past the brass back at the rear, you got no problems. Reporters come and go pretty much as they please out here. Long as they don't interfere with operations. You couldn't be with a better man than Ernie. He knows the ropes as well as anyone."

Maria relaxed a little, taking out her notebook to keep the facts straight. "Mind if I take a few notes?"

"Help yourself."

"I understand you're our number-one ace now."

"So they tell me." Rayburn looked out the dusty window where a flight of P-38s were taxiing out toward the runway. "That could change tomorrow. Don't make much difference one way or the other though. Doesn't mean I'm the best pilot either."

"I don't understand."

"Our main job is to provide cover for the bombers and transports. That means you always keep the formation tight. Teamwork is what counts." He watched the first fighter rev up its engines and roar off down the runway. "There's no room for heroes and prima donnas. You don't go off chasing every German fighter you see. That plays into their hands and gets you a one-way ticket to the graveyard."

Maria tapped the point of her pencil on the pad. "So what you do is fly together over the bombers like an umbrella?"

"You got it." Rayburn grinned slyly. "Except sometimes they turn us loose on strafing missions. Freelancing you might call it. That's where the *real* fun is."

She watched his dark eyes grow intense above his high cheek-bones. "Fun?"

"Yeah, boy! Yesterday we came across a German convoy. It was like Christmas. The trucks were full of men, and they blew out of the sides like firecrackers when we hit one. You'd pop a motor-cycle and the driver'd skid fifty feet before he stopped."

Maria listened, entranced with his story. There was no bra-vado, only a genuine enthusiasm about a job well done. He spoke casually as though he were talking about his best girlfriend or a football game.

"Then a couple of 109s made a big mistake," he went on, de-scribing the action with his hands. "They tried to stop us. Got off one, maybe two bursts before we took them both out. Nothing but black smoke and yellow fire when we got finished with 'em."

"How many planes have you shot down?"

Rayburn was still reliving the dogfight and came back slowly. "Huh? Oh! Six, I think—maybe seven. They're waiting on confir-mation for the last one."

"Well, I guess that just about does it, except for a short bio on you. You're American Indian, aren't you?"

"Half-Navajo," he smiled, "but I look full-blooded. Ol' John Wayne would puke if he knew an Injun was fighting on *his* side in this war, wouldn't he?"

Maria looked puzzled; then it hit her, remembering all the westerns the actor was in. "I think he might be proud of you," she laughed. After getting a few more facts about him, she stood up to leave.

"I sure have enjoyed this, Miss Vitrano," Rayburn smiled. "It's been a welcome break from the daily grind."

"It's been a pleasure for me," she replied. "You might even see your name in the papers one day."

He ignored the remark. "You certainly are a fine-looking woman, Maria. Never saw anybody make army green look so good. If we were back home, I'd ask you out so fast it'd make your head swim."

"Careful, Lieutenant. I just might take you up on it." Maria hesitated, then spoke again. "Would you mind singing another song for me? Music is one thing I really miss out here."

"You must miss it real bad to want to hear me," Rayburn grinned, slipping into a T-shirt. "Let's go outside though. It's getting stuffy in here."

Ernie found them an hour later, sitting under the date palms. Rayburn had his guitar across his lap, eyes closed as he sang "Ghost Riders in the Sky" with a haunting wail to his voice.

"I bet that's what you hotshot pilots think you are, don't you?" Ernie smiled good-naturedly. "Just a bunch of ghost riders in the sky."

Rayburn stopped singing as he continued to strum the guitar softly. "Nah," he answered, glancing up at Ernie. "But we sure are trying hard to make ghosts out of all them German pilots."

"I hear you're getting your fair share of 'em." Ernie turned to Maria. "Looks like the interview went well."

"Better than I expected," she blushed slightly, taking his hand as she got to her feet.

"Got us first-class tickets on the convoy," Ernie continued. "It leaves at dusk."

Rayburn stood up, brushing the sand off his clothes. "How long you gonna be out this time, Ernie?"

"Don't know. Depends on what kind of show they put on for us."

Turning to Maria, he spoke in a solemn tone. "Keep an eye on him, Maria. He tends to think he's bulletproof sometimes. We can't afford to lose Ernie. He tells the folks back home what it's *really* like out here."

"You just keep those Germans in your gun sights, Lieutenant," Pyle joked. "Nothing's going to happen to me."

* * *

Maria scrunched along through the sand next to Ernie, her duffel bag thrown over her shoulder. The hard desert chill settled over them as the sun winked out behind the distant mountains. They were leaving the base to move out with a convoy heading through the mountains toward the front lines. Ahead of them, the trucks were coughing into life and the tanks clanking and rumbling like they were angry at having to stay up all night. Men shouted commands and muttered curses as they made ready to move out in the darkness.

"Won't they use the lights at all?" Maria asked, fearing the thought of driving blind on the mountain roads.

"Can't chance it." Ernie had an edge to his voice.

She had the feeling that he had done this before and feared what lay ahead of them. "Not even in the mountains?"

"There's a risk of losing men when you drive in the dark," he explained. "It's a certainty if you use the lights."

"How will you find the captain we're riding with?" Maria asked, raising her voice to be heard. They walked among the confusion of men. It seemed everyone talked at once and no one knew what he was doing. The gasoline fumes and the grease smell mixed with the odor of thousands of men who were unable to bathe except on rare occasions. *Maybe I should have been a dental assistant. Guess I'll get used to it.*

"He's right over there."

Maria pushed her way through the crowd after Ernie. She was introduced to the captain, a sallow-faced, spare man from Cleveland, and his driver, a sullen corporal from San Diego who reminded Maria of Dr. Frankenstein's assistant. *What a pleasant trip this is going to be. Like spending the night with a grave digger and a ghoul.*

From the time of her arrival in North Africa, Maria had gradually adapted to the rigors of the land—except for one. She could never get used to the bitter desert cold. She wore all the clothes she had with her. Over her long underwear and three pairs of socks, she wore two sweaters, fatigue pants and shirt, a pair of coveralls, and a heavy field jacket. Her combat boots, two wool caps, and goggles completed the outfit. Sitting next to Ernie in the open jeep under a blanket, they waited for their turn to move out in the convoy.

The grinding of the trucks passing them seemed endless. The men sat in the back of the canvas-covered deuce-and-a-halfs, hunched over against the cold like dark wraiths on their way to some sinister celebration of shadows. As the cold settled into her bones, Maria came to see the hundreds of vehicles going by as nothing more than shadows, insubstantial bulks that were only a shade darker than the desert night.

"How much longer?" she turned to Ernie who had just awakened from a nap.

He looked at his watch. "We're supposed to fall in near the middle. It's been an hour now. Probably another hour and a half."

"You mean it takes five hours for this convoy to pass a single point? How long is it?"

"Beats me," he grunted. "I'm just along for the ride."

Maria awakened to the bumping of the jeep as it found its place in the column. She stared up at the biggest, brightest moon she could remember. Its light had a silver quality to it, casting long moving shadows across the desert floor from the convoy. A half-mile further on, she saw the motorcyclists directing traffic as they pulled onto the main road. As her eyes became accustomed to the dark, she could make out the road and the endless line of vehicles in either direction.

Two hours later, they reached the mountains. It was a grueling process to cross them. The heavy trucks growled in low gear as they pulled the steep inclines. On the sharpest switchback turns, the big trucks had to back and fill to get around them. French trucks and buses would block the traffic as they passed the Americans, swinging in and out of the traffic.

Halfway up the mountains they encountered a long delay. The jeep seemed about to slide off the edge of the road where they had suddenly stopped. They finally shut down their engines. The night became blanketed with an unearthly quiet, except for the groaning of the heavy trucks far up the mountain. At times they heard the angry clanking of tanks from below as they took the sharp turns.

Maria sat under her blanket, staring out across the deep chasm of darkness between her and a lower peak. Beyond it, the vast desert floor, surrounded by mountains, seemed to be filling with the cold, silver light streaming down from the moon.

Drifting into sleep, Maria suddenly heard hoarse screams from above—the shrieking of metal being torn apart. Her eyes wide with fear, she saw one of the heavy, canvas-covered trucks tumbling backward down the sheer, moonlit face of the cliff rising from the edge of the road. Each turn crushed and ripped at the truck like some giant hand. Pieces clanged off into the night. It hit the roadbed in front of her with a deafening noise. The screaming stopped as it bounced end over end and crashed down into the darkness.

Silence settled over the road like a dropped curtain. No one moved or spoke in the aftermath of the horror. A hollow *whump* rose from the chasm as the gas tank of the truck exploded. Several men rushed to the edge of the precipice, peering down into the darkness. An orange glow flickered dimly in the night as the flames grew.

16

THE LONELY YELLOW TWILIGHT

Great job, Sergeant." Colonel Ed Gold, a swarthy high school principal from Chicago, shook hands with Chance and patted him on the shoulder. "I couldn't see very much in all that smoke and fire, but I saw *Maria* blasting away at those two panzers. You saved our hides, son—what was left of us to save. Helped get your buddy out of there, too, from what they tell me."

Chance stood in the colonel's tent, pitched in a secluded valley the company had retreated to after the battle. Three days had passed. Replacement crews and tanks had joined them. "Thank you, sir. I had—a lot of help."

"Good! Good! Teamwork is what it's going to take to win this war. Everybody doing his job. Everybody looking out for his buddy." Gold smiled paternally at Chance. "We're having to reassign a lot of men to new crews and new vehicles. You and your crew are going to make up a turret crew for a Lee. You'll be the tank commander. It's got a seventy-five gun on it that ought to put some pretty good dents in Rommel's panzers. We might just have us some Shermans before too long."

Chance knew the heavier tank would put him in the forefront of the battles from now on. His spirits sank.

Puzzled by Chance's reaction, the colonel went on. "I'm recommending you for a promotion, son."

Chance was appalled. "I—I really don't deserve it, sir."

"Sure you do, son. You're just being modest."

Hoping that the other men hadn't found out what really happened, Chance asked, "Could we just keep this quiet for now, sir? I don't want the men finding out."

Gold nodded solemnly. "Certainly. I think I understand. You don't want any of the glory for yourself. It'll be our little secret—for now anyway."

Staring at the ground, Chance burned with shame. He tried to summon up enough courage to tell the colonel what had really happened at the airfield. He despised himself because he couldn't— and he felt a growing rage at Jesse for what he had done. *What did he do? He saved the company from complete annihilation by the Germans. But he took my command—my tank. Made me look like a quitter! Why did I even help Al carry him away?*

Looking at his sergeant's downcast expression, Ed Gold believed him to be a humble man. *Must be all this attention that's causing him to be so uncomfortable. He probably just wants to be with his crew.* "Well, I guess you'd better get on back. I know you're anxious to check out your new tank. I understand Boone's back from the field hospital. Nothing more than a mild concussion."

"Yes sir." Chance saluted and left the tent.

Another winter front had moved in, catching the company licking its wounds after the beating from the panzers. Because they were still close to the coastal belt, the weather front brought with it a cold, steady rain. Chance drew his poncho about him as he trudged through the mud. He glanced about at the men huddled under their canvas shelters, crowding close to their fires. *They must all know by now. They know what really happened at that airfield. I bet Jesse told them. All this misery because of him.*

Through the gray curtain of rain, Chance saw Jesse and Al under the lean-to they had fashioned by tying one end of a canvas shelter to the side of a tank and the other to some poles driven into the muddy ground. Jesse sat on a crude bench of scrap lumber. His face showed the strain of battle, like all the men, but it also held a calmness, a confidence, that gave Chance another reason to dislike him. Squatting before their open fire, Al prepared supper in the bottom half of a five-gallon gasoline can.

"Co-mo-sah-vah, Chance?" Al continued to stir his pot without looking up.

"Hey, Al," Chance mumbled.

Jesse reached for a cup that sat on a blanket with the rest of their mess gear. "How 'bout some coffee? Looks like you could use it. You're not coming down with something, are you?"

Chance took the cup, ignoring Jesse's question. "Where'd y'all get coffee? I didn't think there was any in a hundred miles of this place."

Jesse poured the steaming coffee into Chance's cup. "Al got it somewhere, but he's not talkin'."

"Don't ask," Al volunteered, stirring his pot. "You wouldn't want to know."

"What did the colonel want you for?" Jesse leaned back against the riveted steel of the tank.

"Nothing much, routine stuff," Chance muttered, staring out into the solid wall of rain. *You got a pretty good idea what he wanted already, don't you, Jesse?*

"Y'all jes had a little social talk," Al chimed in. "Some hot tea and them little white sandwiches ain't big enough for one good bite. Maybe a few sugar cookies."

"Knock it off, Al," Chance growled, flinging his helmet to the ground next to the bench. "I ain't in the mood. What are you cookin' anyway?"

"Don't ask," Al grinned, "you wouldn't want to know."

Jesse knew what was troubling Chance. He was brooding himself into an early grave. *He's got to turn loose of this dream of being a big-shot tennis player. Maybe he will—maybe not. But if he doesn't forget about it till after this war is over, he'll get himself and a lot of other men killed.* "Chance, can I talk to you—man to man?"

Chance sat with his back bent, elbows resting on his knees, staring between his legs. He glanced over at Jesse with eyes that were hollow, dark, and desperate. "I ain't much interested in anything you got to say, Jesse. I don't need anybody preachin' to me, and I got a feelin' that's just what you want to do."

"No, I won't preach to you. But I do want to tell you a story about somebody from Liberty." He stared at Chance. His face was gaunt and pale. The almost white, week-old stubble and the haunted look in his eyes made him look ten years older.

At the mention of Liberty, Chance felt a pang of homesickness. "A story? Well, I guess it won't hurt to hear one, long as it's got a happy ending."

"It does," Jesse smiled. "Anyway, this boy went to school at Liberty High. Had a God-given talent for singin'. Some people said he could make it in New York or Hollywood."

Chance was becoming intrigued. "I don't remember anybody like that from school."

Jesse sipped his coffee. "He was a little older than you. Besides, he was so shy he wouldn't sing in the talent contests or plays at school. Nowhere but church—at first that is. When he graduated, he started singing in a few juke joints, a roadhouse or two. To keep from boring you, I'll just say that in two years' time, he ended up with a pretty good part in a Broadway musical."

"That is a happy ending, Sha. I bet he made plenty money, him." Al added some salt to his concoction.

"No. He didn't make a dime. Never sang a note in a paid performance."

"What happened to the happy ending?" Chance snapped.

Jesse spoke reverently, almost as though he were praying. "You see God got ahold of him. He'd been saved when he was ten—confessed Jesus as his Lord and Savior before the whole church, but he was running from God. And his success caused him nothing but heartache." Jesse saw the light come on in Chance's eyes.

"This is about you."

"Yep. God called me to preach the gospel six months after I got saved, but I got caught up in the glitter and the bright lights."

"I kinda like that story, me." Al turned from the fire. "Y'all ready to eat?"

Chance ignored Al. "You mean to tell me you're happier out there in that little run-down church in the hills than you were in New York?" Chance's voice was full of contempt.

Jesse smiled.

Chance already knew the answer to his question, for he had seen few people as content with their life as Jesse Boone. Before Jesse could reply, he said haughtily, "Yeah! Well, you said you weren't gonna preach to me!"

"That's not preachin', Chance. It's just my testimony." Jesse prayed that his words would get through to Chance. "What I'm sayin' is, God has chosen all of us to be His children. The only true happiness comes when we let Him have *His* way in our lives."

"What do you mean, He's *chosen* us?" Chance spat back. "He never chose *me* for anything."

"Yes, He did." Jesse laid his hand on Chance's shoulder. "When He let His only Son, Jesus, die on that bloody cross in Jerusalem,

He chose all of us. He was saying, 'Come, be My children. Come to peace and joy and eternal life through My only Son.'"

Chance knocked Jesse's arm from his shoulder. "I told you, no preachin'!"

"I believe He chose me, yeah." Al smiled at Chance, reaching across the blanket for their tin plates.

Chance glared back at him. "I didn't ask you anything."

"I'm gonna told you anyhow, Sha. 'Cause you need to hear this." Al began spooning the stew into the plates.

"I don't need another story," Chance snorted, but he made no effort to leave.

Al acted as though Chance hadn't spoken. "I listened to what Jesse told my people when he come to see us out in the Atchafalaya. I thought about it a long time, yeah. And, me, I don't think about too much, 'cept where the crawfish are runnin' or the best place to catch some sac-a-lait. But I thought about this story that Jesse called the *gospel*."

Chance stared at the ground. The rain beat steadily on the canvas shelter.

"Anyhow," Al continued, I finally figured out that it had to be from God. A man might make up a story about a little baby, but not one poor as me, born in a dirty ol' stable. And when he grew up, that part about being beat half to death and then nailed to a cross—people don't like to hear about stuff like that, no. That just ain't the story a man would write about the Son of God."

A sudden urge to get up and run hit Chance. Al's words were like darts being thrown at him.

"And the last thing—it's *free*, eternal life is a gift from God. You can't do nothin' to earn it. Jesus did it all for us. It finally come to me—this is God's word, 'cause it ain't like nothin' any man ever writ before. And Jesus wasn't like no man ever lived before."

Chance felt himself trembling—with anger, fear, shame?—he didn't know. He just knew he had to get away from Al and Jesse.

"Have some stew, Chance." Al held the plate out to him. "You gettin' as poor as an ol' stray cat."

Springing up from the bench, Chance knocked the plate to the ground. He grabbed his helmet and stormed out into the rain.

Al began cleaning up the spilled stew. "That boy got him some trouble, yeah."

Chance walked in silence, letting his undefined rage cool down, until he came to a huge boulder on the fringe of the company area. At its base were ledges and grooves that formed natural seats. *Reminds me of the one at the swimmin' hole back in Liberty.* He sat down on one of the flat sections, leaning back against the smooth stone face. Lighting a Chesterfield, he glanced up at the low gray clouds pressing down on him, smothering him. The rain beat a steady cadence on his steel helmet. It sounded like the chattering of machine guns.

All about him, Chance saw the fires of the men in his company. Each crew huddled together under its shelter, trying to draw some comfort from this unforgiving land before they were called again into battle. Their rough voices sounded far away through the steady drumming of the rain. He sat for a long time, listening to them. Toward the western horizon, the clouds began to lift slightly, light seeping in through the seam between the sky and the earth, but the rain continued. And still he sat on the cold stone in the lonely yellow twilight.

For months it had been gnawing at Chance like some kind of monstrous rodent, even before the airfield. It had been growing inside him since Camp Polk. His dream of becoming a tennis star had turned him into a coward. He had prided himself on his courage, on being a man, and now he was mired in shame. A terrible blackness covered him. *I'd rather be dead than go on livin' like this! God, if You're out there, help me!*

It was as though a tiny light glimmered in darkness. Chance remembered a verse from Sunday school so many years before—". . . *Whosoever shall not receive the kingdom of God as a little child, he shall not enter therein.*" He was unaware of the men around him as he spoke the words that came from his heart. "God, as much as I can, I come to You as a little child. I don't know what to say, except I've made a mess of my life and I'm sorry for it. And I need Your help more than anything in the world. I'm not worth much, but I give my life to You. In Jesus' name. Amen."

Chance sat with his head in his hands. He felt hot tears coursing down his palms, his wrists—and he felt the cleansing of them. Everything seemed the same: the rain, like strands of silver in the last light, still beating on his helmet—this strange land so far from his home—and the Germans, out there somewhere with their tanks and artillery, waiting to blow them to bits. Nothing had changed in this wild and deadly country. Yet somehow his anger and shame—and the fear he could never admit he carried with him—seemed to be lifting like the clouds on the western horizon. Somehow he knew—in the deepest part of his being—nothing in his life would ever be the same again.

* * *

"Thank goodness we're out of those mountains!" Maria bounced along in the jeep, watching the sun streak the lion-colored wilderness with shades of pink and orange.

Ernie turned toward her. He looked pale and drawn after a sleepless night of travel. "Never been one of my favorite parts of this job either. I'd almost rather be in the middle of a tank battle."

"Do we get to stop and sleep for a while?" Maria asked, suppressing a yawn.

"I don't know yet. Sometimes, if the commanders think the area's safe, they'll travel in the daytime. It all depends on the situation. And I don't think anybody knows very much ahead of time what they're going to do from one day to the next."

"But surely they have to sleep *sometime!*"

"I've seen men go three days without sleep out here. The Germans don't particularly care whether we're well rested or not." Ernie stretched and yawned widely. "We might as well settle back and try to catch a nap. At least there aren't any mountains to fall off."

The convoy drove all day through the dry, rolling hills. Maria dropped off to sleep and dreamed of falling into a deep crevice, the jeep tumbling over and over with a terrible screeching of metal as it hit jagged outcroppings of rock on the way down. She came out of the dream with a gasp.

"You OK?" Ernie mumbled, half-asleep himself.

"Huh? Sure, I'm fine." For the rest of the day, she dozed fitfully, awakening often to see nothing but rocks, sand, and little dry clumps of bushes. The sun drove her out of her outer layer of clothing by mid-morning. At noon, they ate K rations. The meat tasted like cardboard and the crackers tasted like the meat. Ernie saved her the best they had to offer—pound cake and canned peaches for her dessert. They traveled on through most of the following night.

"Here we are."

At the sound of Ernie's voice, Maria forced her eyes open. They felt like someone had bathed them with acid. Her mouth was as dry and sandy as the desert they had crossed. "Where's here?" she mumbled, struggling up painfully from the jeep's seat.

"Where we're going to spend the last hours of the night." Ernie stood at the side of the jeep, holding out his hand to her.

"I hope there's a bed around here somewhere." As she climbed down, Maria heard the distant boom of artillery. She was closer than she had ever been to that unmistakable sound. From over a rock-strewn hill directly in front of them, she thought she heard the sharp crackle of small-arms fire.

Ernie saw the look of concern, bordering on fear, cross her face. "Don't worry. The front's a long way off. Any patrols the Germans might send out would steer clear of a convoy this size."

Walking next to him toward a tiny, adobe farmhouse, Maria saw the captain go on ahead of them with his driver. They stopped in front of the house. "Anybody in here?" he shouted.

"Who wants to know?" A voice called out from inside, punctuating his question with an oath.

Unquestionably American. The four of them entered the house and found a young lieutenant heating a can of C rations over a gasoline flame. His uniform was covered with blood, but he didn't appear to be wounded.

"You care if we spend the night in here with you?" the captain asked.

"Suit yourself."

The ghoulish corporal started to throw his blanket on the floor when the lieutenant stopped him.

"Hey, watch out for that man over there," he said matter-of-factly, never taking his eyes from his can of food.

Maria stared at the corner where a dead man lay, his face to the wall. He looked more like a pile of old rags than a human being. She looked back at the lieutenant. His eyes were glazed over from fatigue. They had that peculiar hollow stare she had noticed in other fighting men, but never to this extent. He had been surrounded by death that day, immersed in it to such an extent that he neither desired the company of the living nor was he offended by the presence of the dead.

"I ain't sleeping in here," the corporal volunteered on his way out the door.

His captain followed him. "Looks like it's going to be a little crowded. I'll just sleep outside myself."

Ernie threw his blanket on the floor near the wall opposite the dead man, lay down on the edge, and pulled the rest around him. In a matter of seconds, he was snoring softly.

Hesitating a moment, Maria glanced over at the corpse, then lay her blanket down next to Ernie's. She stretched out on the hard, dirt floor, her head resting on her helmet. Unable to sleep, she gazed at the young lieutenant where he stood next to the rickety table, still heating his can of corned beef, still sheltering behind the wall that protected him from the horrors he had seen that day. His light brown hair, matted and dirty, looked as though it hadn't been cut in months. He had a two-week growth of beard, or peach fuzz as the lifers would call it, and his face was as grimy as a diesel mechanic's. The blood on his uniform looked as dark and dry as the desert night.

As Maria stared at the lieutenant, her mind drifted back to the graduation ceremonies at Camp Polk. She sat again in the newly built bleachers while all the shining young men passed in review. Their bright and eager faces were as real and clearly etched in her mind as they had been on that hot summer day. She wondered how many of those faces had lost their shining in the blood and fire and ashes of war.

I wonder where Chance and Jesse are now—and Al. Sure wish I could have followed along with them after they shipped out. Guess there're some things even Duncan with all his connections can't control in wartime.

Chance. I can't explain how you make me feel, even if I only think of you. I still see your eyes that first time when you were on the tennis court in Liberty, and that lean, tanned face and hair bleached almost white. When you touch me the warmth goes all through me like dark music flowing in my veins. But there's a—restlessness in your spirit that frightens me, some kind of longing I fear will never be satisfied.

Jesse. I feel so safe with you. Like nothing could ever harm me again. And there's a joy in your life beyond my understanding. You think so little of yourself and so much about others. I think you must be very much like Jesus was when He lived here on this earth.

Al. My Cajun fisherman and kid brother. My friend who loves life and makes me laugh.

Maria looked again at the young lieutenant, eating from his can, his eyes staring at something far away. *How can the folks back home stand the agony of this separation from their husbands and sons and daughters, knowing they could be killed at any moment? Knowing that terrible telegram could come any day. Praying that it never does. Oh, God! Let this war end soon!*

For the first time in years, she prayed and drifted off to sleep with prayer still on her lips.

*   *   *

From the turret of his Tiger 1E tank, Lieutenant Kurt Einstadt of the Tenth Panzer Division peered ahead of him, barely able to see through the sandstorm that had come up so suddenly. His division rumbled through the Faid Pass of the Eastern Dorsal toward the Arab village of Sidi Bou Zid. "What a break this sandstorm is. We'll be on the Americans before they know it."

Einstadt, born in Wolfsburg, Austria, was brought up in the Prussian tradition of discipline, courage, and honor. The traditional dueling scar decorated his left cheek. With ice-blue eyes and blond hair, he looked like a poster advertising Hitler's Aryan race. Although he believed in an Austria separate and apart from Germany, his life was dedicated to the Fatherland.

Raised in cool, green valleys beneath snowcapped mountains, Einstadt hated the bleak and dry desolation of North Africa. He longed to see the edelweiss growing along the clear, cold streams of his homeland. Instead, all that lay before him were cactus and ugly clumps of dry bushes. The driving force in his life was to defeat the Allies and secure this barren desert for Germany so he could be free of the place.

The Germans broke out onto the plains west of Faid Pass just as the Stukas gave the American forces their first taste of the screaming hell of dive bombing. German artillery followed with a barrage like a firestorm of hot steel.

Einstadt rushed full speed into the fray, giving instructions for his gunner to hit any target of opportunity. With his main weapon, an eighty-eight-millimeter cannon, he possessed far more firepower than anything in the Allies' arsenal. The hundred-millimeter armor plate of the Tiger made it practically invulnerable to their guns.

Positioning his tank on a slight rise on the right flank of the American defense, Einstadt launched his deadly attack. The first round from his cannon blew apart a Lee that was advancing on him. He saw the commander fly out of the turret like a rag doll as the tank burst into flame. Only two of the seven crew members escaped. One of them beat furiously at his coveralls, trying to put out the fire as he scrambled from the turret. Einstadt watched them flee, never having a thought of machine gunning a helpless enemy.

The combination of artillery, dive bombers, and tanks cracked the will of the Americans. The first to flee were the artillery crews that supported the tanks. Trucks of German infantry drove hard on the heels of American ground troops, sending them into a pell-mell scramble to the rear. The Tigers roared through the midst of the battle, invincible with their armor and firepower, blowing the American tanks apart like so many children's playthings.

By mid-afternoon the American forces had been driven back six miles beyond the village. The attack came so suddenly and unexpectedly no one in headquarters could believe it. The command post started retreating when the forward troops were almost upon them. By then it was almost too late. Command cars, jeeps, and half-tracks started across the valley floor and through the Arab fields, because the main road to the north had been cut off.

Einstadt's company bypassed the main battle, seeing that victory was theirs, and pursued the enemy along their eastern flank. They positioned their Tigers behind a low range of hills, waiting for the command post to pass by them. When the lightly armed vehicles were in sight, they commenced a blistering attack.

After launching several volleys from a distance and knocking out the few accompanying tanks, they charged in among the lighter vehicles. Flight was the only alternative left to the headquarters company. Every jeep and car was on its own. All they could do was run and try to dodge their ponderous attackers. There was no front. The fighting was scattered across miles of desert sand.

Only darkness saved those who escaped. Fifteen miles behind its first position, the command post reassembled in a cactus patch. All night long stragglers wandered in from the desert. That same night the Germans withdrew from the territory they had taken. The next morning the Americans sent trucks out to bury the dead and tow in any salvageable vehicles.

At midnight Einstadt and the men of his company sat on their tanks, listening to a briefing. Rommel, the Desert Fox himself, stood in the firelight, his hands clasped behind his back, talking to his officers. Suffering from jaundice and desert sores, he allowed his men to slouch on their tanks while he spoke to them. It foreshadowed the loss of passion for command, a hallmark of the legendary man.

Rommel stood erect, the flickering light shadowing the hollows of his gaunt face. "Tomorrow the Americans will counterattack. We will defeat them again. Then we press on to Kasserine Pass, the gateway to Algeria and the town of Tebessa."

Einstadt felt a sense of dread come over him for the first time in the African Campaign. *Why should I feel this way? Today we won a great victory.*

"Tebessa is one of the most vital Allied communications and supply bases. The north-south roads are excellent. From there, our armies will sweep virtually at will to the Algerian coast." After a brief coughing spell, Rommel continued. "We then sever Allied supply lines and hit the British from the rear. After the British are defeated, the Allies will either retreat or face the same fate."

It sounded like the perfect strategy to Einstadt. Their tactics had been proven in today's battle. *Why then do I feel this terrible sense of impending . . . ? Enough of this!*

Rommel made a slight motion to raise his arm, thought better of it, and left it at his side. He gazed at the faces of his men with eyes that had lost their fire. "Long live the Fatherland," he said, more in a tone of farewell than encouragement. Hands folded behind his back, shoulders slightly stooped, he walked slowly away into the darkness.

17

DAY OF THE TIGER

We're gonna kick their butts today!" The general paced back and forth inside the white Arab farmhouse. Like many other farmhouses, shells had shattered sections of the walls and roof.

The general's red face and shock of white hair, along with the blue veins in his bulbous nose, gave him an especially patriotic appearance. "Nobody expected that many men and tanks coming through Faid Pass, but we're ready for them now. And we've got the stuff to blow them back to Cairo."

"Where'd be the best place to get a good look at the battle, General?" Ernie Pyle sat in a camp chair taking notes.

The general spread out a large wrinkled map, explaining the battle plan to Ernie and Maria. "Here or over here would be good spots. High ground."

"How dangerous would it be today?"

"Since when do you worry about danger, Ernie?"

"It's not about me." Ernie nodded toward Maria.

"Hmm—I see," the general sniffed. "Well, the only danger I can see is if they circle around behind you and cut you off. But that'd only happen if the battle goes against us—and it ain't. Not today!"

Ernie thought about the previous day when the Germans had come barrelling out of Faid Pass in their Tigers and Panzer IVs and thrown the whole army back fifteen miles. "Maria, you stay with the general here in the command post."

"But . . ."

"I mean it," he barked.

Maria pouted, but said no more.

Later that morning, Ernie caught a ride to the front in a deuce-and-a-half that was hauling supplies. Maria stood in the whirling dust, watching him wave out of the tailgate of the truck. When he was out of sight she immediately began trying to hitch a ride up to the battleground. Everyone seemed to have left already, those who were going at all. The few who hadn't refused to take her.

Toward noon, Maria sat on the dusty ground, leaning against the wall of the command post. She ate some British crackers with blackberry jam and drank hot tea that someone had made over an open fire. The day was mild and dry and the sky a bright Prussian blue. Lying in the sunshine, she soon fell asleep.

"I hear you're looking for a ride up to the front."

She groaned wearily, opening her eyes a little at a time until she squinted up at the corporal. His pale skin *(How could he stay pale out here?)* made his buckshot eyes look even darker than they were. The uniform looked like he wadded it up in his boots at night while he slept. "I am," Maria groaned, feeling a weariness in her bones.

"Let's go then." He headed for a jeep parked in front of the command post.

Following him, she saw that it was empty. "Where's the captain?"

"Dead."

Maria scrambled into the front seat next to the corporal. "I don't even know your name. Mine's Maria."

"Marnet. Francis Marnet." He glanced at Maria with a surprisingly pleasant smile.

The jeep lurched out onto the road, throwing her against the back of the seat. She leaned forward so the windshield would keep the choking dust clouds out of her face. "What kind of business do you have up at the front?"

"None." Marnet raised his voice above the road noise. "I don't have any business at all right now. But I do have this jeep, and I heard you needed a ride. I don't have anything better to do."

They turned off the dirt road, speeding east along the highway until they came to a crossroads. It was high ground and they could see for a great distance in all directions.

"Dive bombers," Marnet said flatly, pointing to several large craters near the crossroads. They were still smoking. "Not more than fifteen minutes ago."

Maria looked at a smashed tank near a crater. It burned with an oily black smoke. "When will the counterattack begin?"

"Soon." He pointed to their right.

The treeless expanse of the valley looked very much like the American Southwest. Clumps of dry bushes grew randomly among the stands of shoulder-high prickly pear cactus. In the irrigated sections, the small stucco farmhouses of the Arabs sat among their cultivated fields. In the distance, purple mountains rolled gently along the horizon.

As far as the eye could see, American equipment and men covered the length and breath of the valley. Tanks, half-tracks, artillery, and infantry—thousands of vehicles and tens of thousands of men—extended miles and miles in every direction. They were all as still as if the whole scene were nothing more than a painted landscape. Some ten miles or so to the east, the Germans had taken position, but there was absolutely no activity—no smoke on the horizon, no rumble of artillery, no planes roaring through the skies. The silence, in its own insidious fashion, was more unbearable than the clamor of battle.

Maria was mesmerized by the scene before her—all that destructive power waiting to be unleashed. The mostly unseasoned soldiers seemed to her more fragile than newborn babes as they waited on the brink of the impending firestorm.

"What are they waiting for?" She felt as though a band were tightening around her chest.

"Orders," Marnet mumbled. "Want to go down and take a closer look?"

"Sure. Why not?" Maria replied, trying to sound nonchalant.

Marnet put the jeep in low gear, driving down the slope from the road and into the valley. As they moved among tank after tank, they saw each commander standing rigid in his turret, the drivers at their controls.

Stopping next to one of the Lees, Marnet hailed the commander. "What's the delay?"

The man pulled his dark goggles up and squinted down at them in the bright sunlight. His face was still blackened with smoke from the previous day's battle. "Waiting for orders."

"What's the plan?"

"Nobody knows. The company commander'll radio us when

he gets the order." He pulled his glasses back down and grinned at them. "I don't think the general has any idea what he's doing. Only thing we all know is nobody wants to face them Tigers again."

Marnet stopped at several other tanks, but no one knew the battle plan. "Let's get out of here. I don't want to be in the middle of these monsters when they move out. I hear this is supposed to be the biggest tank battle ever fought in this part of the world."

Easing the jeep across the sandy valley floor through the endless rows of tanks, Marnet bounced over gullies and ditches toward a high rocky hill. He headed up its side, the engine growling and the gears grinding painfully until he located the commanding colonel standing beside a radio half-track. Marnet pulled along close beside him just in time to hear him give the attack order. He seemed unaware of their presence.

Marnet killed the jeep's engine. "I won't be long." He walked toward a group of men huddled together over a map spread out on the hood of a jeep.

Maria saw below her, all over the floor of the valley, the tanks pouring out blue smoke from their engines. Then they all began clanking and roaring across the desert, dragging their dust trails along behind them. They were a hundred to two hundred yards apart in no apparent formation, followed by artillery and the armored infantry in half-tracks and jeeps.

Through the heavy field glasses she found in the jeep she saw their destination, Sidi Bou Zid, its green trees standing out against the bare brown desert. She swept the glasses slowly across the valley, stopping at an Arab farmhouse below her. A small girl, her long hair dark against her tattered white robe, led a sack-laden burro toward the fields. Tanks clanked along beside her. She waved up to the drivers. Passing a herd of camels, driven along by an older boy, she stopped her burro at the edge of a field where a man was plowing.

Taking a brown sack and a clear glass bottle from the burro's back, the child walked into the plowed field toward the man. Suddenly she vanished in a brown geyser of earth. Maria gasped but held firm to the glasses. The shell's concussion knocked the man to the ground. He struggled up, running frantically across the plowed ground. All that remained was a gaping crater, smoking like a crack in the iron gates of hell. *Oh God! Oh God!* Dropping the glasses on the seat beside her, Maria took deep breaths, fighting to gain control.

Shells began exploding all over the desert floor, followed by the distant boom of the big guns. Maria took the glasses and looked back toward the town. The Germans were bearing down on them. All she could make out in the distance were their dust trails.

Chance must be down there somewhere—and Jesse and Al. *God help them! God help us all!*

* * *

Kurt Einstadt raced along in the front rank of the Tenth Panzer Division. He was eager to finish the work they had begun yesterday—the annihilation of the American forces. Far ahead of him, he could see their dust trails. Glancing to his left and right, Einstadt marveled at the invincible phalanx of Tiger tanks, pride of Rommel's Afrika Korps, sweeping across the desert. Their scouts had advised them that the Americans had given their first Shermans to the British. The Stuarts and Lees would be easy marks for the Tenth Panzer.

Tempered by two years of desert warfare, Einstadt smiled as he remembered how, only two hours before, they had defeated the American outposts stranded on the hills of Djebel Lessouda and Djebel Ksaira outside Sidi Bou Zid. He looked again at his comrades in arms, at the glaring sun and the high blue dome of the sky. *What a perfect day for battle! How can Rommel look so . . . defeated when we're crushing the Americans like so much chaff under our feet?*

Then the Stukas came shrieking out of the sky ahead of Einstadt like birds of prey in the bright shimmering air. He saw the flashing orange blossoms of direct hits on American vehicles, the columns of black smoke billowing upward in the still afternoon, and heard the rolling thunder of the bombs.

As the massed armies collided, he steeled himself for the blood and destruction of battle. The massive Tigers, less maneuverable than the Stuarts and Lees, ground to a halt, taking up defensive positions, moving only when they became vulnerable. They fired their deadly armor-piercing shells at the advancing rank of American tanks, destroying fully one-third of them with the first volley.

In a matter of seconds all the carefully laid battle plans were useless in the mass confusion of tank warfare. The desert became a killing field of orange and yellow flame, roiling black smoke, and the lumbering bulks of the tanks. The screams of the wounded and dying were drowned in the continuous reverberating explosions and the clattering, clanking, roaring sound of the tanks.

Launching round after round from his cannon, Einstadt crippled three Lees and destroyed two of the lighter Stuarts. He used his advantage in firepower and armor with practiced and deliberate precision. In his element now, he had focused all his concentration on winning the game, for that is exactly how he saw warfare, as a game where the stakes were eternal.

In the shuddering hell of battle, Einstadt's trained eye spotted an American commander guiding his tank with unerring instinct among the clumsier Tigers. He had crippled two of them by blasting away their tracks so that they were easy targets for his fellow warriors. Momentarily captivated by the skill of the commander, Einstadt suddenly realized he must stop this man at all costs. He had seen lesser adversaries than this American turn the tide of battle before.

Einstadt barked his orders into the radio and the massive Tiger moved deliberately into firing position. Launching his first round, he saw it shatter the left track of the American tank. As the tank ground helplessly to a stop, Einstadt fired again. His shell hit dead center, crumpling the armor plating and ripping a jagged hole through the front of the tank.

*   *   *

Half-blinded by the smoke of battle and the sweat streaming into his eyes, Jesse had just positioned the Lee for a broadside at a Tiger when the first shell hit. It felt like an earthquake as the heavy projectile rocked the tank around on its tracks. He flew out of his seat, banging his head against the gun mount. Dazed, he struggled back into the driver's seat, staring out through the slit. The last thing he saw was the bright flash of the Tiger's muzzle.

Jesse felt a tremendous blow slam into his chest with an unbearable and instantaneous pain. With the pain gone almost as soon as it began, he found himself as a ten-year-old boy, walking barefoot on the pine boards down the aisle of the little church he had grown up in. He saw his mother, her face glistening with tears of joy—felt his father's arm around him, strong and comforting, as the tall man walked to the altar with his son. They passed Abner and Mattie Collins, standing side by side on the front row, their hands raised toward heaven.

Kneeling next to his father at the altar again, as he had done so long ago, Jesse felt an ineffable peace sweep over him. Then the church was gone—his mother and father, the friends of his child-hood—all vanished. Before him stood a figure clothed in white and His brightness outshone the sun. And a voice like rushing waters came to him out of the light. "Welcome home, Jesse. We've got a lot to talk about."

* * *

Stunned by the impact of the second shell, Chance regained his senses quickly. His left foot felt numb. His combat boot was shredded on the outside of his ankle. Blood seeped out, staining the leather. Throwing his helmet aside so he could see in the smoke and dust below, he dropped down into the turret. Al lay in a pool of blood, his face pale as chalk. A jagged hunk of steel jutted from the center of his chest. Four other crewman were dead.

Chance turned to Jesse, slumped over in the driver's seat. He pressed his finger against the throat and felt a faint pulse in the ca-rotid artery. Bracing himself on his good right foot, he caught Jesse under his arms and dragged him up to the turret and out onto the top of the tank. In the blinding fury of battle, he saw an armored half-track wheeling among the tanks. As it passed close by, he yelled and waved his arms. The driver spotted him and pulled his vehicle alongside the shattered tank.

* * *

Einstadt saw the half-track stop next to the tank he had just destroyed. Letting helpless crew members escape was one thing. Allowing an armored vehicle to leave was something else entirely. He bore down on the wounded tank, bringing his lethal weapon to bear on the half-track next to it. Twenty yards away, he opened his mouth to give the order to fire when the American commander who had so captured his imagination in battle turned toward him.

As though Einstadt were confronted by his own Doppelgänger, he stared in rapt fascination. The man was a mirror image of himself—the same bright blond hair, blue eyes, and features that were fashioned by the same craftsman—even the same dueling scar beneath the left eye. Emotions Einstadt never knew existed hit him with a rush. In his mind the American sergeant became the brother he had always longed for and never had.

The two men stared at each other across the national walls that separated them. But the bond between them was far stronger—it was of the blood.

The image of the American commander, holding his wounded comrade amid the battlefield's fire and death, was forever fixed in Einstadt's mind. In his old age as he sat by the fire in his cabin, looking out across the valley toward the snowcapped mountains, he would call back that memory and it would comfort him like an old friend.

Einstadt barked an order into the radio. The massive tank swung away from the helpless Americans, grinding and clanking its way back into the battle.

* * *

The second retreat from Sidi Bou Zid had begun. This time there was no talk of a counterattack, no boasts of what the American tank battalions were going to do to the Germans. The retreat began sometime before dawn after the second day's fighting and continued unabated for twenty-four hours across the vast Sbeitla Valley and on through Kasserine Pass. Carried out calmly and efficiently, it appeared no different than any ordinary convoy.

The kitchen trucks and engineers left first in order to prepare the way for the remainder of the convoy. Next the rolling guns and some infantry moved out to set up protection along the roads. Then came the field hospitals, command posts, ammunition and supply trucks, infantry, artillery, and finally, as a rear guard, the tanks. It was one of the few times in history that American forces were forced to retreat in large numbers in a foreign war.

"What time is it, Ernie?" Maria sat with him in another of a seemingly endless number of jeeps. She no longer cared whose it was or what anybody's name was.

Ernie scowled at her. "I shouldn't even be speaking to you after what you did yesterday. It's a miracle you weren't killed. Four o'clock."

Maria stared up at the night sky, so clear she felt she could reach up and pluck a star out of it like some king of shining fruit. "They beat us, again. Didn't they?"

"Yep."

"Is that all you have to say?"

"I'm so tired I have to restrict myself to monosyllables."

She sat up, a troubled expression darkening her features. "You certainly seem unconcerned about the whole thing."

Ernie rested his head on the back of the seat, his eyes closed. "It's only one battle, Maria. And a rather insignificant one in the whole scope of things."

"The men don't think so."

"They never think so." He opened his eyes. They reflected the fears and everyday cares of the common soldier, the men he felt most comfortable with. "That's because they get killed just as easily in the little skirmishes as well as the great battles."

"Well, why aren't you concerned then?"

"I am—for the men. Not for the outcome of this campaign in North Africa or about who's going to win the war, for that matter. I already know what the end will be."

"How can you be so sure?"

"We believe we're in the right." Ernie closed his eyes and lay back again. "I'm not saying we're the only country who believes it's right. We're just the only one with the capability of production strong enough to make that big difference."

Succumbing to a bone-deep weariness, Maria began to consider the rise and fall of nations as inconsequential when compared to individual human suffering. "Why don't the other countries just give up and end it all right now then?"

A trace of a smile crossed Ernie's sad face. "Hitler's insane. The Japanese don't want to lose face. An oversimplification of course, but a truer reason than any politician would ever give you for fighting a war."

Maria's last thoughts before falling into a troubled sleep were of Chance, Jesse, and Al. Her last words were, "Ernie, I'm going home."

EPILOGUE

*T*he Germans only held Kasserine Pass for one day?" J.T. sprawled next to Maria on the bleachers, wearing khakis and a dark blue pullover shirt. The sun's April warmth felt like the caress of a young girl on his face.

Maria had gained most of her weight back and the nightmares no longer troubled her. "That's right. They left the next night after they took it. Rommel managed to pull their retreat off so discreetly, though, it was almost another whole day before the American commander even knew the Germans were gone."

"Well if you believed what the newspapers said over here, Kasserine Pass was the worst defeat this country ever had." J.T. attempted an indirect glance at Maria's figure in her white shorts and pale green knit shirt that flowed softly along the curves of her body.

"They beat us, all right," she continued, "but it was only one battle and a minor one at that, if you look at the whole picture. We'll have the Germans whipped in North Africa in a month or two now that Rommel's gone home."

"You sound like a real seasoned pro, Maria."

"I'm not, but I spent some time with one."

J.T. squinted across the startlingly green grass of the court. "You think Chance's ankle is ever going to heal?"

Maria frowned, her eyes taking on a different light when she looked at Chance. He pounded the ball off the backboard with the same beautiful, fluid strokes, but his gait no longer had that perfect combination of speed and grace that had taken him to the semifinals of the national championships at Forest Hills. His left leg twisted awkwardly with each step. "Not enough to play world-class tennis. And once a player reaches that level, all the other tournaments pale in comparison."

"You think he'll take the teaching pro job they offered him here at Pine Hills?" J.T. studied Maria's face. He thought the slight aging he saw reflected in her eyes and the tiny wrinkles at their corners made her even lovelier than when he had first seen her.

"I think so. You should see him with the children's classes. I think it's the happiest he's ever been."

J.T.'s eyes narrowed in thought as he gazed at Chance. "Something's really changed him. I guess it's the war."

"Probably," Maria responded, but she knew it was something other than war.

"You know, there's a rumor going around town that he's gonna preach up at Jesse's church on Sunday." J.T. shook his head slowly. "Never know what you're gonna hear next."

"It's not a rumor. I don't know if you'd call it preaching or not. I think Chance calls it his *testimony*." Maria found herself coming to Chance's defense. "After he spoke at Jesse's memorial service, Abner Collins asked him to come back."

J.T. looked back at Chance. "I knew there was something different about that boy. Did he just up and tell 'em he'd do it?"

"No. He told them he'd pray about it."

"Chance Rinehart—preacher and tennis pro. Well I reckon that's better than J. T. Dickerson—part-time lawyer and professional drunk," he smiled.

Maria sat quietly, watching Chance move painfully about the court, one shattered ankle standing between him and the dream he had carried most of his life.

"You love him don't you, Maria?"

"I guess I have since that first day." She smiled at J.T. "You remember when we came out here. He was playing a match with Billy Christmas. There was something about him that frightened me back then."

"But not anymore?"

"No. Not anymore."

J.T. looked into Maria's dark eyes, wishing that the different light he saw in them was for him. "You think there's any chance you'll settle down here in Liberty?"

"I don't know. I'm still not in any shape to make long-range plans right now."

"I heard you talked to ol' Dobe Jackson over at the *Liberty Herald* about goin' to work for him."

"Is there anything in this town you don't know about?" Maria laughed.

J.T. smiled. "There's worse places to live than Liberty." He lay back on the bleachers, his face turned toward the sunshine. In a few minutes he was snoring softly.

Maria opened her purse, taking out a brown leather Bible. Keeping her promise to Chance, she continued her reading, *"But as many as received him, to them gave he power to become the sons of God, even to them that believe on his name . . ."*

Chance finished his practice session and sat in a chair next to the net post holding a paper cup under the spigot of the water cooler. He breathed heavily, sweat pouring from his body. His ankle felt like it was on fire.

"Buy me a drink, soldier?" Maria stood next to him, her left hand on the curve of her hip.

He squinted up at her in the bright sunlight, noticing the tendrils of damp hair curling darkly at the edge of her ears. "Sure thing. You're that famous war correspondent, Maria Vitrano, aren't you?"

"Yep," she smiled haughtily. "Thought I'd come slumming down here in this little hick town."

He smiled, handing her a cup of water.

Maria took it, staring into Chance's smoke blue eyes. She knelt beside him, tracing the white scar under his left eye with the tip of her little finger. Letting her hand rest against the side of his tanned face, she bent to him, felt the taste of his salty lips against hers, felt his warmth flowing through her body. A tingling sensation began at the sides of her neck and ran down her spine. She felt herself trembling. "My goodness!" she gasped, pulling back breathlessly.

Chance took a deep breath, expelling it with a rush of air. "Me too," he grinned.

Maria took the chair next to him. She took his hand in hers as they sat together for several minutes, enjoying their nearness.

"I wish Jesse and Al could be there to hear you preach Sunday," she murmured, finding it difficult to speak of them.

"I don't know if I'd call it preachin' or not. I don't even know what I'm gonna say yet." Chance turned toward her, thinking how much she looked like a little girl. "I got a feeling they'll know all about it some way or another though."

Maria remained silent, her eyes bright with the beginning of tears.

"You know, Jesse used to tell me that this world wasn't his home. That he was only a stranger and a pilgrim here." Chance reached down and rubbed his painful ankle. "I think I understand now what he meant."

"I've heard him say that." She gazed into his eyes. "Pilgrims. Maybe that's what we're meant to be."

"How'd you like to make the journey with me, Maria?"

She nodded, tears glistening on her face. She thought of the dark years of war still ahead, but her fear of them was gone. "I think I'd like that," she whispered.

"You know, I never thought I'd say it, but I'm actually glad to be back in Liberty." Chance looked about the courts, freshly clipped and shining greenly in the sunlight. "I thought being the teaching pro here at Pine Hills would be the worst thing that could happen to me, but I'm startin' to like it. Especially the children's classes. Never paid much attention to kids before. Sometimes I think they help me a lot more than I help them."

Knowing what he was leading up to, Maria realized she had no answer for him.

"Maria?" He paused for a moment. "You think you could ever settle down here in Liberty?"

She glanced down at his twisted ankle and felt his pain. "I don't know, Chance. It's so—different from everything I've ever known." She suddenly stared into his eyes. "I just thought of something! You could be a teaching pro at Forest Hills! With your reputation they'd take you in a minute!"

Chance's eyes narrowed in thought. "It never occurred to me, but I expect you're right."

"Well?"

"I just don't know. For the first time since I can remember, I like livin' here in Liberty. It feels like home now."

Maria felt her brief hopes fading. "Well, I may be sent back overseas, anyway. I'm still a war correspondent. I guess this isn't a good time for either of us to make any decisions."

A shadow seemed to cross Chance's face. He turned to her as if to speak, but said nothing.

She held tightly to his hand, felt the back of it lying warmly against her thigh and, in that ordinary moment of time, knew that she couldn't bear losing him. "I'll do whatever you want me to."

I can't make this decision for her—force her into something she might regret later. "There's an old German saying, Maria. *'Ich bin du nah, und wär Ich noch so fern.'"*

She looked puzzled.

"It's about the only thing my daddy ever taught me," Chance smiled. "It means, 'I am with you, no matter how far away I might be.'"

Glistening in the sunlight, a single tear moved down Maria's cheek and dropped on her hand where it was joined with his.

Chance put his arm around her, pulling her closer to him. Maria lay her head against his shoulder and, for the first time since her mother had died, felt that she was no longer alone in the world.